More Than M

Endwell Investigations, Volume 3
fJ Donohue

Published by Frank Donohue, 2024

MORE THAN MURDER

First Edition, February 1, 2024

Written by fj Donohue

Prologue

He was parked in the lot of the EnJoie Golf Course on a Sunday in August. It was late in the afternoon, but he was able to find a bit of shade along the side of the lot under a row of trees. Jason Belvedere was getting impatient as he'd been waiting for close to thirty minutes. *These guys always jerk you around with meetings and times,* he thought, *I told him I can easily meet any time next week in New York City. What's the rush? I'm trying to fix it; shit give me some time.*

A large Lincoln SUV pulled up next to him and parked on the driver's side of his car. The driver got out of the car and walked around to Jason Belvedere's car. He made a hand gesture for Jason to roll down his window.

"Mr. Marcucci is still tied up in a meeting. He asked me to tell you he'll be along shortly."

Before Jason could respond, the man pushed his head down towards the steering wheel with his left hand and with his right hand put two bullets in his head behind his left ear. It was a small caliber pistol; there weren't any exit wounds.

The cops were never able to close the case. After a year and a half, they were no further along than when they started.

All they knew was a man was killed in his car in the parking lot of the EnJoie Golf course. No witnesses and a clean crime scene. The victim was local and didn't have a police record. The hit was done by a professional. Two shots with a twenty-two-caliber pistol. No mess, no fuss.

For sure, the victim was the target. Nothing was disturbed in the car. His money and credit cards were not taken.

What did you do Jason to make this bad boy shoot you?

Chapter 1

It was a typical late August Sunday in Broome County, New York. Hot and muggy, sometimes referred to as the dog days of August. Thunderstorms were forecast for the early evening. Lieutenant Elton Hendricks and Detective Todd Adams of the Binghamton Police Department along with Alastair Stewart the boss of Endwell Investigations regularly played in the Wednesday golf league at the EnJoie golf course and on the weekends when they could find the time.

They were a Sunday foursome today. Todd's wife Judy who taught at Binghamton High School had introduced their math teacher, Abe Shapiro to the group. Originally from the Bronx; a city guy for sure. He graduated from Binghamton University where he met his future wife, Kerry. He majored in math, obtaining a master's degree. The upstate New York lifestyle suited him and he stayed. Abe had been teaching at the high school for six years now.

Abe taught all the AP or advanced placement math classes. He also ran a math lab after school which was open to everyone. Although the kids jokingly referred to it as 'dumb school,' it was very popular. Abe would put the kids in groups depending on what courses they were taking, so he could go from group to group working with the students. There was an added benefit to the lab that Abe had never anticipated; the kids would help each other. He never saw it coming. As the school year progressed, they became a tight knit group. Dumb school was cool! Although the math lab only ran from Monday through Thursday, it was not uncommon to find Abe working one on one with a student on a Friday.

Abe was about five foot eight, slight of build but not skinny. Todd referred to him as a sneaky strong guy. He was new to golf, this being only his second year on the tour as he liked to say. The best way to describe his game according to Todd was that Abe was an eager golfer. He bought a level of intensity to his game. He would go to the practice range with Todd who spent a lot of time getting him to slow down his swing.

"Let the club do the work Abe, that's why you have them."

They were a nicely balanced foursome. Todd and Abe teamed up against Alastair and Elton. Abe was the worst player in the group and Todd was the best. Alastair and Elton played at about the same level, somewhere between Abe and Todd. It was a good balance.

When they finished the round, it was fairly late in the day and everyone had family commitments so they decided to head home. Todd had parked at the far end of the rectangular parking where he could pick up the late afternoon shade from a line of trees along that side of the lot. It would keep the car a bit cooler. At least he wouldn't be getting into a sauna.

Todd opened the tailgate of his Nissan Rogue and the driver's side door to get some airflow in the car. He was sitting at the rear of his SUV changing out of his golf shoes when he noticed a car parked about ten feet to the left of his car. There was a guy sitting in it. He wasn't moving and seemed to be tilted forward. Not dramatically but it just seemed odd. When he looked over at the car again after he finished changing shoes and stowing his clubs, he noticed that the man had not moved at all. Was he sick? Asleep?

Todd's cop side kicked in. *Let me see if the guy is okay.*

He went over to the driver's side of the car to check on him. His window was down.

As he bent down to get a better look, he said, "hey mate, you, okay?"

Todd put a hand on his shoulder to try and get his attention. As he did so all the weight from the guy shifted away from Todd. He could see two bullet holes behind the man's left ear along with gunpowder residue. He stabilized him and looked around the parking lot for Lieutenant Hendricks, but he'd already left.

He quickly called him on his cell phone. "Elton, you gotta get back here. There's a guy in the car next to me that's been shot. He dead; looks like a professional hit."

"Okay, turning around. Just came off the bridge. I'm on the Vestal side of the river. Give me five minutes. Call it in and get a crime scene crew over there. Don't let anyone near the car. Are Abe and Al still there?"

"No, they left right after you did. Should I call them?"

"Later after we finish. You call Abe and I'll call Al. Maybe they saw something."

Chapter 2

While waiting for Lieutenant Hendricks to return to the parking lot, Todd took some time to look over the victim's car. The parking lot was not crowded at this time of day so he didn't have to worry about keeping people away from the crime scene. First, he checked the ground around the car. No shell casings or anything that might be related to the shooting. The parking lot was paved so there weren't any foot prints or tire marks.

The victim was driving a Nissan SUV similar to Todd's. The back seats were folded down so he had a good view of the interior of the car. The first thing he noticed when he looked inside the car was that there weren't any golf clubs in it. EnJoie was a public course so the players usually didn't store their clubs at the golf course. Everyone brought their clubs and shoes with them. The other thing that caught his attention was the victim was not dressed to play golf. His attire was business casual.

Why are you here? he thought, *strange place for a meeting. What would bring you to this place? Were you picking up or exchanging something? This wasn't a social call.* As he was finishing up his assessment of the car and surrounding area, Lieutenant Hendricks arrived.

"What do we have Todd?" asked the lieutenant.

"Two clean shots behind the left ear. Up close; there's gunpowder residue at the entry points. I don't think the guy came to play a round of golf. No clubs or shoes and he's not dressed for golf."

The two men walked over to the SUV and stood by the driver's side looking into it. Neither one said anything; they were trying to assess the situation. After a few minutes, Elton spoke up.

"I see a guy coming to the driver's side and talking to the victim. He rolls down his window and at some point, the shooter jams the gun behind his left ear and pumps two shots into his head."

"Yeah said Todd," and he's probably right-handed. Just lean in and fire. If he was left-handed, he would have to turn the victim to shoot him behind the left ear."

"So, he probably knew him or was expecting him. It had to be a meeting of some kind. Why else would the victim show up at the golf course if he wasn't going to play."

"Maybe he wanted to ask you for some golf tips," laughed Todd.

The crime scene team and the coroner, Doctor Carlucci arrived along with an ambulance as the detectives were finishing their initial look at the victim and car. The detectives briefed them on the situation.

"I'll need his wallet and whatever else he has in his pockets," said Elton, "Todd and I will inform the family as soon as we leave here. I think everything happened on the driver's side. Check the outside of the driver's side door for prints."

The crime scene team was very thorough. After looking in the glove compartment and under the seats, they vacuumed the interior of the car and dusted it for prints. The two detectives spoke with Doctor Carlucci. He was on the short side with an expanding waist line. His hair was thinning and the good doctor was trying to comb over the remaining hair over the top of his head to hide the loss. Todd remembered he had a neighbor who tried to do the same thing. Never works.

"Gentlemen, looks like two shots to the head. I don't see any exit wounds; the bullets are still inside. They're probably pretty beat up so don't expect much to work with. I don't see any trauma marks on the hands or head. We'll know more after the autopsy but at this point, it looks like a professional hit. Quick and clean. I'd say the victims in his mid-fifties and appears to be in good shape.

When they recovered the victim's wallet, his driver's license identified him as Jason Belvedere and he lived in Endicott, not very far from the golf course. *Interesting* thought Todd, *what did you do? Jump in your car for a short drive here to meet up with someone?*

As they were standing near the victim's car a Toyota Prius was driving down Main Street parallel to the parking lot. The car quickly slowed down and turned into the parking lot. The driver, a middle-aged women headed directly towards the victim's car. Todd was able to get between the Prius and the victim's car forcing her to stop about ten feet away from the car.

"What's going on? That's my husband's car! I recognize it from the decal on the rear window. Has there been an accident. Why is there an ambulance and police cars around his car?"

Fortunately, by this time, Jason Belvedere had been removed from the car, placed in a body bag, and moved to the ambulance. The doors to the ambulance were closed so it was not possible to see much of the inside. Marion Belvedere looked toward the ambulance and said, "is my husband in there? I want to see him!"

There is no easy way to communicate this type of loss to someone. Not only was her husband dead, but he had been murdered. Lieutenant Hendricks walked up to Marion and said, "I'm so sorry to have to tell you this but you husband is dead madam. He was shot while sitting in his car. We don't know much more than that now. Can I offer you a ride home? My partner will follow us in your car."

Marion Belvedere was overwhelmed. She struggled to process what had happened. Jason shot and killed? Who? Why? What am I supposed to do?"

"Do you have any family nearby?" asked the lieutenant.

"We have a son who lives in Vestal. I'll call him. He'll know what to do."

"Ask him to meet us at your house," replied Todd.

Chapter 3

Marion Belvedere's house was located at the bottom of a tree lined cul-de-sac. Most of the trees were oak, probably planted when the houses were built in the mid-1970s. There were seven two story houses on the street, well maintained over the years with energy upgrades, new roofs, windows, and siding. Being at the bottom of the cul-de-sac, Marion's house was on a larger lot.

Her son had not arrived yet so they sat in the living room and waited. There wasn't much to say at this point. They were in the initial stages of the investigation; more questions than answers.

"When will you know why this happened and who did this?" asked Marion.

"I don't know at this point," replied the lieutenant, "we're gathering information and I'll keep you informed as we move forward. I know this is not the best time but when your son arrives, I'd like to ask you both some questions. It's important to get information as early as we can."

"I'll try," replied Marion.

They'd been at the house about fifteen minutes when her son Steve arrived with Carol his wife. Both were in their late thirties. No doubt Steve was her son; hair color, eyes and chin were the same. The detectives left the three of them alone in the living room and waited outside as they wanted to give them some time to talk amongst themselves and comfort each other.

"We'll be outside, call us when you feel ready," said the Lieutenant.

When the detectives joined the family, Elton said, "I'm Lieutenant Elton Hendricks and this is Detective Todd Adams. We're with the Binghamton Police Department. We were at the golf course today. After finishing our round of golf, Detective Adams found Mr. Belvedere. We've contacted the Endicott Police Department as your father was killed in Endicott and they've asked us to take the lead in the investigation as we have more extensive resources. We'll try to answer your questions and as I mentioned to your mother, we need to ask you some questions now to better understand the case."

"When can we see our father and plan for the funeral?" asked Steve.

"He's been taken to Binghamton General Hospital. They'll do an autopsy either Monday or Tuesday. After that we can release the body to the funeral home."

Elton could see both Steve and Marion react to the word autopsy. It's a common occurrence. Many people expected the procedure to be highly invasive and disfiguring.

"We understand your concern," said Todd. The doctor will respect your husband. Given the circumstances of his death, the law requires an autopsy. Have the funeral home contact the hospital and they'll call them when they can release the body. I would expect it to be later in the week."

"Will this be a media circus?" asked Steve.

"It's hard to keep like this out of the media," said Elton, "However, this was late on a Sunday afternoon. The parking lot was pretty deserted. I don't think they've picked up on it yet. You may have a few days of quiet but plan on this going public before the end of the week. This is a small town and the circumstances of your father's death will be a big news story. Once this breaks, the media will be pulling out all the stops to get information. I'd suggest not talking to the them. I don't think you can gain anything by it."

"Is my mom in any danger?" asked Steve.

"I don't think so but you may want your mother to stay with you for a few days. I can let the Vestal Police know and they'll provide increased coverage around your neighborhood."

"I'd like that Steve," said Marion, "I don't want to be here by myself."

"Mom, you can stay with us as long as you want," replied Carol, "the kids will be happy to have you with us. When things settle down, I'll help you deal with the house and Dad's things."

"Can Detective Adams and I ask some questions now?" said Elton.

"I'm not sure what help I can be but I'll try," said Marion, "Steve and Carol can help me."

"What kind of work did your husband do?" asked Todd.

"He worked independently most of his life," said Steve, "He mainly put together real-estate deals. Larger ones like shopping centers, office buildings and housing developments. He worked mostly in the Northeast not often south of Washington DC. He usually worked with investors rather than banks. If you have a sufficient number of investors, you can limit the banks participation or don't even have to use them. It's cheaper money but it does come with some strings attached as you have to manage the investor's expectations."

"Sound a bit risky," said Todd.

"Well, nothing's a lock in that business. Many things are in play. The project may not be a success, investors may try to pull out or the market changes from inception to completion. I know managing their expectations was a problem at times," replied Steve.

"Did he ever have projects go south or fail to put it bluntly," said Elton.

"I'm sure he did," replied Marion, "but he never talked about his business. I think the investors wanted confidentiality. My husband was a very private person. He avoided any publicity. Sort of the man behind the scene I guess."

"Did he have an office in the house?"

"Yes, in one of the spare bedrooms."

"I'd like to get a tech team to search the office and the house," said Elton.

"I can be here when your teams conduct the search," replied Carol, "but please don't trash the house. We've nothing to hide and want to help."

"I'll come over with the tech team," said Todd, "we'll respect your property. If we take anything back for analysis, we'll provide you with a list. Time is critical, can we do this tomorrow?"

"Yes, I can be here by nine-thirty."

"Should I be here also?" asked Marion.

"No Mom, stay at our place. It's too soon for you to start going through the house. If the police have any questions, they'll call you."

"Was he working on a project at this time?" asked Elton.

"He was always busy on something," said Steve, "I think he always had a couple of things in play."

"And yet he never talked about it?" asked Todd.

"No, not really. It's always been like that. I remember as a kid asking him what he was doing and he never really told me anything specific."

"Did he ever meet with any potential investors here?" asked Elton.

"No, never. As I said earlier, I think the investors wanted to stay out of the limelight. If a project was ever reported by the media, there would be a nondescript name for the group. Maybe Oak Street Development or something like that."

The detectives felt they had taken this about as far as they could for today. Hopefully the autopsy and search of the house would open things up a bit. When they got back to the golf course parking lot,

Jason Belvedere's car had been towed to the police garage for further analysis. The detectives sat in Todd's car and discussed the situation.

"Elton, I can hear the gears turning in your head. What are you thinking?"

"I've not comfortable with this guy Jason," said Elton, "why all the secrecy? Lots of companies do real estate development. What the big deal? We need to understand the money behind these projects. I don't like it. Do you remember that case we worked a few years back over at Sunrise Terrace off Upper Front Street. The guy was laundering money in the Caribbean?"

"Yeah, I do. You called the case the Caribbean Laundry. Do you think he was doing something like that?"

"I don't know but all this secrecy is a real concern. Somethings going on here."

Chapter 4

Elton and Todd called Abe and Alastair to see if they noticed anything unusual in the parking lot when they arrived or were leaving.

"No, Abe and I were parked at the other end of the lot. When we finished, I drove out of the exit up there. I didn't notice anything. Maybe Abe saw something?" said Alastair.

Abe had the same reply, He hadn't noticed anything unusual.

The autopsy did not reveal any new information. The two slugs removed from his skull were` identified as twenty-two caliber snub nosed bullets but were damaged and not expected to provide any additional ballistics information. The search of the house did not turn up anything new. Their home office was used for paying house and living expenses and their joint bank account held a reasonable amount of money. Clearly Jason had another office or work place but they could not find it though the detectives guessed it was around town so as to give him easy access to it. The same with the money. They knew he handled a lot of it dealing with investors but could not find it. An offshore bank?

Jason didn't have any close friends that the detectives could identify. They felt he had some 'associates' he worked with but could not find any. His Federal and State income tax filings appeared to be normal and did not identify a large revenue stream over the years. His son Steve said his father had a mobile phone that was used for family purposes. However, he had seen other mobile phones around the house.

"I think he must have had a separate mobile phone for each project. I asked him about it once and he just laughed and changed the subject. He never let me get close to his business. I know Mom was frustrated with his ways but I guess she learned to live with it. Dad was always good to us but there was a line we couldn't cross."

The case was very active for about six months. Lots of things to run down and understand. But the reality was that they needed a break in the case and they couldn't find one. Jason Belvedere lived a very secretive life. Even his family couldn't help. And then the thing all detective fear happened; the case went cold. Not all at once. But over time it dried up as the cops like to say.

Elton kept the case on an open status but it was now well over a year and the trail was cold. Very cold. It was clear from looking at completed projects that in many cases, the investors probably were not pillars of the community. Their money was invested in Jason's projects through shell companies. Find me if you can they seemed to say. The police were never able to find a way into Jason's business dealings.

Over at Endwell Investigations, it was a busy place these days. They were still only a team of four investigators. Chantal, Randy and Gil, and Fred Dublonsky a retired detective living in Scranton Pennsylvania was also doing part-time work for the agency. Alastair was still looking for another team member for the Endwell office but for now they were able to cover the workload. Surprisingly, they were about to get a new investigator———Sherlock, Alastair's dog!

Gil had taken a call from a Mrs. Gilday who wanted to set up an appointment to meet with Alastair as soon as possible. Alastair had planned to take the afternoon off to fix an electrical problem at home, but the caller was an elderly person and clearly worried. Alastair asked Gil to have her come to the office at one o'clock. He would deal with it and then go home to sort out a troublesome circuit breaker in the kitchen. The joys of home ownership.

Chantal met Mrs. Gilday in the reception area. She appeared to be in her late seventies and slim almost to the point of being skinny. She was early for the appointment and had come prepared. She had a picture of the problem; her missing cat! When she showed Chantal a picture of the cat, she asked her to wait in the reception area while she told Alastair that she had arrived.

"Al, Mrs. Gilday is here and she wants you to find her missing cat! She's really worried about it."

"What? Are you kidding?" said Alastair, "I don't even know where to start. But, we can't just blow her off. Let's meet with her and maybe we can help her find the best way forward. *Is Ace Ventura still in business? he* laughed to himself *thinking back to the comedy movie Ace Ventura Pet Detective starring Jim Carey.* "You best join the meeting too Chantal; I need some support!"

When Chantal went back to the reception area to bring Mrs. Gilday to Alastair's office, she found her patting Sherlock who had also been in the reception area with Chantal.

"I'll be joining the meeting Mrs. Gilday. Let's bring Sherlock with us; looks like you found a friend."

They all sat around the low coffee table in the corner of the office surrounded by four comfortable chairs. Sherlock stayed close to Mrs. Gilday.

After greeting her, Alastair said, "Would you like some coffee or flavored water? I'm going to have some coffee. Last one of the day for me or I'll never sleep tonight."

"Thank you, some coffee would be nice. No sugar please."

"Chantal, any coffee?" asked Alastair.

"Okay, you talked me into it Al." she responded with a broad smile.

Alastair bought in three cups of coffee along with a selection of small cookies. Mrs. Gilday was clearly impressed with the surroundings and atmosphere.

"Now, what can we do for you?" asked Alastair.

Well, I'm a good friend of Marilyn Leonard. I'm sure you remember her. You found her son Raymond who had been missing for a number of years."

"Sure I do. We still keep in touch. I usually see Marilyn and Raymond when he visits his parents. We were very fortunate to find Raymond and reunite him with his family."

"When Barney, that's my cat, had gone missing, I called Marilyn and asked her what I should do. She told me to put notices all around the neighborhood. Hopefully someone would see Barney. I called her the next day and asked her if I should hire a detective also. She wasn't sure but suggested I call your office for advice. Maybe you could help find Barney? He's eight years old and has never been away from the house. He's all I have now Mr. Stewart; I have to find him. My husband died last year. We were married over fifty years."

Alastair and Chantal briefly made eye contact both wondering the same thing. *What can we do? Where do we even start?*

"Mrs. Gilday, may I be candid with you?"

"Certainly, and please call me Norma."

Thank you. Please call me Al; you've already met Chantal, one of our investigators."

Where to start? thought Alastair, *what do I say to her? I guess I may as well come right out with it.* "Norma, I don't know how to find a missing animal. We have never done this kind of work before. Putting a notice around the neighborhood is a good first step. Maybe leaving some food or treats outside might help. Other than that, I'm at a loss on what else to do."

Chantal nodded in agreement and asked, "How long has he been gone Norma?"

"This is the third day and I wonder if he can survive much longer. He may be hurt and not able to take care of himself."

Everyone was quiet trying to come up with the next steps. "Norma, do you have woods near your house? asked Alastair."

"I don't but my neighbors on both sides do. Not too deep, just extensions to their property. Why?"

"Has anyone looked in the wooded areas?"

"I don't think so."

"Okay, let's try this. We live fairly close to each other. When we finish here, let me take Sherlock and we'll look in the woods and around the neighborhood. Can you give me something of Barney's so Sherlock can get a scent. She's never done anything like this before but who knows. Maybe she'll connect the dots."

"He has a small stuffed squirrel that he plays with. I'm sure that will work."

Chantal joined the conversation. "Al, my son Bobby is headed this way. He's going to the super market for me this afternoon. Let me have him follow Norma home and join the search party. He can be another set of eyes and ears."

"Good idea. He'll help us cover a lot more ground. Norma, no promises on this. If Barney is not in the immediate area, I'm afraid all we can do is try to expand the search with more notices."

"I understand. Poor Barney, he's not a wanderer, I know something's happened to him."

"Bobby should be here soon and we'll get started," said Chantal.

Chapter 5

While they were waiting for her son Bobby to arrive, Chantal and Alastair took the time to look at the current cases and upcoming appointments. One in particular caught Alastair's eye. Marion Belvedere had called the office and scheduled a meeting. He remembered the name from the murder in the parking lot at the EnJoie Golf Course.

How long ago was that? he thought, *must be close to a year and a half now.* He thought about calling Lieutenant Hendricks or Detective Adams to let them know she was coming to the office but decided to wait until after he met with Mrs. Belvedere. He assumed it would be about the murder of her husband but maybe not. He hadn't thought about the murder for some time. *I wonder if they closed the case yet? I don't remember anything recently in the media about it. Must have gone cold by now.*

"Did Mrs. Belvedere say anything about why she wants to meet with us?"

"Gil took the call, he didn't say anything about it," replied Chantal.

"He's out on a case now, I'll send him a text to see what he can tell me," said Alastair.

Gil called back about twenty minutes later but he didn't have much to add. When she called to schedule the appointment, she had told Gil it was personal and would discuss it when she came to the office. By this time, Bobby had arrived and Chantal went to brief him on the search for Barney.

"Wow! Sherlock and I are your new investigators. How cool is that?" exclaimed Bobby.

"Mrs. Gilday is really worried about her cat so be patient with her and follow Al's lead. This is very important to her, and the chances of ever finding the cat are pretty slim. All you may have for her at the end is bad news."

"I understand Mom."

When they arrived at Mrs. Gilday's house, Alastair was surprised at its size. It was a large two-story house with an attached two car garage. Alastair guessed it was built in the mid-fifties. *It must take a lot of horses to keep this place running,* he thought, *she needs a good support network. I hope somebody is talking to her about downsizing. You can really get trapped in these big old houses. Well, for now it all seems to be working.*

"This is a really nice house," said Bobby, "does she live here all by herself?"

"I think her children are grown and have left the nest," replied Alastair, "her husband died recently so I think it's just her and the cat."

"We have to find Barney, he's all she has now," replied Bobby.

"That's what she said too."

Alastair and Bobby stood in the backyard, just off the steps and looked around the area and adjacent woods. Sherlock was nearby close to Mrs. Gilday who was on the back deck. Bobby wasn't sure how they should conduct the search. Split up or work in some kind of team arrangement.

"How do we do this Mr. Stewart?" asked the lad.

"I think it's best if we work as a team. There aren't a lot of woods here but we need to make sure we cover them thoroughly. Barney isn't very big and we could easily walk right by him. You and I should stay about six feet apart and we'll let Sherlock run free. I don't know if she'll really understands what she's supposed to be doing. We'll keep the cat's toy squirrel with us and keep letting Sherlock sniff it. Maybe she'll figure it out."

"Do you think some animal killed Barney?" asked Bobby.

"Well, we do have coyotes around here and he'd be a good catch for them. I don't think there are any other animals that would go after him. Maybe a fox, I just don't know."

Alastair turned to Mrs. Gilday who was standing nearby with an anxious look on her face. "We're going to start now Norma."

"Thank you so much for doing this Al. I guess I'm just a silly old lady. I know you have better things to do."

"Sherlock and I are happy to help," said Bobby, "we'll do our best."

As they entered the trees to the left of Mrs. Gilday's house, Alastair saw that this would not be a simple search. The wooded area had not been managed or taken care of and was now overgrown with vines, weeds, and bushes. Seeing anything in there would be difficult. Just walking through it was a challenge. They did their best to make it around the various obstacles but were not able to search the area as thoroughly as Alastair wanted. On top of that the wooded area on the other side was the same. Sherlock stayed close to them but didn't understand her role in the search. Together they spent over an hour looking through the wooded areas without success.

When they came out of the second wooded area, Bobby asked, "What do we do now Mr. Stewart?"

"I really don't know at this point. This isn't working, that's for sure."

By this time, Bobby was sitting on the ground patting Sherlock who was playing with the stuffed squirrel.

"Mr. Stewart, can we get something else of Barney's for Sherlock to sniff. She thinks the stuffed squirrel is just a toy. I don't think she's made it past the squirrel being just something to play with. Maybe something Barney sleeps on."

"Good idea, let's give it a try. Let's put the squirrel on the back deck."

Mrs. Gilday gave them a small blanket that Barney slept on. They put the blanket about ten feet from the wooded area on the left and stood next to it with Sherlock by their side. The dog sniffed the blanket and then got the scent and started moving towards the woods.

"That's it, good girl," said Alastair, "go find it."

Sherlock stood at the edge for a few moments before entering the woods to follow the cat's scent. Alastair and Bobby followed her but not too close. They didn't want to distract her. As best they could see Sherlock made a wide arc into the woods and then stopped. When they caught up to her, they didn't see anything right away, but then in the underbrush just to the right of Sherlock they saw Barney. He was all tangled up in the brush. He must have panicked which only made it worse. He wasn't moving; probably exhausted and dehydrated, maybe even dead.

Suddenly Bobby exclaimed, "look Mr. Stewart, he just blinked and I saw his ear twitch. He's alive!"

"Let's be very careful getting him out. His right hind leg is at a funny angle and extended. I think it's broken or dislocated. He probably did that struggling to get free. Go back to the house and tell Mrs. Gilday we found Barney and bring back the cushion he sleeps on. We need to get him to the vet."

When they came into the yard with Barney, Mrs. Gilday was standing by the wooded area, a big smile on her face and certainly a tear or two.

"Al, Bobby, you did it! You found Barney!"

"Sherlock found him, she's the best rescue dog ever!" exclaimed Bobby.

"We need to get Barney to the Veterinary Hospital in Endwell right away," said Alastair. "We can all ride over in my car, plenty of room. Norma, you hold Barney."

The poor cat looked as if he had fought the last war single handed. His fur was all matted and his legs were caked in mud. At the hospital, Doctor Quinn took the cat to an examination cubicle to check him out.

"Just wait here in reception. I I'll come back shortly."

When the doctor came back, he was all smiles. Mrs. Gilday quickly read his expression and knew that Barney was going to be fine.

"He looks a lot worse than he is," said the doctor, "he has a dislocated hind leg but we can sort that out. He's also quite dehydrated but that's easy to fix. I'd like to keep him here for two to three days. We'll sort out the leg, clean him up and get some food and fluids into him. By that time, he should be back in fighting form. You can come and visit him Mrs. Gilday. That will help in the recovery."

Mrs. Gilday was very quiet on the ride back to her house. Most likely trying to absorb the recent events. Bobby saw her wiping some tears from her eyes. He didn't say anything at the time but would talk to his mom about it later. As they were pulling into her driveway, she perked up and reminded Alastair that she expected a bill from him.

"Sure Norma, but I need to check with Sherlock and see what her rates are for search and rescue! I'll get back to you."

Mrs. Gilday knew that Alastair would never bill her for the services, so she took matters into her own hands. She sent Chantal a check for a hundred dollars and asked her to make sure Bobby got it. When Bobby got the check, he was thrilled.

"This is a lot of money Mom; can I keep it?"

"Sure you can. I don't think she'd accept it if you tried to return it. but make sure you send her a nice thank you letter."

So, Sherlock was now a major player in the office. Chief rescue dog, saver of cats and Bobby was a budding investigator!

Chapter 6

Alastair had never met Mrs. Belvedere though he had followed the murder case in the media and occasionally it would come up in conversations with Lieutenant Hendricks or Detective Adams. However, as it was an open case the two detectives did not discuss it in any detail. From what they did say though, Alastair could tell they were frustrated with the case progress. Hitting the wall as the cops liked to say.

Mrs. Belvedere and Alastair met in his office on a warm sunny day. Sherlock followed them into the office and sat next to her. They met around the coffee table in the corner of the office. This was his preferred spot as it allowed for a more casual atmosphere. Much better than looking at someone over the top of your desk. He felt this was important to help the clients more openly discuss their cases. The corner of his large office was covered with an oriental rug about ten-by-ten feet. It was under the coffee table and chairs so the area had its own identity. Maybe a conference area within the office. He had recently found the large rug at an antiques show in Syracuse. It was a Tabriz and in great condition. *Maybe made at the turn of the century,* he thought, *prices for oriental rugs are so good these days, you couldn't get these low prices ten years ago. A bit like antique furniture, the bottom had fallen out.*

Alastair guessed Mrs. Belvedere was in her late sixties. She was on the tall and lean side and he thought she probably spent a fair amount of time with a personal trainer and followed a structured exercise routine. *I need to get serious with my exercise game,* thought

Alastair, *I talk about it more than do anything about it. I gotta up my game.*

"Mrs. Belvedere, I remember your name from the incident at the Enjoie Golf Course a few years back. I was actually at the golf course that day playing a round of golf with Lieutenant Hendricks and Detective Adams. I don't know much about the case other than what I've read in the newspapers and heard on TV. How can I help you?"

"The police were never able to find the person who killed Jason. I know they worked very hard to solve it but they weren't successful. I'd like to have an outside source take a look at this now. Maybe fresh eyes and a new perspective will make a difference."

It was always a concern to Alastair that new clients often expected immediate gratification. Pay the money and get quick results. Also, many of them did not have the resources to support an extended investigation. So, it was important to explain how their case would be handled. Randy, one of his investigators called it defining the rules of engagement. It was not that uncommon for Alastair to turn down a prospective client because of unrealistic expectations.

He opened the conversation with an explanation of how his agency works. "Mrs. Belvedere, let me be candid with you. These kinds of investigations can be very expensive and there are no guarantees of a good outcome. You could spend a lot of money and end up no further along than where you are today. Also, these types investigations typically take a fair amount of time."

"I understand Mr. Stewart. I have the resources. My husband was well insured and he also left me a trust fund. About two months after he was killed, I got a letter from an attorney advising me about the fund. My son Steve also got a similar letter regarding a trust fund in his name."

"Before I can decide on taking the case, I want to speak with the police. If the case is still open, they may have an issue with another party getting involved. This only works if my agency and the police can cooperate. They have a lot of case history which I'll need to review. I don't think there will be a problem but I want to make sure they can support me. Assuming we do go forward, I'll bill you monthly. If you're not satisfied with the progress, you can shut us down at any time. Also, as I said, if I don't feel we're making sufficient progress, I may decide to stop the investigation. I don't want to waste your money. By the way, have you spoken to your son about retaining us?"

"No, not yet."

"Please do, we need everyone onboard. I'll need to speak with him and it's important that both of you support this. Are there any other children, brothers or sisters who need to be informed?"

"No, it's just me and Steve. Jason was an only child and his parents died a number of years ago. I have a brother in California but we don't see much of each other. I haven't seen him since Jason's funeral."

"Okay, let do this. I'll call the police and let them know of your interest in having a third party look at the case. Speak with your son and let him know what you plan to do. If the police and your son will support this, then we can move forward."

"I'm going over to his house for dinner tonight, I'll talk to him then. Do I owe you anything for your time today."

"Not at all, it was a pleasure meeting with you and I think Sherlock is happy with her new friend. I'll call you early next week after I've reviewed it with my investigators and spoken with the police. We have a weekly staff meeting this Friday, so I can brief my team."

That finished the initial meeting. Chantal and Mrs. Belvedere left the office with Sherlock close on their heels. *Interesting*, thought

Alastair, *the dog really likes Mrs. Belvedere. I wonder what the attraction is between them.* Alastair always found Sherlock to be a good judge of people. There was certainly a bond forming between Mrs. Belvedere and Sherlock.

When Chantal came back to Alastair's office, he said, "let's put this on the agenda for the Friday wash-up. What did you think of her."

"I liked her and think she's a strong person. Sherlock certainly liked her."

"Yeah, I noticed that too. What do you think about the case?"

"Well from the brief exposure, it's the kind of case I like. Plenty of digging for sure. I do think we need to be very careful and manage her expectations. This could go on for a long time. The fact that the cops could not close the case is telling. We're sure not going to find the answer hidden in a shoe box in the back of Jason's closet!"

"Amen," said Alastair, "I think monthly billings will allow us to gauge the case progress and also give Mrs. Belvedere a metric to assess our performance. I don't want to take her money unless we're moving forward. I'll call Lieutenant Hendricks and see what his thoughts are."

Chapter 7

All the investigators were able to attend the weekly staff meeting or wash-up as they called it. Someone was usually out on a case and would have to call in. However, a full house today for a change. Chantal, Randy, Gil, Alastair and of course Sherlock. They used the conference room instead of Alastair's office as Gil had some photos, he wanted to show the group regarding an insurance fraud case he was working on. It was much easier projecting the data on the large conference room screen then passing around paper or leaning over a small computer screen. Although Mrs. Belvedere's case was at the top of agenda for the Friday wash-up, Sherlock and Bobby's recent adventure finding Barney the cat took center stage.

"Bobby is so happy the two of you found Barney. He talked our ears off at dinner the other night. He's so proud of Sherlock too," said Chantal.

"Bobby broke the code in our search for Barney. Once we got away from the stuffed squirrel toy and used the cat's sleeping blanket for a scent, Sherlock was able to understand what we wanted her to do. Without that change, I don't think we would have found Barney. He was barely visible under all the brush." replied Alastair.

"Good-on-ya Sherlock," laughed Randy, "no more chasing bad guys and deadbeats; search and rescue is our future now!"

"Well maybe one more bad guy," laughed Alastair, "I met with Marion Belvedere the other day. You may remember the last name. Her husband was murdered in the parking lot of the Enjoie Golf Club about a year and a half ago. I was there that day along with Lieutenant Hendricks, Detective Adams, and Abe Shapiro from

Binghamton High. We had finished our round and were leaving the parking lot when Todd discovered the body. She wants us to take a look at the case."

"Yeah, I remember that," said Gil, "got a ton of media coverage. It's been a while, did the cops catch the guy?"

"I don't think so," said Randy, "I think the case is still open. Maybe not active though."

Alastair replied, "I like this case; it's a good fit for us. It's complex and touches a lot of different areas such as the murder itself and the money behind the real estate development. This has always been a shady area, open to a lot of games for want of a better word, but I need to speak with Lieutenant Hendricks first. The cops have all the case information and we'll need access to it or we'll have to start from scratch and I don't want to do that. I told Mrs. Belvedere that if we took the case, we would bill her incrementally, based on progress. If we can't move it forward, we'll shut it down. She can also stop the investigation at any time.

"Will the cops let us review the files?" asked Gil.

"I think they will," replied Alastair, "we'll certainly share all our findings with them. Maybe we can move things along. I think it's been a tough case to crack, it's been open for some time now and as you know, time's not your friend in an investigation. I have a call into Lieutenant Hendricks. He's in court. If He doesn't get back to me today, I'll see him on Sunday. We're playing in a golf tournament at Hiawatha Links over in Apalachin."

The Friday wash-up didn't take very long and by four-fifteen they had completed the review of active cases and financials. No major problems with the current cases and the financials were solid. Alastair sent the team home early as it had been a long week for everyone. When an investigation is hot, the eight-hour day work day goes out the window so, take the time when you can get it. He remained in the office with Sherlock as he wanted to check on some plane reservations to Fort Walton Beach, Florida. It was getting close to the anniversary of the death of his wife and unborn child, killed in a mob hit in Miami during his FBI days. He always tried to see Emmi's parents Nigel and Marie once a year and visit his wife and baby's grave. Emmi and the baby were buried near her parent's home. A visit to the grave was still an emotional experience for him. Although a number of years had passed, standing by her grave brought back so many memories of what happened and what their life could've been like. He had no regrets regarding his new life. Time and good friends had provided the support he needed to recover after the murders. *I've been so lucky,* he thought, *I couldn't have put a new life together without all their care and support.*

As he was checking flight possibilities on his computer, Lieutenant Hendricks returned his call. "Al, glad I caught you. Sorry to call so late in the day. What's up?"

"Thanks for calling back. You sound tired, long week?"

"Not too bad except for today, I had to spend all day in court and only got called to the witness stand at the end of the day. On top of that I think my testimony lasted less than ten minutes. So, I just sat there all day thinking of all the stuff I needed to do and couldn't get to. The assistant DA made a meal of the trial today. Damn, we got the robber on video in the store and getting into his car outside. Dumb-ass even looked into the surveillance camera outside and smiled. The assistant DA is pretty new and didn't want to make any mistakes so he was slow and methodical. I could see the judge was getting a bit tired of it all too. But I guess I have to cut the kid some slack. Better this way as opposed to blowing up the case."

"Elton, I was calling about the guy who was murdered in the EnJoie Golf Course parking lot about a year and a half ago. His name is Jason Belvedere. The guy's wife or widow now I guess, wants us to take a look at the case and see if we can do anything with it. She doesn't have a problem with the police work. In fact, she mentioned

Todd and Tony saying they worked hard to solve the case. Is it still active?"

"Well, open but not active. We still have it on a weekly case review. We worked it hard for six months but could never make any real progress. I'm pretty sure Belvedere was operating his business on the fringes of the legal side but could never get to him. He had a separate life that his wife and son were not a part of. His home was clean, nothing in the house or home office. He had a simple joint savings and checking account for living expenses. Like I said, we could never get close to him. I think he had a bolt hole somewhere around here and ran the operation from there."

"What about legal filings and permits for his projects? He had to register them, didn't he?"

"He did and that's where an odor comes in if you know what I mean. The projects were all incorporated under different development companies. Each one had a new name. For example, State Street Development, Sterling Development, Oak Street Development, names like that. The participating investors also had similar companies that did not have a public identity. Sort of like shell companies. Frankly, it smelled like money laundering to me."

"Were you ever able to find out where he did his banking?"

"No, but I'm sure it was off-shore somewhere. Maybe the Cayman Islands or somewhere in the Caribbean. Not in the States, we would have been able to find it."

"Did he have any associates? Local guys?"

"He had a local attorney, guy by the name of George Adamo. Small practice, mostly corporation stuff some wills and estates. Belvedere kept him on a retainer. One hundred twenty-five thousand a year."

"Not bad. I wonder why he didn't just pay him by the job."

"It's not uncommon for corporation work to be paid that way. As long as you're not going to trial, it seems to work."

"What do you know about the lawyer?"

"Not a hell of a lot. He's okay with the Broome County Bar Association; never been in trouble. He doesn't appear to have a large clientele or stable as Todd calls it. I think Belvedere was one of his big-ticket clients."

"Did he move any money for him?"

"No, just corporate filings, legal notices, and incorporation documents. We really worked it but could never open the door into his other life. Belvedere was not kosher Al, and his wife and son don't have a clue about what he was doing. I wonder why she wants you guys to look into the case now?" asked Elton.

"I've only met her this one time but my sense is the family wants closure. I agree that they know little or nothing about him. They just want to know what was going on with him. Reading between the lines, when I met Mrs. Belvedere, I got the feeling that she had real doubts about his working life. She didn't say anything directly but I got the sense that she wants to know what he was up to."

"So, no search for a large safety deposit box or two filled with money?" laughed Elton.

'I don't think so, but if this guy was operating on the fringes, I bet he had money squirreled away somewhere. Are you okay with us looking at the case files? I don't want to take on the case if we have to start from the beginning. It would be too expensive. I'm worried about the cost. I don't want to take her money without a way forward. Maybe after we take an initial look into it, we may have to shut it down. You guys spent a lot of time on it and came up short. That really worries me. Maybe there's no way in."

"I'm happy to have fresh eyes looking at this. Todd will be out most of next week. We caught the guy who robbed those convenience stores awhile back and the trial is set for next week however, Tony Ronaldo is in the office. Call him and set up a meeting. I'll let him know you'll be in touch."

Chapter 8

On the way home from the office, Alastair stopped at the dog park near his house so Sherlock could touch base with her canine buddies. Some of the dogs knew each other from previous visits and greeted their friends with lots of sniffing and tail wagging. Sherlock seemed to have bonded with one dog in particular. They always looked for each other at the dog park and when they met, they spent a lot of time together. It was an interesting relationship between the two dogs. After an initial greeting, if you can call it that, they would stay in close proximity to each other. The other dog was not very large and appeared to be a mix of breeds. A real mutt was the best way to describe the dog. They always made Alastair smile. *The odd couple,* he thought.

While he was at the dog park, Alastair gave Marty Fitzgerald a call. She was still at work at The Samaritan Counseling center in Endicott. They had been together for about three years now, having first met when Alastair was working on a missing person case Involving an autistic young man. Alastair didn't understand the condition so he met with Marty for advice. The relationship grew from casual meetings for drinks, to something more serious. After the loss of his first wife and unborn child some years back, he was now at the point where he could move forward.

"Late day?" asked Alastair.

"I just finished," she said, "I usually meet with this client on a Friday afternoon. He stops by on the way home from work. He's at the point now where we could do this on a Zoom call but I prefer face to face meetings. It's much more telling."

"I know what you mean. I don't think there's any substitute for face time. Zoom calls or anything like that on a virtual platform are not my first call. No pun intended," laughed Alastair.

"Yikes, don't get started on the puns, you'll get into a groove and do it for weeks!"

"Okay, I'll be careful. Maybe you can line me up with a good therapist who can wean me off puns."

"Not possible," laughed Marty, "you're hooked and too old to train. I'll have to live with it. Oh, by the way, we can still do dinner at your place tomorrow but I can't stay over. Bobby's coming home on leave from the Air Force late Saturday night so I'll need to be home."

"Sure, why don't we all go out for dinner while he's home. We can go to Bud's over in Apalachin. "

"He'd like that."

"Have you told the boys about us getting married around the end of the year?"

"He and his brother have already figured it out. They want to interview you to make sure you're solid and responsible," laughed Marty, "be ready to make a full disclosure."

"Yikes, my secret life will finally be revealed. Sort of sounds like a case I may be taking on."

"I'll come over mid-afternoon tomorrow with the desert. I'm making a fruit salad."

"Deal, I'll pick up a couple of New York strip steaks, baking potatoes and try again to make a decent creamed spinach. Last time was a bust but hope springs eternal."

"Do you want me to make the creamed spinach?"

"No, I'm getting close to making a good one; one more try."

"Okay tough guy, see you tomorrow."

The meal on Saturday was a success. Dry gin martinis to start, followed by steaks grilled medium rare, with slowly baked potatoes and finally the cream spinach with just the right balance between the sauce and spinach all washed down by a bottle of cabernet sauvignon. Franciscan Vineyards was the brand Alastair preferred. It was a medium-priced cabernet, consistently good. After the meal, they talked about the upcoming case regarding Jason Belvedere. Alastair didn't go into any specific details. He was more interested in discussing Belvedere's apparent double life.

"How could he pull that off?" asked Alastair, "his wife and son must have wondered about what he was doing all those years."

"Maybe they did but it doesn't seem to have been an issue with it them, said Marty, "they must have accepted it. Doesn't make them part of the crime but I think the way he was killed raised a lot of questions and maybe confirmed some suspicions. I can understand them wanting to know the full story now."

"I guess if she knew anything about his business dealings, she wouldn't have contacted me looking for answers."

"Did you tell her she might not like whatever you find."

"We've not discussed it yet but if I do take her case, it has to be a major part of the conversation."

The following Monday Alastair called Detective Tony Ronaldo at Binghamton Police headquarters. Lieutenant Hendricks had already spoken with Tony so he was expecting the call. Alastair had met Tony a few times over the past two years and although they had not cooperated on any cases, they were familiar faces to each other.

"Tony, I guess Lieutenant Hendricks briefed you on my interest in the Belvedere murder."

"He spoke with me last Friday. How can I help?" replied Tony.

"Can I come over to your office and discuss the case and review the case files?"

"Sure, does Tuesday morning work for you? I'm in court this afternoon and have to prep with one of the assistant DA's this morning."

"Sure, I'll bring the donuts. Say ten o'clock?"

"Great, you know cops love donuts! I'll have the files and case notes ready for you along with coffee."

When Alastair arrived at police headquarters the next day, he met with Tony in the conference room next to Lieutenant Hendrick's office. Tony had already brought in the files which were much larger than Alastair had expected.

"Looks like it took three trips to carry all of this in here," he said.

"I used a rolling cart and made it in one trip," laughed Tony, "it just keeps growing but we don't seem to ever make any progress. I had hoped for something to break the case open but so far, no joy. Did this ever happen to you?"

"For sure, especially during my FBI days. We had cases that ran for a couple of years with lots of agents working them. Sometimes we had to stop and regroup. My boss used to say working a big case was like herding cats. Lots of agents on the case, but little or no progress. We come up against the same thing today at the agency. Chantal, one of our investigators calls those cases 'head bangers.' You stand up against the wall and just keep banging your head on the wall to break it down."

"Well so far, this wall is made of bricks. Just like the story of the three little pigs. Wish the wall was made of straw," laughed Tony.

Before diving into the files, the two men discussed the background of the case. Alastair needed a good understanding of the investigative trails that the police were following. In his mind, there were two crimes. The murder of Jason Belvedere and then, his secret life and business dealings. Solve one and you probably solve the other. Alastair didn't know which way to go at this point. The murder was clearly a professional hit. Clean crime scene and so far, no trail. The lab couldn't recover anything useful from the bullets and there were no finger prints on the car other than Jason's, his wife, and the expected assortment of extraneous prints. The driver's side door had been wiped clean; most likely by the shooter. The golf course did not have any security cameras; why would they? To say the crime scene was clean was putting it mildly. It was antiseptic!

"So Tony, you didn't get anything from the crime scene?"

"Nothing, not a scrap. We got a list of the tee times that day and checked with the golfers. It was a slog. We had the names of the guys who made the reservations and contacted them and they connected us to the other players. We were able to cover most of them but nobody saw anything in the parking lot. One guy thought he saw two cars parked away from the others on the end of line by the trees but he was not sure about what he saw. Could have been golfers. Nobody heard any shots or any kind of disturbance. We didn't get a thing."

"Were there any security cameras on the street by the golf course or nearby?"

"No, there aren't any cameras in Endicott. We checked with both the Town and County. My opinion is we have to unravel his second life. I doubt if we're going to catch the shooter. Todd has some good sources around town and the feedback suggested that it was probably outside talent; not local. One of his sources checked up in Syracuse too. Nobody knew anything. The speculation was that the shooter was possibly from New York City but Lieutenant Hendricks is ex-NYPD and he checked with his contacts. Nothing came back. We need to catch a break to move this side forward."

"Okay, let's talk about Belvedere's hidden life."

"He was a property developer. Shopping malls and office buildings both new and major renovations. He didn't secure a lot of loans from banks. It appears that he relied on private investors to raise capital."

"Was there ever a blend of private capital and bank loans," asked Alastair.

"I need to check," replied Tony, "I remember a few but as I said, mostly investor capital."

"What about his State and Federal tax returns?"

"He paid himself a modest salary from his companies that fronted his various development projects. The last few years showed a salary of around two-hundred thousand a year. Good money for this part of the State. We had a CPA office in town take a look at his returns. They didn't find anything unusual. Once a project was completed, his development corporation for the project was dissolved; end of story. The investors companies ran the operations and sold them off over time. Belvedere probably got his money out of the investor's corporations. Maybe a phony listing as an investor or a kickback from the investors. Where he parked the money is a mystery. The people investing were never named in the projects, just obscure company names. They were not public companies either. Lieutenant Hendricks thinks that it was a money laundering scheme. Maybe mob money or worse, drug money."

"What about the trust funds he set up for his wife and son?"

"What trust funds?" asked Tony.

"They came into play about five months after he was murdered."

"Damn, she never said anything to us about any trust funds. Where are the payments coming from?"

"She didn't say and only mentioned it when I met with her. I was concerned about the cost of the investigation and wanted her to understand that this type of investigation can get expensive. She said Jason had very good life insurance and that she and her son were also covered by trust funds. I don't know any more than that. I'll run it down and get back to you guys."

"If they have trust funds, then there has to be a stash of money or investments somewhere," said Tony, "maybe a trail there? Damn, wish she said something earlier."

Alastair felt he had taken the conversation as far as he could at this point. He spent the next few hours looking over the case files mainly trying to understand the scope of the investigation by the cops. The files were comprehensive and well documented. Clearly Todd and Tony had put a lot of time into the case. But as Tony said, they had not moved forward.

He decided he needed to think about the case in terms of agency staffing and come back to look at the files again. Most likely he'd bring Chantal into the mix. She was a good detail person, comfortable sifting through a ton of paper. Maybe bring Randy on board also to help him carry the load. There were lots of points to run down. He made a list of people he needed to speak with such as the local lawyer who did Belvedere's corporation work and the bank who handled the trust fund. He also had to find a good forensic accountant, when they started looking into the trust funds. But, he needed something solid for them to dig into. Right now, all he had was intuition and speculation and the accountants want numbers.

As he was finishing the initial review, Lieutenant Hendricks returned to the office and poked his head into the conference room. "Got them bad boys yet?"

"Give me another day and I'll have them all here in handcuffs," laughed Alastair, "it's a pretty simple case for a master-detective like me! I just need to check my facts with Sherlock!"

"What are your thoughts?" asked the lieutenant.

"More questions than answers at this point. It seems as if the murder side has dried up. I think I'll put the emphasis on Belvedere's business dealings. We may have a better shot there. By the way, about five months after he was murdered, a pair of trust funds started paying Mrs. Belvedere and her son on a monthly basis."

"Really! I don't think she ever disclosed that. I wonder if she was trying to hide that from us."

"I don't think she knew about it. The way she told it to me, it just started showing up one day. By the way, I'll be back with Chantal tomorrow to dig deeper into the files."

"Sure, you can use the conference room, it's available all week."

Chapter 9

Before calling Marion Belvedere, Alastair met with his investigators, Chantal, and Randy to discuss the case. He didn't want to start it without them being on board. There were a lot of moving parts so the team needed to be on the same page.

"Guys, we don't have any solid leads on this case yet. The murder trail is cold. Actually, it's been cold from the start. I think the financial side may offer us the best way in. There's an odor to Jason Belvedere's secrecy regarding his business activities. I spoke with Lieutenant Hendricks the other day and he's of the opinion that it may be some sort of money laundering operation."

"Who does he think Belvedere's investors are?" asked Randy.

"He's got no idea at the moment. It could be anyone but it smells like mob or maybe drug money. The mob is always trying to get into main stream businesses and this would fit that. I'm going back to take a harder look at the files. I only glanced through them the other day. Chantal, I'd like you to come with me and take the research lead on this. And Randy, I know we're probably chasing ghosts but take a look at the murder again. I'm not questioning the earlier police work, just want some fresh eyes on it. When I was meeting with Detective Ronaldo the other day, he said that neither the town or county have any security cameras installed in Endicott. But I wonder if there's any cameras at our Lady of Good Counsel Church or Meals on Wheels across the street from the golf course. I didn't think to ask about it when I was with Detective Ronaldo and there may be other cameras on the street too."

"I'll check it out and also talk to a guy I know who's the Endicott town engineer. Maybe he has some ideas," replied Randy.

"Okay, Chantal and I will go back to Police Headquarters and dig into the case files. Maybe we can get lucky."

After the meeting, Alastair called Marion Belvedere.

"Mrs. Belvedere, we'll be happy to take the case and as I said before, we'll look at it incrementally. If we're making progress, we'll continue. If we're not making any progress, we may want to shut it down and not waste your money. Also, you can stop the investigation at any point. As we move forward, we will be sharing our findings with the police. Although we have no evidence at this point, we are of the opinion that your husband was probably operating outside of the law. Are you prepared for a less than positive outcome for him?" asked Alastair.

"I spoke to my son Steve about all of this and we're on the same page. Steve thinks he was killed by a professional hit man and that says a lot. I always felt uncomfortable with his business life. Shame on me for not speaking up sooner. But he was a good provider and I chose to look past it and ignore my concerns. Over the years we learned to live with it. When Jason was murdered, it all changed. For better or worse, Steve and I want to know the truth."

"Our first efforts will be to review the case files and one of my investigators will take another look at his murder. I'm not very hopeful about that side of it but we need to look at everything. Regarding the trust funds, what kind of information do you have about them?" asked Alastair.

"Well, I have the initial letter from the bank and monthly payment receipts."

"I need copies of them. Can I stop by later today and pick them up?"

"Actually, I'll be over your way today, I have a dental appointment nearby. I can drop them off if you like."

"That would be fine and also any other papers or correspondence you may have regarding your husband. At this point everything has value."

"Okay Mr. Stewart, I'll stop by in the early afternoon."

"Please call me Al, first names are a lot more comfortable."

"Oh yes," she replied, "first names for sure; please call me Marion."

When they finished, Alastair briefed Chantal on the trust fund information that Marion would be dropping off at the office in the afternoon. Alastair would be out. He finally had a meeting set up with Belvedere's lawyer, George Adamo who had handled his corporate affairs. When he initially called his office, he had been reluctant to meet with Alastair. Not an outright refusal but certainly not cooperative. Maybe he just didn't want to get involved or he was involved more deeply in Belvedere's business activities. He had worked for Jason Belvedere for ten years which meant that he had a significant amount of knowledge of the corporation filings. Names and addresses and maybe banking information. Alastair had to have this information to move the case forward. When he called Adamo again, the conversation was less than productive. Although it started out on friendly terms, it quickly degenerated into what Alastair called a slow-roll. Adamo was evasive and said he really hadn't had much to do with Belvedere over the years. After about fifteen minutes, Alastair got fed up with Adamo's tactics and pushed back.

"Look Mr. Adamo, we can do this one of two ways. One, you and I meet and have as the Japanese say a 'frank and sincere' conversation about the work you did for Jason Belvedere and provide access to the work. Or two, I'll go to the police and request they issue you a subpoena and we can deal with it at Police Headquarters. I've already met with them and have their support for my investigation. I'm not trying to threaten you sir, but we need to understand each other."

At this point, Alastair had Adamo's attention and the meeting was set for the afternoon. The lawyer's office was in a small office building on the Vestal Parkway across from a large car dealership. Both the reception area and his office were well appointed with modern furniture and decorations. Alastair had expected something more pedestrian and dated. *Maybe the guy has a reasonable practice,* he thought, *I may have misread him. I thought Belvedere was his main client but maybe not.*

Alastair started by explaining that he'd been retained by Marion Belvedere to take a new look at her husband's murder. He also told Adamo that he would be sharing his findings with the police. This seemed to set a more even tone for the meeting.

"I wasn't trying to avoid you earlier Mr. Stewart. Client confidentiality is always important, even if they're deceased. I've had a number of meetings with Detective Adams over the past year or so. I trust this information is available to you."

"It is. I had an initial look at the case files the other day and I'll be back at the police headquarters tomorrow with one of my investigators who handles our research. Can I be quite candid with you?"

"By all means."

"I respect your position on client confidentiality. We deal with the same thing at the agency. I also believe you answered Detective Adams questions truthfully but if he didn't ask the 'right question' so to say, you didn't volunteer any information. I probably would have done the same thing if I was in your position. However, I need to move past this and ask you questions that require more than a simple factual answer. I need your insight and thoughts. I believe Jason Belvedere was operating outside of the law or if not, certainly on the fringes. He lived a life of secrecy as far as his business dealings were concerned. His wife and son want to put this all behind them and need to know the truth about the man."

"Okay, ask your questions, I'll do my best."

"Specifically, what did you do for Jason Belvedere?"

"I handled the formation and dissolution of his development companies. Every development deal he put together had a separate company which would be active until the project was finished and then dissolved. All his investors were corporate entities; he had no identified private or personal investors. Once the development was finished, one or more of the investor companies would take over the operation of the developed property. If there were multiple investors, I believe that one of these investment companies would take the lead and the others would fall in line behind it. I never got involved with the formation of any of the investor companies on the projects. I only worked for Belvedere."

"How did Belvedere get paid?"

"Sometimes a fee was defined in his development company incorporation documents, other times not. When a payout was not identified in the incorporation documents, I assumed he had something worked out with his investors. I was never a part of that."

"Why the two different ways to get paid?" asked Alastair.

"Well sometimes banks were involved in the project. When that was the case, Belvedere's compensation was called out in the incorporation documents."

"Why?"

"The banks wanted a more complete disclosure. They were always subject to audits; so I suspect they insisted on Belvedere's compensation being disclosed. When it was one or two private companies, the incorporation documents were a lot simpler."

"Did you ever wonder about this?"

"Yeah, I did but I can't tell the man how to do business. I made sure my participation was up front and legal."

"But you did wonder about it all?"

"Yes," said George, "most of the banks were from Florida and he never had any development projects there. His projects never went south of Washington DC."

"What did you think about that?" asked Alastair.

"Usually, investment money is never too far away from the projects. Of itself it doesn't ring any alarm bells but with all of Belvedere's secrecy, it raises some questions."

"How did Belvedere pay you?"

"Monthly deposit to my office account."

"From a Florida bank?"

"Bingo, from Miami," said George.

"So, what do you think was going on?" asked Alastair.

"I have no proof and this is just my opinion but I think his investors were shady."

"Mob money?" asked Alastair.

"Could be anyone but clearly folks who don't want the rest of us to know much about them."

"A couple more questions George. Were you involved in the trust fund or payments to Mrs. Belvedere and her son?"

"Not at all. I got a call from a Miami bank about a year or so ago regarding the trust funds asking where Mrs. Belvedere and her son banked. I called them, got the information, and passed it on. Never heard from either party again."

"Did you tell this to the police?"

"No, it happened after they interviewed me. I didn't think it was important."

"Really? I would think they'd be very interested. Do you know if Belvedere kept an office around here?"

"Never came up. All of his development incorporation documents listed his Endicott address. I assumed he worked out of the house. He never mentioned an office and we always met here."

"Thanks for your time, George. I'd like to keep in touch; I'm sure we'll be talking again."

"No problem, call anytime."

Count on it George; you've more to tell, thought Alastair.

It was now fairly late in the day so Alastair decided to go back to the office, pick up Sherlock and take her to the dog park on the way home. He was looking forward to a quiet evening at home. Recently, he had started to read a series of detective stories by Donna Leon set in Venice, Italy and following the adventures of Comisario Guido Brunetti. They were great fun to read. Well written with tight plots. He also found a TV series based on her books produced by a German company. So, he would be watching the series set in Venice, spoken in German with English subtitles. Surprisingly, quite enjoyable. Who would know! The show was very well cast and fit the characters in the books. *I was in Venice once and loved it,* he thought, *maybe Marty and I can go there for our honeymoon?*

Chapter 10

Alastair was usually the first one to arrive at the office as it was not far from his house in Endwell and with only himself to look after, it was easy to be up and running early in the morning. Sherlock was always awake first and ready to go. She was familiar with his routine and would sit by his bed by six-thirty in the morning making small barking noises to wake him up. *No rest for the wicked,* he laughed to himself. He liked to get to the agency early and have the coffee ready when the others arrived. However this particular morning, Gil Jensen was already there and hunched over his computer.

"Be careful Gil, that thing might swallow you if you get too close."

"I need to get my eyes checked," said Gil, "after a bit of time on the screen, I need to keep moving in and out to keep it in focus."

"What brings you in so early today? Don't you have a meeting with the insurance company."

"I do, this afternoon. It's pretty much a status review. But this fraud case may not be as straightforward as we think. So far, I've only been looking at the one claim filed here. However, I found another one filed in Carbondale, Pennsylvania about two years ago, almost identical to this one. Same MO, a van used in the guy's heating and air conditioner business full of expensive tools and test equipment was stolen, never recovered."

"How do you know it's connected to our guy here in town."

"Simple, it's Marcel, his brother!"

"Wow, how did you find that out?" exclaimed Alastair.

"I just stumbled on it. I was talking to one of Adam's customers and he mentioned that he had a brother in Carbondale who was also a heating and air conditioning contractor. I called, Fred Dublonsky in Scranton and asked him to take a look at it. He checked the guy out and found the claim from two years ago. But it gets better!"

"Oh?" replied Alastair.

"The guy is still in business and driving an eight-year-old van, not a newer one you would expect him to buy with the settlement money. Fred managed to check the VIN number while the guy was at a diner having breakfast. Guess what?"

"I think I can see this coming," laughed Alastair.

"Yep, same VIN number as the van reported stolen on his claim. He probably had the van hidden somewhere until the claim was settled."

"Wouldn't the insurance companies and Department of Motor Vehicles coordinate with each other regarding VIN numbers?"

"I don't know yet. Fred is looking into how Pennsylvania and the insurance companies handle this. However, it looks like the brothers Marcel and Adam Burris, ace heating and air conditioner contractors have found a way through this. I bet the same thing is going on here. Adam Burris is hiding the van somewhere until the claim is cleared."

"Same insurance company?" asked Alastair.

"Yes, Northeast Insurance and Indemnity," replied Gil, "

"Take a look around and see if you can get an idea of where Adam Burris might be hiding the van, but don't put yourself at risk. Maybe we can get lucky. Once we contact the insurance company, I'm sure they'll bring in the police. Nice work Gil."

Gil was not sure how to try and find out where Burris might have hidden his van, if that was actually the case. So, the best way forward was to speak with Chantal who had just arrived at work. She was the best researcher at the agency.

"I think the guy I'm looking at in my insurance fraud investigation filed a false claim that his van and work tools were stolen. He has a brother in Pennsylvania who worked the same scam about two years ago. I think my guy is hiding his van until the claim settles and he can collect the pay-out. Then the van will appear again. That's what his brother did. I'm trying to find out where he might hide it. I can check around his house and business but I doubt he'd be dumb enough to hide it in one of those places. I'm wondering if he had a second home or vacation place where he could stash the van. Any idea where to start on this?"

"Why did the insurance company ask us to look into this in the first place," asked Chantal.

"Seems our boy has a long history of filing claims for one thing or another. The current one is fairly large and the insurance company is not comfortable with it."

"Makes sense," replied Chantal, "if he has a second property in New York, we should be able to find it from his tax records. If it's not in New York State, it gets harder as we have to look at other records and filings. Ask Fred Doblonsky to take a look around his brother's place. He could have stashed it there."

"Good call, never thought of that."

"I'll check the tax records here and you turn Fred on to do the same thing in Pennsylvania," she said, "let's see what it gives us, we can sort out the next steps after that. I don't think these guys are very smart, it's probably in one of those places. Tell Fred to check both the city and county tax records in Pennsylvania. Start local and branch out if nothing shows up."

Gil called Fred on his mobile and found him at the library branch near his home finishing up some work for Alastair.

"I can get to this the day after tomorrow, I gotta finish this project Al has me on."

"That'll work, Chantal is running the brother's tax records here. Once we get this finished, we'll pass it on to the insurance company. I guess they'll call in the cops."

"Count on it. They'll also try to recover the past settlements from both of them. These guys will never see this coming. Surprise, surprise! Nobody will ever sell them another insurance policy and then you have the criminal part of this. They're toast! Happy hunting Gil, back to you soon."

Chapter 11

Alastair, Chantal, and Randy met in Alastair's office to review the Belvedere case. They sat in the corner of the office in the comfortable chairs around the low glass topped table, their morning coffees in hand. Chantal had baked some cookies for her boys the night before and had brought some to the office. Marion Belvedere had dropped off her trust fund information the previous day, so Chantal had an opportunity to look it over. After the meeting, Alastair and Chantal were going to police headquarters to look deeper into the case files. They were not looking for anything specific, just a trail to follow. Randy would be meeting with the Endicott town engineer in the afternoon to see what he could tell them about security cameras around town if any.

"Okay let's start with the trust fund material. Chantal, what does it look like?"

"Well, the monthly receipts are pretty standard. The money is paid into her account at Key Bank in Endicott from a bank in Miami called Third Dominion Bank. I think it's a regional bank, never heard the name before. I don't know if the money originates there or is an onward transfer from somewhere else. I met with her briefly when she dropped off the information. She said her son Steve has the same arrangement with his bank. She said it's TD Bank."

"Will the banks talk to you?" asked Randy.

"I'm sure the local ones will. We already have that information; they're just a deposit station. The Miami bank is a different story. We may need some support from Lieutenant Hendricks but I'll try them on my own first."

"What's your day look like Randy?" asked Alastair.

"I'm going to meet Ollie Henderson. We went to school together. He's worked for the town since graduation. I've driven up and down Main Street a number of times and I'm sure there are security cameras in some of the businesses. There's Key Bank, a large auto repair shop and a United Health Care Walk-In which appear to have cameras. There may even be some cameras from houses along the street. The problem is that even if there are security cameras, we're looking for footage that's well over a year and a half old. I don't think anybody keeps their data that long. The town doesn't have any cameras except at the town office and that's no help. So, all in, a bit of a fishing expedition. Maybe Ollie can turn me on to something else."

"Do you think it's worth the effort?" asked Chantal.

"It's an easy trip and I've not seen Ollie for a bit so maybe just a social call. But you guys know the game, 'if you don't go fishing, you don't catch anything.' "

"We have to keep looking and see if something opens up. I'm encouraged by the trust fund information. Maybe we can get closer to Belvedere's pot of gold," laughed Alastair.

"Al, what if we do find his money, will Marion and her son Steve inherit it," asked Randy.

"Good question; I don't really know. Maybe the money is 'dirty' and would not pass to them. Sort of like fruit from the poisoned tree. That term usually means evidence illegally obtained, but the analogy is similar to money illegally obtained or made from investing it. Sort of like robbing a bank and giving the money to the Salvation Army or some other charity; they can't keep it. We just don't know where the money is coming from to make the call yet. I think the accountants will take a long hard look at it all. But first we have to find the money."

They spent a little more time talking about other open cases at the agency and then were on their way: Alastair and Chantal to police headquarters and Randy headed over to the Endicott town offices to meet Ollie Henderson. Chantal would call the Miami bank from police headquarters. She wanted to wait until mid-morning as calls to banks early in their day were not usually productive in her opinion. When they arrived at police headquarters, Todd Adams met them at the reception. They signed in and went to the conference room next to Lieutenant Hendricks office. All the files were stacked on a roller cart in the corner of the conference room waiting for them.

"Let me get you guys a cup of coffee and maybe we can talk for a bit before you start. Tony and I are happy you all are taking a look at the case. We could never catch a break." Tony's in court this morning.

"I can understand not catching a break," said Alastair, "after speaking with Belvedere's attorney, his wife and taking a quick look at the files. I don't really see an obvious way forward. I think you guys may have been blindsided by the trust fund Marion and her son have. George Adamo didn't tell you, and I don't think Marion Belvedere intentionally withheld the information. We know the money comes in monthly to their local banks from a Miami bank named Third Dominion. We don't know if the account resides with them or if they're also a transfer station. We're going to try and run that down today and may need a bit of muscle from you to get them to talk."

"Sure, let us know what we can do," replied Todd, "money coming out of Miami sounds a bit unusual for an Endicott guy."

"Maybe he likes remote banking?" laughed Chantal.

Alastair and Chantal spent the better part of the day reviewing the files which were clear and well documented. They didn't find any missing threads or neglected areas. They couldn't find any areas that needed to be revisited. *We've got to find a new path,* thought Alastair, *plowing old fields is not going to get us anywhere.* Late in the afternoon, they decided to call it a day. They stopped by Todd's office to thank him and Tony for their support and headed back to

Endwell. Randy had not called in and Gil was in Scranton meeting with Fred Dublonsky on the insurance fraud case so they didn't expect to see anyone. However, when they got to the office, they found Randy sitting in reception drinking a cup of coffee.

"I've got something stronger back in my office if you need a lift," said Alastair.

"No this will do it for now. I'm just beat; been a long day."

"Any joy?" asked Chantal.

"Well, no and maybe yes."

"How so?"

"I checked with the bank, auto repair shop and the United Health Care Walk-In. They all have cameras and in fact the auto repair shop has the best installation. But nobody keeps the surveillance info more than a year. Whatever, they may have had is long gone. By the way, nothing at Our Lady of Good Counsel Church and Meals on Wheels across the street from the parking lot."

"So that's it?" asked Alastair.

"Maybe not," replied Randy, "do you guys remember the hit and run at the intersection of Main Street and Grippen Street right near the golf course? It happened around two years ago."

"Sort of," replied Chantal, "didn't a kid get killed?"

"Yeah. That intersection had been an accident hot spot for years. They tried to get by with a stop sign on Grippen Street but it never worked. The traffic was too strong on Main Street. After the lad was killed, the town and County decided to install traffic lights and pedestrian crossing walks. Part of the project was to do a proper audit of the intersection. The company doing the work installed video cameras and traffic strips on the road to record the traffic throughout the day and night. The County had a similar project going with the same company over on the west side of Binghamton so they just added Grippen Street onto their project. When Ollie and I checked the dates for their work, it coincided with Belvedere's murder. Here's where it gets interesting, Ollie thinks there's a regulation that the company that did the analysis has to keep the traffic data for five years. Something to do with liability issues if there's another accident. From what Ollie told me, it seems they had cameras installed in both directions on Main Street and Grippen Street."

"So, four camera angles and this company may still have the traffic data?" asked Alastair.

"Ollie called the engineer he worked with back then and is waiting on a call-back. He was out on a job and wouldn't be back in the office for the rest of the day. The intersection is close to the parking lot so maybe we can get some coverage assuming the company has the data."

"Who are the guys who did the analysis of the intersection?" asked Chantal.

"Empire Traffic Analytics. They're located just outside of Horseheads near Corning, not too far from us. They've been around for a long time. We should know something pretty soon. So, what did the Miami bank have to say?"

Chantal hadn't had time to call the bank in Miami when they were downtown at police headquarters. The review of the case files took a lot longer than planned and it did not make too much sense to call a bank late in the day.

"I'll get onto the bank tomorrow and see what they can tell us."

By this time, it was getting close to six o'clock and everyone was ready to call it a day.

"Let's get out of here," said Alastair, "we can slay the dragons tomorrow and I need to pick up Sherlock at my sister's. So, we've got two balls in play, the Miami bank, and Empire Traffic Analytics. Let's see where we can take this."

"What's on tap for you tonight?" asked Chantal.

"I'm still streaming the Donna Leon detective series set in Venice, Italy. I'll watch one or two of them tonight. The main character, Detective Guido Brunetti is the best, we gotta hire him. He always catches all the bad boys!"

"Wow, Endwell Investigations with offices in New York and Venice Italy, how cool is that!" laughed Randy.

Chapter 12

Gil had decided to go to Scranton to meet with Fred Dublonsky and see what luck he had checking out Adam's brother Marcel. He couldn't find a vacation property for Adam Burris so; it looked like there was no second location to hide the truck and equipment in New York. Adam had a garage on his property in the town of Union next to Binghamton which he used to store his work tools, equipment, and his truck. Gil was able to see inside the garage one day when the doors were open but the truck was not there. He could be hiding it with a friend but Gil thought this was too risky and he would keep it in the family.

Gill called Fred and the two men agreed to meet in Carbondale, Pennsylvania where Adam's brother Marcel's business was located. Fred had finished his research assignment for Alastair so he asked Gil to take the files and data back to the agency.

"There are two large boxes Gil and much easier for me if you can take them back. You can be the office courier."

"Great, I've been looking to move up in the organization!"

"I'm waiting on a call-back from my contact in the County Tax office. They don't have the tax data for Carbondale online so he has to do some digging but I should have the information pretty soon. Carbondale is a nice little town, nothing like it's coal mining name. I know a good restaurant there, all home cooking. I'll buy you lunch, then we can drive by Marcel's place and see what's happening.

"I'm sort of partial to the food that comes in frozen on a truck and finished off in a microwave oven. You can eat the food and the packaging too; it all tastes the same, laughed Gil."

"I know what you mean, reminds me of soggy French fries in reheated grease from the fast food joints."

The drive from Endwell to Carbondale, north of Scranton was an easy run. Gil got off I-81 south about fifteen miles from Scranton, then used county roads for the rest. They met at Sisko's Restaurant on Main Street about eleven thirty, ahead of the lunch crowd. Fred was already there nursing a cup of coffee. Gil thought highly of Fred. His experience as a detective with the Scranton Police Department and approach to working a case was impressive. Fred was a skilled detective and Alastair gave him as much work as he wanted.

"Al has me looking into a CPA firm in Scranton that may be cooking the books for a few companies. Two here and one up your way. I'm pretty much finished with my work on it."

"Are you an accountant too?" asked Gil.

"Hell no; just doing some basic research on the CPA firm and the companies in question. Al is interested in the entries for various costs associated with the companies here. Looks like they're being used as dummy accounts for some expenses so I've been working on a spread sheet for him to show the companies and amounts charged and cross-checking lots of tax records. It's a lot of detail work, not my strong suit. I don't really know what the CPA firm is up to but it sure has an odor.

"You mean the companies don't know they're being used?"

"I don't really know: we're in the early stages. At this point, it looks like their names are showing up on the books of other companies as expenses. It may be they're trying to play some game with the IRS like claiming phony expenses. Al may be getting close to opening an investigation."

"Who turned the agency on?"

"One of the law firms in Binghamton. Apparently, one of the companies suspected that they're being compromised. I don't really know much more about it than that."

The two men talked about other cases being handled by the agency and then ordered the lunch special; homemade split pea soup and a meatloaf sandwich.

"Gil, this is an important question and will impact our relationship in the future. Think carefully before you answer. Are you a ketchup or mustard guy with meatloaf?" asked Fred.

"Has to be ketchup," laughed Gil.

"Amen! You have excellent taste my boy. By the way, I got a call this morning from my contact regarding property owned by Marcel Burris here. Seems he only has his house and garage. No vacation home, at least not in Pennsylvania. We'll snoop around his place after lunch."

"I don't think Adam would hide the truck with a friend," said Gil, "seems sort of risky."

"You're probably right, let's see what the house and garage look like."

It was a short drive over to Marcel's place. The house and garage were on a large lot on the edge of the town, with views over the surrounding countryside. Almost a rural setting. This was common in the small towns. Once you left them, it was pretty much open country. There were two other houses near Marcel's place, also on large lots. Marcel had a three-bay garage, with a long driveway leading from the road. Over the garage there was a simple sign that said 'Marcel Burris, Heating and Air Conditioning' along with a telephone number.

"Seems sort of silly having that sign over the garage," laughed Fred, "what's he trying to do, capture the walk-in traffic?"

Two of the overhead garage door were open and they could see a light on and somebody moving inside the garage. It was hard to get a good look inside as the garage was set off of the driveway so the viewing angle was not optimal.

They drove onto the property and Fred parked near the garage. "Stay here Gil, I'm going to talk to whoever is inside. I'll say I'm looking at some property around here and will need some electrical and heating work soon. It'll give me a chance to look around the garage a bit."

Damn, thought Gil, *I would have never thought of that.*

When Fred entered the garage, a young lad was working at a bench off to the side installing a fan in what appeared to be a rectangular heating duct. Fred called out from the door as he didn't want to scare him.

"Excuse me, I'm looking for Mr. Burris, is he around?"

"Sorry, he's out on a job and won't be back until late in the afternoon. Can I help?"

"I'm looking at buying some property near here and wonder if Mr. Burris has time to take on some work. It won't be for a few months. I saw your door open as I was driving by and thought I'd stop in and ask."

"I'm sure he can, but best call him. The number on the sign outside is good."

As they were talking Fred casually looked around the garage. It was fairly large and had space for three or more vehicles. At the back was a white GM panel truck that was modified with a roof rack to hold ladders and piping. On the side was a sign saying 'Burris Heating and Air Conditioning.' No first name. But it had a telephone number and the area code was 607. *Bingo* thought Fred, *that's Gil's area code.* Fred did not want to take any more time and risk being caught snooping, he had what he needed and had also managed to get a picture from his cell phone by pretending he was making a call. When he got back to their car, he was all smiles.

"It's there Gil, and I got a picture. I think you've got all you need now. The case is a wrap! Al will contact the insurance company and they'll take the next steps. They'll be happy campers. We got them both!"

From there, the two men went to Fred's house to pick up the boxes to take to the agency. As they were driving back to Fred's house, Gil sent Alastair a text letting him know they had wrapped up the insurance fraud investigation.

"You know, I learned a lot today about investigations. You broke the case wide open going into the garage and getting that picture. I never would have thought about that approach."

"Private eyes can do things the cops can't do. Makes the work a little easier," laughed Fred.

When Gil got back to Endwell, he stopped by the office to drop off the boxes and found Alastair and Sherlock still there. It was close to six o'clock.

"Al, you're putting in some overtime," laughed Gil, "bucking for a promotion?"

"Just trying to wrap up some work on the Miller arson case. We closed it last week and I need to finish the report so we can bill the client. Your text sounded good, got all you need to finish the case?"

"Sure do, Fred is so clever. He got a picture of Adam's van in his brother's garage. I'll write it all up tomorrow. Do we also report this to the cops?"

"No, the insurance company will run with it. They'll deal with the cops. We may be called to provide testimony later on. Looks like you caught bad boys on both ends; the insurance company will be happy with your work."

"Don't forget Fred, he got the picture of the van and that sealed the deal."

"Fred's a good detective; wish we had him here full time."

Chapter 13

Over the weekend, Randy got a call from Ollie Henderson, the Endicott town engineer.

"You want to go to Horseheads next week and look at some movies?"

"You mean they've got surveillance video on the date of the murder?"

"Yeah, but I don't know how good it is. It could be a lot of crappy beat up tapes or discs. The camera angle wasn't set for the golf course so I really don't know if it's worth anything but there were four cameras involved. One looking each way on the two streets. We gotta look at it and you make the call. The good news is it's well organized as to time and date so we should be able to go right to the day and time in question."

"Let's do it! When do you want to go?"

"Has to be Monday," said Ollie, "My guy will be available then and I need him to walk us through all the stuff. That's why I'm calling you on the weekend. He's on travel for the rest of the week after Monday."

"I'll meet you at your office at seven on Monday," replied Randy, "I'll stop by The Bagel Factory near the Price Chopper in Johnson City and get some coffee and bagels. Road warriors need to be well fed!"

Randy sent Alastair and Chantal a text message letting them know he would be at Empire Traffic Analytics in Horseheads on Monday looking at security footage near the golf course. *Back in the hunt,* thought Randy.

That Monday Chantal called Third Dominion Bank in Miami to see what she could find out about the monthly trust payments to Marion and Steve Belvedere. As she anticipated the bank was less than helpful. A call from an out of State private investigator did not get their attention or cooperation. *Okay,* she thought, *you guys are definitely off my Christmas card list, time to move on.* She called Detective Adams to see if they would be more forthcoming to the Binghamton Police. Todd called back later in the morning to let her know he didn't get much further.

"I got the usual litany of customer privacy concerns and the bank's strict adherence to policy. Sort of yada, yada, yada," he laughed. "End of this sad tale is we'll probably have to get a subpoena to get them moving. I can get started on that today."

"Sit on it for a bit," replied Chantal, "let me talk to Al. I want to be sure how hard he wants to push it at this time."

She found Alastair in his office finalizing his plane reservations to Fort Walton Beach to visit Emi's family and visit her grave.

"Al, the bank blew me off. I probably would have had better luck trying to sell them the Brooklyn Bridge. Todd also made a run on them and was told to get a subpoena before they would take any action. How do you want to play this?"

Alastair sat quietly for a few minutes thinking about options. The subpoena would take some time. Although the DA could issue it quickly, he felt the bank would drag their feet responding to it. They needed to get the bank's attention.

"You know, I'm headed to Fort Walton Beach later in the week to visit with Emi's parents. It's a reasonable ride to Miami. I still know some guys in the FBI field office there and my old boss is retired and still lives in the area. I'll make a few calls. Maybe it's time to visit some old friends and see if they can help in getting the bank to cooperate. Nothing like a call from the BBI to help get things moving."

"BBI?" asked Chantal.

"That was what my wife Emi used to call us back in the day," laughed Alastair, "It stands for Big Bureau of Investigation. It always made me laugh."

Alastair called his old boss, Chris Collins. When Alastair was with the FBI back then, Chris had been worried about retirement and what he would do. His children had stayed in the Miami area after graduating from college so he and his wife wanted to be near them. Chris and Alastair had discussed a number of career options after retirement but that's not where Chris ended up. He took a completely different path. One that was not in his game plan. The week after he retired, he got a call from a company looking for consulting services on security issues for both their computer systems and buildings. His years at the FBI served him well. He knew where to go to find the talent to address the company's needs. It was a great fit and from there his business grew. He brought people into his company who were experts in security and computer issues; a tight knit organization was in place. Chris Collins Security Consultants or CC Security as they were known in the business was well respected and the company was expanding to other southern States.

"Al, come down to Miami on Sunday and come over for dinner. I'll set up a meeting at the field office for Monday and you can head back north on Monday night or Tuesday morning. I'll pick you up at the airport."

I have a rental car booked. I'll be in Fort Walton Beach on Friday visiting Emi's parents. I'll get an early start and drive to Miami on Sunday; thanks for the help setting up the meeting."

"Easy to do. The new office chief, Gordon Marella, is a good friend, he'll be happy to meet you. You know they still talk about you in the office. I was still on the job when you found the shooter who killed Emi and the baby. I remember you said you found him in a hospice in New Jersey. I told the guys about it during a staff meeting and everyone stood up and started clapping. It was quite emotional."

"Thanks Chris, I'm hoping that the FBI can punch the bank in the nose and get some cooperation. The bank by the way is called Third Dominion. They have branches in south Florida."

"I know the name. They were on our radar at different times when I was there. We suspected they were involved with a couple of banks in the Caribbean moving money around."

"You mean money laundering?" asked Alastair.

"We thought so and had them audited a couple of times but couldn't nail it. Money was coming out of the Caribbean to Third Dominion but by then it was all corporate company transfers, not individuals. At that time we were up to our ears with a big racketeering case and did not have the horses to continue chasing the bank so it was put on the back burner. I'm not sure if Gordon is doing anything with it these days."

After the call, Alastair briefed Chantal and asked her to call Detective Adams. *If the FBI can't light a fire under these guys, we can always get a subpoena,* he thought.

"This is great Al, maybe a way forward?"

"I hope so, the banks always want to stay on the sunny side with the FBI. When you call Todd, also let him know that Randy may have found some video of Main and Grippen Street near the golf course. He'll be checking it out today."

As they were wrapping up their conversation Gil came into the office.

"Al, I finished the report on the insurance fraud investigation. I'll leave it with you to review."

"Happy to take a look at it. I let you know when I'm finished and you can take it over to their office."

"Don't you want to do it?"

'Not a chance. You did all the work; time for a victory lap!"

This was typical of Alastair. He could have easily taken Gil's report and briefed the insurance company on their findings but he chose to let Gil get the credit. *He's a good kid,* thought Alastair, *I don't want to steal his thunder. Northeast Insurance and Indemnity don't know how successful this investigation has been. We have one brother for the recent bogus claim and now the other brother for the past claim. Gil made all this happen; time to shine!*

"When you meet with them, I expect they'll have the regional manager and his investigator at the meeting. Make sure you're comfortable with everything in the report. I can imagine these guys asking a lot of questions especially when they find out you've connected his brother to the claim. You hit a home run my man."

"Should we send them a copy of our findings ahead of the meeting?"

"Yeah, that's a good idea. This is much bigger than they're expecting. Also, put together a brief Power Point presentation to summarize the findings. That will help them understand the case. The fact that Marcel was hiding the van in Carbondale for Adam is important, it ties the brothers together. Also, Marcel's van was never stolen, he still has it and uses it. Interesting days ahead for the Burris brothers."

Gil was pumped! He was the lead on the investigation and now would close it out with the client. *How good is this* he thought, *When I first came here, I had no idea of where this job would lead me.*

Chapter 14

Randy was early picking up Ollie at his office. Two bagels, medium size cups of coffee in hand and ready to go. On the way over to Horseheads, the two men talked about the traffic cameras and what they might show. It was a lucky break that the intersection analysis and upgrade had been going on at the time of Belvedere's murder. Randy had not been successful in finding any other cameras on the street that had retained data from the time of Belvedere's murder and had mixed feelings about their prospects with the traffic cameras from Empire Traffic Analytics. Those had been trained mainly on the intersection so he didn't think they'd have a large field of view. But they couldn't ignore anything at this point.

"Don't jump off the ledge yet," said Ollie, "I know they were mounted fairly high off the ground to get coverage of the intersection and approaching traffic. Maybe the field is bigger than you think."

"I hope so," replied Randy, "the businesses on the street were a bust. Cameras yes, but they didn't have any data we could use."

The drive to Horseheads took well over an hour as the traffic through Elmira was slow due to road works. When they arrived, they parked in a visitor's slot in the front of a standalone two-story building in a small industrial park. Gerry Bachand the lead engineer met them at the reception desk in the lobby. He and Ollie had not seen each other for a while so they caught up on their work and local news as Gerry took them back to the lab.

"Let me explain what we've set up for you guys," said Gerry, "Main Street runs east and west and Grippen street north and south.

When we did the intersection analysis, we set up four cameras so we could look in each direction independently. I'll run them all on the same time clock so you'll see how the traffic flows at the intersection. Take your time looking at this and you make the call on which cameras offer the best coverage. As the golf course is west of the intersection and on the left side of Main Street, I think you'll be interested in Grippen Street looking south and Main Street looking west."

After looking at the video streams for a few minutes, Randy decided that they wanted both directions on Main Street in case they spotted something interesting and wanted to follow it for a bit. Gerry was right; Grippen street south and Main Street west gave them the best look at the golf course parking lot.

"So," Gerry said, "three cameras in play; what time of day are you interested in?"

"We're pretty sure Belvedere was whacked later in the afternoon, but let's run the cameras from twelve o'clock just in case it was earlier," replied Randy."

"I can speed them up so you don't spend the rest of your life here," said Gerry, "The cameras are all synced to a joy stick so the time line stays the same for each camera. You can also back them up if you want to look at something again."

"Can we zoom in on anything?" asked Randy.

"You can, but you need to freeze the frame. I'm not sure how good the pictures will be, as it was wasn't needed in our analysis so I suspect it may not be the best resolution. I can have one of the techs take a look at it if you do decide to zoom in, maybe we can enhance the image, if needed. Why don't you play around with the system for a bit to get the hang of using it while I make a phone call and then we can zero in on the date and time you're interested in."

Randy and Ollie spent the next twenty minutes getting used to the system and displays. It was pretty straight forward although the joy stick was very sensitive and it seemed to go from slow to take-off speed in a heartbeat. After a while, they had it under control.

When Gerry came back, he said, "Okay guys, cleared for launch?"

"Yeah," replied Ollie, "I think we're in good shape. We only crashed twice!"

Gerry entered the date and time and they were off on the hunt. Nothing much happened until three in the afternoon. Randy recognized Jason Belvedere's SUV as it came down Grippen Street and turned right onto Main Street followed by a quick left into the parking lot of the golf course.

"Shit!" said Randy, "the trees along the side there are blocking a good view of his car. I can't see the driver's side. Neither the Grippen Street or Main Street camera gives a complete view. Damn, damn, damn."

"The cameras are set to look straight down the streets so I'm not surprised that anything in the lot or off to the sides might be compromised. Sorry guys, but we have to work with what we have. Let's keep looking, said Gerry."

"You're right, I was looking for a home run," said Randy, "we may struggle to get a single in this game."

About fifteen minutes after Jason Belvedere came into the lot, a black Lincoln Aviator came down Main Street, went through the intersection and turned into the parking lot. It pulled up next to Jason Belvedere's car.

"Hey, can we get that plate number?" asked Ollie.

"Sure, freeze the frame at the intersection. You'll get a good look at that point," replied Gerry.

They easily read the plate, a Pennsylvania registration. The license plate had a frame around it showing the dealership where it was purchased. Ray Price Lincoln, Stroudsburg, Pennsylvania. Unfortunately, like Belvedere's SUV, they couldn't see much of the

Lincoln either when it parked in the lot. Pretty much the same situation as with Belvedere's SUV. They could see the back but not much more. Shortly after the Lincoln parked next to Belvedere, they saw a figure walk behind the Lincoln and go up between the two cars and stop by Belvedere's window. They couldn't see a clean picture but they could see that he was at Belvedere's- window and had reached into his car. Then, he quickly came back around again, got in his car, and drove away.

"That's when he killed Belvedere" said Randy, "let's slow everything down and see what we can get. Maybe frame by frame and zooming will give us something."

When the shooter walked behind his car, Randy and Ollie could not get a good look at this face. They went frame by frame but no joy. His face was obscured by the trees. But they could see that he was on the short side. He was wearing a yellow short sleeve polo shirt. In some of the frames, they could see something on his right arm. Possibly a tattoo. They couldn't make it out but clearly, he had something on his forearm.

When the shooter left the parking lot, he turned right onto Main Street heading east and joined two cars waiting at the Main Street and Grippen Street intersection for the light to change. When the light changed, they were ablet to get a look at the driver's side of the Lincoln from the Grippen Street camera. His window was down as he threw out a cigarette butt and they got a good profile view of him as he started to drive through the intersection. Black hair and probably in his early forties. Not a kid for sure. And then, for whatever reason, maybe traffic or someone crossing the street. he turned and looked down Grippen Street. This gave Randy and Ollie a full-face shot.

"There you are!" exclaimed Randy, "we've got your sorry ass!"

"This is great Gerry," said Randy. Although we didn't see him shoot Belvedere, we can connect all the dots and it's compelling.

High fives all around the room!" he laughed, "Gerry, can I have a copies of the good stuff?"

"Sure, I'll get one of the techs and you tell him what you want. Pretty easy to do. I'll also give you a letter explaining where the video came from in case you end up submitting this as evidence or something like that."

"Good idea, this will end up with the Binghamton cops and who knows where it will lead. They're frying some pretty big fish on this one."

Randy sent Alastair a short text message. *'Got the shooter; back in the office in a couple of hours. You're going to like this Al. I made copies of the interesting stuff.'* He and Ollie hadn't had lunch and both were quite hungry so they stopped at The Blue Dolphin Diner in Apalachin for a quick lunch on the way back to Endwell Investigations. Randy was a creature of habit and always ordered the same lunch. Tuna toasted on whole wheat, tomato, and no lettuce. Ollie was more adventuresome checking out the lunch specials.

As they ate lunch, Randy exclaimed, "Ollie, this is great. If you hadn't remembered the traffic analysis, we would never have found it. Talk about catching a break. You're the man!"

"Glad I could help. Who would know that some road work could play such an important part in your investigation. I guess I shouldn't say anything yet about what we found?"

"Yeah, please keep this close-held. This is an active investigation. When you get back to your office, please call Gerry and thank him again for all his help and also ask him to keep this quiet for now."

Chapter 15

Northeast Insurance and Indemnity is located in downtown Binghamton near the County Courts on Hawley Street. It's an older building dating to the 1970s. Gil had chosen to dress carefully today in a suit and tie as they were a new client and he didn't want to take any chances with a dress code. When he arrived around ten o'clock on a rainy Monday morning, the receptionist called Adrian Hall, the regional manager to let him know Gil had arrived. As is the style these days, Adrian's office attire was business casual.

When the two men looked at each other Adrian broke into a broad smile and said, "even stodgy old insurance companies have made the change to a more casual business attire. Look at me, mid-fifties and riding the wave," he laughed.

"I wasn't sure Mr. Hall, and didn't want to take any chances."

"You look fine Mr. Jensen; follow me, I have a room full of people waiting to meet you."

They went into a large conference room with leather chairs and a large mahogany and walnut veneer conference table. Seated around it were ten people. Gil didn't know what to make of the number and wondered who they all were. Adrian assumed the role of master of ceremonies and introduced Gil to the multitude. A little bit of everything as it turned out, lawyers, investigators, accountants, and claims adjusters.

Adrian started out the meeting, "Your findings were quite a surprise to us. We initially thought we were dealing with a questionable claim based on the history of his prior claims but you've opened up a much more comprehensive pattern of fraud. Our compliments to Endwell Investigations for pulling this all together. Please walk us through your investigation. We're curious as to how it all unfolded."

Gil had anticipated a series of specific questions from his report but it seemed that the group was more interested in the mechanics of the investigation.

"I have a short power point presentation of about eight slides that summarize our investigation. You have it all in much more detail in our report, but let me go through the slides first so we're all on the same page and then I'll talk about how we ended up with much more than we expected. *The presentation took about fifteen minutes and did not elicit any questions from the group. I guess they bought into everything* thought Gil, *they're more interested in the boots on the ground side of it.* When he finished, Adrian said, "so tell us how this all unfolded. As you mentioned, I'm sure it's all in your report but we want to hear it from the detective in charge."

Hey, thought Gil, *detective in charge, that's me!*

"When we started, we were only looking at Adam Burris as that was our mandate from your company. We looked into his tax records and work history and found that he'd done some work for the city and county so there were good records to review. He had a viable business and it seemed to be stable. We reviewed all his prior claims against your company and felt that there were quite a lot of them which seemed out of the ordinary. Although the vehicle and tools were reported stolen, we didn't believe it. We thought he might have hidden them somewhere. A check of the county tax records didn't show a second property where he could have hidden the truck and we didn't think he would hide it with a friend as that would be too risky.

At that point we were still on a fishing expedition so to say, trying to open up the case. We didn't have any concrete evidence. We spoke with a number of heating and air conditioner contractors in town to see if they could provide any information about Adam Burris and also spoke with past clients when we could find them. During one of these conversations, it was mentioned that Burris has a brother in Carbondale, Pennsylvania who was in the same business. We didn't think much of it at that time, just a data point, but I asked Fred Doblonsky, our investigator in Scranton to check out his brother Marcel. Candidly, we didn't think he had any role in the claim. That's when we came back to you to see if you provided any insurance coverage to Marcel Burris. Turns out you did and Marcel had filed an identical claim about four years ago with your office in Wilkes Barre, Pennsylvania. When Fred was checking out Marcel, he noticed that his truck was about eight years old which was surprising as you had previously settled his claim for a stolen van and tools. Wouldn't he buy a new one or at least a later model van? Fred was able to check the VIN number on the van when Marcel was in a diner; a quick photo shot through the front window of the truck with his mobile phone camera. The VIN was on a metal tab on top of the dashboard of the truck in the left corner. When we ran the VIN, we found out that it was the same van he had reported stolen.

By this time Gil had everyone's attention. No questions from the group; they were all ears!

Gil continued, "we decided to take a closer look at Marcel thinking that he had a role in Adam's claim. We checked to see if he had a second property where he could have hidden Adam's van but could not find one. Marcel's business in Carbondale, is just outside of town and has a large garage next to his house where he keeps his van and tools. Along with our investigator from Scranton, we went to Marcel's place to look around the property. Fred spoke to a young lad working in the garage. He told him he was looking to buy some property nearby and asked if Marcel might be available to do some work on the house in a month or so. While he was in the garage, Fred noticed a van parked in the back of the garage with the company name Burris Heating and Air Conditioning. It didn't have Adam's name on the van but it had a telephone number, with our 607-area code. So, we had found Adam's van. Fred pretended he had to make a phone call and stepped away from the workbench where the young lad was working and was able to get a picture of the van. Adam was hiding the van in his brother's garage and claiming it was stolen."

When Gil finished, the room was quiet for a bit and then one of the investigators spoke. "This is a great outcome; we rarely get these kinds of results. Are you satisfied with the outcome? Are there any loose ends to tie up?"

"Well, there's a disconnect here that we don't fully understand yet. It appears that both brothers reported their vehicles stolen to the police and to Northeast Insurance and Indemnity. We don't understand how Marcel could register a stolen vehicle. You would think that the VIN number would be cross-checked by the Department of Motor Vehicles against VIN numbers of stolen vehicles when you register a vehicle. It seems as if this was treated as another registration by the DMV and there wasn't any cross-checking between the police and DMV."

"You mean it fell through the cracks?" asked Adrian.

"We don't know for sure at this point. I think you need to discuss this with the police when you present the case to them," said Gil, "for sure it was a new registration, Fred checked the plates on Marcel's van and they were new, not the same plates when the van was supposedly stolen."

"Do you think Adam and Marcel knew about this possible loophole regarding coordination between the police and DMV," asked one of the attorneys.

"I don't think they knew anything about the protocols between the police and DMV," said Gil. "I've not spoken with the Burris brothers but from what Fred and I observed, I wouldn't put them at the head of the class. I think Marcel filed a claim in Pennsylvania and got lucky. Then a few years later, brother Adam in New York tries the same scam."

"You're probably right," said Adrian, "but we have a problem and need to sort it out quickly. We always check the police reports to make sure there is a record of a of a stolen vehicle before we settle a claim, but I wonder do we need to do more? We have no access to DMV registration information unless we ask for it on a case-by-case basis" He looked over to one of the attorneys, "Jeff, you take the lead on this and let's put it to bed."

"Do we need to take any further action?" asked Gil.

No, we'll contact the Scranton and Binghamton police and report the fraud. You and Mr. Doblonsky may be called to provide a deposition or even testify at some point; we'll keep in touch and let you know."

Gil spent a bit more time with the group but the conversation was general in nature. Most of them had little contact with a private investigation agency so the questions were more about what kind of cases Endwell Investigation handled.

As Gil drove back to the office he thought, *so that's it, case closed. How quickly cases can move at the end. At one point, I was digging for information not knowing where this was headed and all of a sudden things fall into place and then, game over! I wonder when the cops will arrest the Burris brothers? Stay tuned,* he laughed to himself.

Chapter 16

Randy got back to the agency around three o'clock. Chantal was in the reception area working on a spread sheet for one of the ongoing investigations which had been running for almost a year. All the agency cases were now tracked on spreadsheets to show both billings and activity so that the client could see measurable progress. This was especially important in longer running cases where everyone's memory of events gets a bit fuzzy over time.

"Looks like you're drowning in data mate," laughed Randy, "want to see some interesting video my main man Ollie and I got from Empire Traffic Analytics?"

"Sure, I'm almost finished with this, why don't we use the video system in the conference room, that way we have a big screen. Al and Sherlock are in his office, I'll get them. Want some coffee? I just made a fresh pot"

When Alastair and Sherlock came into the conference room, he was all smiles. "Is this as good as I think?" he asked.

"Probably better," laughed Randy. "We got a picture of the shooter and his license plate number too and even know the car was purchased in Stroudsburg, Pennsylvania.

Randy had all the data on a DVD and as he ran the video, he talked them through the events. "We don't actually have him firing the shots, some trees were in the way; but look at the sequences. He drives into the lot and parks next to Belvedere; goes around to the side of his car, leans into Belvedere's SUV, stays there less than a minute, and quickly leaves. Nobody went near Belvedere when he arrived other than the shooter and nobody came near him until

Todd got there. The time line is solid; he's the shooter. We got him coming and going from the parking lot and a picture of him in his SUV. The DA can make this case.

"Great pictures of the guy by the way. He may want to frame them!" laughed Chantal.

"Who would have thought we'd get any video," said Alastair, "this is really good stuff. I'm sure the DA will run with it."

Randy looked over towards Alastair, "What do you want to do with this now?" he asked.

"We need to get this over to Lieutenant Hendricks and Detective Adams but I'd like to give them a more complete package. I'm headed to Florida in a couple of days and will be back early next week. I need you guys to dig into this and let's see what additional information we can put together. For instance, I'm wondering if the shooter works for an organization or is a contract employee. We need to get a full picture. Give Fred a call in Scranton and ask him to look into it with you. He still has good contacts around the State. When I get back, we can lay it all out for the cops and take the next steps."

"Do you think he's connected?" asked Chantal.

"I don't know. If he has a New Jersey address or one near New York City, I would say he's probably mobbed up. That's where a lot of the bad boys hang out. But if he lives in Stroudsburg, Pennsylvania who knows? It's an easy commute to the New York-New Jersey metro area so anything's possible. We need to sort it out."

After the meeting, Alastair made two calls; one to Marion Belvedere and the other to Detective Adams. He wanted to tell Marion they were making progress but could not go into any details with her at this time. Their investigation should continue and he'd keep in touch. The other, a call to Detective Adams was to let him know about Randy's success. Although Alastair had a close personal relationship with Lieutenant Hendricks, he did not want to go around Todd Adams as he was the lead on the case and he wanted to stay in channels as the FBI liked to say.

Marion answered on the second ring.

"Marion, you run a tight ship, two rings!"

"I was sitting at the desk paying some bills, the phone was right nearby. Did you catch the guy who shot Jason?"

"It's best if we don't discuss this in any detail at this point. I'm satisfied with the case progress and recommend that we continue the investigation."

"I understand Al; it's been so long, I guess I just want to know."

"These things take time, they always do," replied Alastair.

After the call with Marion, he called Detective Adams, "I want to give you an update on our investigation into Jason Belvedere's murder. We found the shooter."

"Are you shitting me!" exclaimed Todd, "Chantal told me Randy was checking on some video. How'd you find him?"

"I'd love to tell you it was by persistent investigative examination of the case files and great skill, but actually, we got lucky. You know how the games played; work hard and hope you catch a break. Well, Randy was checking the security cameras on Main Street as there are a number of them at the businesses and also some home installations. The problem is none of them kept the security data more than a year. So, no joy there. However, Randy knows the Endicott town engineer; they went to school together, so he went over to see him to talk about the business security installations. Maybe there were some he missed. Turns out Randy had covered them all but there was a temporary one that was set up by a company called Empire Traffic Analytics over in Horseheads. Do you remember the big traffic accident at the Main Street and Grippen Street intersection next to the golf course a year or more back?"

"Sure, I think a kid was killed in a multi-car pile-up," replied Todd.

"That's the one. The accident happened about two months before Belvedere was murdered. Part of the process of redesigning the intersection was do a traffic analysis; that's where Empire Traffic Analytics comes in. They set up four video cameras on Main Street and Grippen Street. Two of the cameras gave a good view of the Enjoie Golf Course parking lot."

"And they still have the tapes?" asked Todd. "

CDs, actually," replied Alastair," they converted the tapes to CDs for easier storage. the law requires them to keep the CDs for five years. Liability issues, I guess. Randy was at the company on Monday and got copies. It's really good stuff."

"When can I see them?" asked Todd.

"Give me a few days to finalize the findings," said Alastair, "We got his license plate number; it's a Pennsylvania plate and we know where he bought the car. It's a kick-ass Lincoln SUV. I have a retired Scranton detective who does part-time work for us and I want him to run the guy down and see what he can find out. We only have his plate number at this point but I think he lives in Stroudsburg, Pennsylvania or close by. I'm off to Fort Walton Beach soon to visit Emi's parents. We'll keep in touch and I'll be back next week. Oh yeah, as you know Belvedere did a lot of banking in Miami. I'm going to see some friends at the FBI field office there and see if we can light a fire under the bank. It's been a few years since my FBI days there but some of the agents are still around. I know the bank stiffed Chantal and slow-rolled you. When I get back, we can put it all on the table."

"You still keep in touch with your wife's parents?"

"Oh yeah, when Emi was murdered by the mob, we grew much closer. I guess the grief and tragedy of it all brought us together. I try to visit once a year and visit Emi's and the baby's grave. When I'm with her parents now, we don't dwell on the murders but remember the good times."

"Okay, I'll close the loop with the Lieutenant. He'll be a happy camper. Al, I know you and Elton are tight and you could have easily called him; thanks for keeping me on point."

"It's my old FBI training. Take care, see you next week," replied Alastair.

Chapter 17

The arrest warrants for Adam and Marcel Burris were executed in Binghamton and Carbondale on the same day with both brothers being taken into custody. Not guilty pleas were entered and bail was set at fifty thousand dollars for Adam and thirty- five thousand dollars for Marcel. The brothers posted bail using property bonds. Trial dates would follow shortly. Although the media picked up on the arrests, it wasn't a major story, just another insurance scam Their coverage lasted for a few days but would pick up again when the cases went to trial.

When the brothers were arrested, the Binghamton Police Department obtained a search warrant for Adam Burris' home and business. The police suspected that other scams might be in play. The fact that he had been arrested was sufficient grounds for a closer look at Adam's activities.

The search not turn up anything new. He had run a small, stable business over the past twelve years. His wife was the bookkeeper for the company and used Quicken Books, a bookkeeping system for homes and small businesses. The police took all the business records so they could take a closer look at the operation and Todd's partner Detective Tony Ronaldo was given the job of looking into them.

"Tony, we'll get the accounting department over at the county offices to take a look at this but first, why don't you look through it and see if there's a smoking gun. Maybe he's a secret agent funneling money into a large international drug trafficking ring?" laughed Todd.

"Or he's just an idiot, trying to scam the insurance company," responded Tony, "let me apply my sharp accounting and forensic analysis skills and sort this out!"

The year-end balance sheets did not show anything as far as Tony could see. The accounts balanced and the company made money. The records went back seven years. Tony guessed they used a different accounting system earlier. The current system had a journal showing the bills submitted to clients and payments received. Tony was not an accountant so the balance sheets did not tell him much. However the journal was interesting as it was a historical archive of company activity over the past seven years.

Tony had the accounting records spread out on the conference room table next to Lieutenant Hendricks office. As he was looking at the journal entries from three years earlier a name caught his eye. He called Todd into the conference room.

"Hey crime stopper, take a look at this. Jason Belvedere; isn't that the guy you and Al Stewart are chasing?"

"Same name, what's the address?"

"Plaza Drive, it's over by the shopping plaza on the Vestal Parkway that has a Starbucks. I think it's called University Plaza. Must be a business address, I don't think there's any housing around there other than student apartments for Binghamton University. I'll look it up."

Tony did a Google search and found a property office called Valley Real Estate at the address.

"What's this all about?" asked Tony, "was he in the real estate business?"

"I don't think so, he was in property development, big stuff. I'll give Al a call and let him know what you've found."

When Todd called Alastair, he caught him just leaving the office to go to the Syracuse Airport to catch his flight to Atlanta and then connect to Fort Walton Beach.

"Al, you know that case Gil just closed? The insurance scam that involved two brothers; one here and the other in Pennsylvania."

"Sure, the guys were arrested the other day."

"We got a search warrant for the guy's house and business here. We didn't find anything dramatic but we took his business records and Tony was going over them and we found a name that surprised us. Three years ago Adam Burris did some work for a property firm called Valley Real Estate on Plaza Drive over in Vestal. Looks like a heating and air conditioning installation job costing twenty thousand dollars. The guy who paid for it was Jason Belvedere."

"That's odd, seems like that would be a landlord issue," replied Alastair. "Why is he involved? We checked around when he was murdered and he didn't own any real estate in town other than his house."

"What do you think?" asked Todd.

"So far, the guy's a mystery; we don't know much about him other than his name. Let's make sure there aren't any other Jason Belvederes in town. Can you and Tony pay the place a visit and see what you can find out? You guys have more horsepower than a private detective agency. I'll call Marion Belvedere and see if she knows anything about this. Let's put it on the agenda for our meeting when I get back. Make sure Lieutenant Hendricks is on board."

"We're peeling back the layers of the onion," laughed Todd.

Alastair was able to call Marion Belvedere on his way up to Syracuse. His Nissan Murano had a great hands-free calling system and he used it all the time.

"Hi Marion, I'm calling you from my car, I'm on the way to Syracuse and I'm between Marathon and Cortland. The signal may drop off in this area so if I lose you, I'll call back when I get to Cortland."

"Okay, I can hear you fine now. What can I do for you?"

"Did Jason do business with, or have any interest in a real estate business here?"

"Not that I know of. Actually, he never did any projects in Broome County so I don't know what use a business here would do for him. I know he didn't have a real estate license. Steve asked him once if he needed one for his business and he laughed and said he was fishing in a bigger pond than selling local properties. Why are you asking?"

"It's speculative at this point. I need to dig a bit deeper. These investigations always have a lot of dead ends so give me some time and let's see where this takes us."

Alastair felt he they were getting closer to Jason Belvedere but they still didn't have anything concrete. His relationship with Third Dominion Bank in Miami was unusual as was this new connection with a real estate firm in Vestal. Nothing solid yet, but maybe some cracks in the wall?

You're out there Jason, you sly dog, and we're going to find you, he thought.

Chapter 18

Alastair arrived at Fort Walton Beach around four in the afternoon, after an uneventful flight from Syracuse to Atlanta and a connection to Fort Walton Beach. After that, a short drive to Emi's parent's house. Nigel had cocktails ready and Marie had prepared an assortment of olives and cheeses.

"I guess you're still a Ballantine's scotch man, so I made sure we had some ready for you," said Nigel.

"Old habits die hard," said Alastair, "I think the distillery may give me the loyal customer award. I realize how old I'm getting when I think about how long I've been drinking this scotch."

"I think I'm the same way with gin," replied Nigel. I don't like these new gin blends, too sweet and fruity. Beefeaters has been on my shelf for years."

"I guess we're too set in our ways to retrain," laughed Alastair.

Alastair helped Marie carry the trays with the cocktails and snacks to the lanai. Although the weather was warm, it was comfortable sitting in the lanai as there was a pleasant on-shore breeze from the Gulf. He looked over at Marie and said, "You and Nigel look great, I trust no health issues."

"No, we're doing okay as long as I can get Nigel out of the house, then I can have some peace and quiet," she laughed.

The murder of their only child and unborn baby had taken a toll on them but they had resolved to not give in to their grief. Not an easy thing to do but like Alastair, they found a way to move forward. After cocktails, they sat in the lanai and talked about Emi.

Their overwhelming grief had passed and now the memories were of the good times they had shared together. Marie had taken over Emi's document editing business and was as busy as she wanted to be. Initially she took it on to complete the projects Emi had on contract but she found she liked the work and it grew from there. Nowadays, she still edited research papers for the faculties at the University of Miami and Florida State University but now, much more of her time was spent dealing with novels. "I find the research papers tedious at times. If the author does not know how to prepare footnotes, it can be a long slog getting it all in order. I really like editing novels and have had some good success these past few years."

"Is the money different between the two?" asked Alastair.

"Not really, I bill by the hour so it all works out. The academic papers are more mechanical and I don't usually understand the content so I'm mainly looking at grammar and presentation whereas the novels require an assessment of the story as well as the layout of the book."

They sat quietly for a bit and then Alastair smiled and said, "Remember how Emi used to refer to the FBI as the BBI, the Big Bureau of Investigation? it still makes me laugh."

"I sure do," said Nigel, "she had an ability to turn a phrase. "She used to refer to my golf game as 'whack and smack.' I think she nailed it," he laughed.

They rounded off the evening with stuffed crab cakes served with coleslaw and garden peas. Nigel added a bottle of Sancerre wine to compliment a great meal and they retired in a mellow mood.

Alastair spent the following morning with them and later on Saturday afternoon went to the cemetery to visit the grave of Emi and her baby. He sat on a nearby bench and let his mind wander back to their days together. The murder would always be with him, but was manageable now. He was planning to marry Marty Fitzgerald later in the year and felt that at some level he was abandoning Emi. When he got back to the house, he spoke to Marie about it.

"I don't know Marie; I feel as if I'm moving away from Emi. I don't want to lose her."

"Al, your life is in front of you, not behind you. Emi will always be a part of your life but you need to move forward. I'm so happy that you found someone; don't forget to invite us to the wedding."

The following day, he got an early start for the drive to Miami to meet with Chris Collins, his boss when he was with the FBI. Chris and his wife Barbara still lived in Miami in the same large four-bedroom house, all on one floor, which sat on a large lot with an ample garden.

"I thought you'd have a fancy condo down on the beach by now," said Alastair.

"Maybe in the future, but we're not ready for vertical living yet. We like it here. It's home, and I don't think the kids would let us move," he laughed.

"I'm starting to feel the same way about my place in New York. It's home. Right now it's just me and Sherlock my dog, but I'm getting married around the end of the year."

"That is such good news! Congratulations, you've built a successful business and a new life. After everything that happened, you survived, sometimes we never make it back."

"I couldn't have done it alone. So many people were part of my recovery. It was a team effort."

The next morning Chris picked Alastair up at his hotel which was near the FBI office in North Miami. The meeting with Gordon Marella, the agent in charge was set for nine o'clock. When men arrived, they were taken to the large conference room. They were surprised to find it full. All of the agents and support staff stood up and clapped as they entered the room.

Al leaned over to Chis and whispered, "I hope I don't have to make a speech; I'm overwhelmed, I don't think I can hold it together."

Alastair walked around the conference room greeting everyone. Handshakes and hugs were the order of the day. The welcome back reception lasted about an hour and then folks drifted back to work. Gordon took Alastair and Chris back to his office.

"Al, I understand you're chasing a bad boy up in Binghamton who may have banking connections here in Miami and maybe south of here also."

"Correct, Jason Belvedere was murdered about a year and a half ago. The police were never able to close the case. The guy's widow came to our agency and asked if we could take a look into it. She and her son are receiving a monthly check from a trust fund that either comes through or originates with a bank here. My sense is it comes from another bank and Third Dominion in Miami is transferring the money. Belvedere probably has a significant amount of money in one of the banks either here or somewhere in the Caribbean."

"What are you looking to do Al?"

"We tried to get information from Third Dominion but they blew us off which we expected. The Binghamton Police called them but the bank will not cooperate without a subpoena and you know what that means. They'll slow roll them forever and a day. I'd like to find out what kind of banking Belvedere did with Third Dominion. Maybe they just transfer the trust account money from another bank or he did a lot more business with them."

"Third Dominion is always on our radar," said Gordon, "I can set up a meeting with them and maybe they'll be cooperative. We don't have an active case going on with them now and I bet they'll want to keep it that way. I'll have Cisco Riviera go with you. He's our finance lead and they're afraid of him," laughed Gordon, "do you want to do this today?"

"This afternoon or tomorrow morning would be great."

"Okay, let's see what we can do."

Chapter 19

While Alastair was in Florida, Todd and Tony decided to make a call on Valley Real Estate so they could brief everyone when they met later in the week. Before going over to the company, Todd did an online search of the business. It had a very good website with pictures of current listings and recent sales. The owner, Marjorie Monette, who had been in business about twelve years, was listed as a broker and had two agents on staff. When Tony checked the tax records for the firm, he found that she also owned the building.

"This seems to be a successful company," said Tony. "It's a lot more than someone working out of their house."

"Did you see Jason Belvedere's name on any of the tax records?"

"No, so far, he only shows up on that one invoice. You know when we found him in Adam Burris' books, we never asked the next question: How did he pay? Cash, check, casino chips? I need to get back to Burris and see what he can tell me before we visit Valley Real Estate."

"You're right," I never got past Belvedere's name. We should have looked deeper into it."

Tony called Adam Burris and set up a visit for later in the afternoon, arriving just as Adam was returning from a job. Tony walked up to him as he was getting out of his van.

"Nice van," said Tony, with a smile.

"You're a barrel of laughs," said Adam, "what are you going to tell me next? Make sure it's well insured?"

"Sorry Mr. Burris, I was being a smart-ass. I take it back."

"I got bigger problems than that, what do you want?"

"As I mentioned on the phone, you did some work for Valley Real Estate on Plaza Drive a few years back and the work was paid for by a man named Jason Belvedere. We need to know how he paid for it."

"Why is it so important? Are you investigating him?"

"Yes, he was murdered."

"Wow, I didn't see that coming," said Adam, "but first, let me ask you a question. I'm pretty jammed up on with Northeast Insurance and Indemnity. I know I'm not going to escape the charges, but I want to try and protect my business if I can. My son is a partner with me and can run the business if I end up going to prison. I'll take whatever is coming my way but I don't want to lose the business."

"I'm sorry, Mr. Burris, I'm not able to offer you any relief or cut a deal. Those issues rest with the DA. What I can do for you is let the DA know of your cooperation. I can't put a value on it but from what I've seen with other cases, it could be worth something."

"All right, let's go inside and look at the books. You said the work was done about three years ago?"

"Yeah, over at Valley Real Estate, and the work was paid for by Jason Belvedere."

"Okay, we've got pretty good historical records. It should be in the journal."

The two men sat in the office at the back of the house. Tony was surprised at how well everything was organized. Neat and tidy for sure. Adam noticed Tony looking around the office and smiled. "My wife, not me. I'm sort of a messy guy."

It didn't take long to find the invoice and payment for the work.

"Yeah, here you go. Invoiced and paid within thirty days, $15,562.49. New aircon and heating system. I remember that now. The boss lady was a real looker. Just a professional observation detective; nothing more to add."

"How did he pay for the work?"

"By check."

"Can you tell me what bank he used?"

"Give me a minute, I need to look in another place."

Adam went online and appeared to be looking at some history of past bank deposits in what Tony guessed was an income statement or invoice summary for the year in question.

"Here it is. A Florida bank named Third Dominion."

"Can I get a copy of the check?" asked Tony.

"Hang on, I need to turn on the printer."

Two minutes later, Tony was holding a copy of a check written from Belvedere's account. The check gave the sort code and account number. *Great,* thought Tony, *got the check and account number, this is really good. Jason you sly fox, we're getting closer to you!*

"Thanks Mr. Burris, this is helpful, really helpful."

"Please make me sure you let the DA know I helped you guys."

"I will. For what it's worth, get yourself a good lawyer. If you go to trial, make sure it's someone who knows their way around a courtroom."

Once outside of the house, Tony called Todd. "Hey, Belvedere paid by a check from Third Dominion in Miami. I got a copy of the check. We have his account number and even the sort code if we need it."

"Great. I'll send Al a text and let him know what we got, but he may already be headed back here. I'm not sure about his itinerary. He was going to Fort Walton Beach and Miami."

Alastair got a text message from Todd at five thirty on Monday afternoon. As it turned out, he was too late to get a meeting at Third Dominion that afternoon. However, along with Cisco Riviera from the FBI, they were scheduled to meet with the bank at nine o'clock on Tuesday. *Nice work guys,* thought Alastair, *no way the bank can tell us they don't have any record of Belvedere. I'll call Cisco and let him know about this.* When Alastair spoke with him, he laughed when he heard the news.

"This is great Al; they'll think we know a lot more than we do. It should help."

Alastair texted back to Todd to let him know they would be meeting with Third Dominion the next day and he would be heading back to Binghamton after the meeting. Todd scanned the check and e-mailed it to Alastair with a note saying, "just in case the bank has memory issues or denies Belvedere was a customer."

Chapter 20

Todd called Valley Real Estate on Tuesday and was able to set up a meeting for the early afternoon. When they arrived, Marjorie Monette was finishing a meeting with a customer, so the detectives waited in the reception area looking at the property listings.

"Do you ever think about moving to another house?" asked Tony.

"Not really, our little guy, Ben is just three and we have plenty of room. I like the west side, nice neighborhoods. Maybe later if we have another kid. What about you?"

"It's just me, but I keep thinking I need to get on the property ladder. It's getting pretty serious with Julie, maybe time to do something."

"You mean like plan ahead?" laughed Todd.

"Yeah, I'm so lucky to have found her. She's a keeper."

When Marjorie came out of her office, she smiled and said, "My, two detectives, I hope I'm not in serious trouble gentlemen."

Todd introduced Tony and himself and explained the reason for the visit. "Ms. Monette, we're interested in some heating and air conditioning work done on the building which was paid for by Jason Belvedere."

When Marjorie heard Belvedere's name, her smile became rigid and Todd saw some rapid eye movement. Clearly the detectives hit a nerve and she was on high alert. She did not respond immediately and seemed to be trying to sort out an answer. *We caught her by surprise,* thought Todd, *she's scrambling for an answer.*

After some time she said, "Oh yes, I remember now, I bought the building from Mr. Belvedere and part of the sale was replacing the heating and air-conditioning system."

"When did you buy the building from Mr. Belvedere?" asked Tony,

"Oh, maybe six or seven years ago. Before that I rented the building."

"And he only replaced the hearing and air-conditioning system about two years ago. I thought you said it was part of the purchase, said Todd."

Marjorie Monette was digging a hole and she would not be able to get out of it. The detectives did not get confrontational with her as they wanted to keep the conversation going.

"I'm confused Ms. Monette," said Tony, "why wouldn't the system be replaced when you bought the building?

At this point Marjorie was circling the wagons. With both detectives asking questions, she was losing control over the situation. "Maybe I should consult an attorney? I don't understand all these questions."

"That's your decision Ms. Monette. You can get an attorney and we'll continue the conversation down at police headquarters. Let me be very candid with you," said Todd, "I'm sure you know that Jason Belvedere was murdered. We're trying to find out who killed him. If you know anything that can us help find his killer, I strongly suggest you tell us. Withholding information in a murder investigation is a serious matter. We're not comfortable with your answers to our questions so far. They do not confirm our investigation results. Let me explain. We checked the county tax records and Jason Belvedere never owned this building. His only property was his home in Endicott. You bought the building from a Mr. Harry Morgan a local CPA, not from Jason Belvedere."

Marjorie was overwhelmed at this point and started sobbing. "I didn't murder Jason; I loved him."

Todd was surprised; he hadn't considered a relationship between Belvedere and Marjorie Monette. But once she made the statement, the detectives knew the secret life of Jason Belvedere was finally opening up.

"Ms. Monette, you're not a person of interest in his murder. However, your relationship with him is important to our investigation. We need your cooperation. You can speak with us now or as I said earlier, get an attorney. It's your decision," said Todd.

"I've done nothing wrong detectives. I'll try to answer your questions but if I think I need or want an attorney, I'll stop the discussion."

"Fair enough," said Todd, "let's start at the beginning; how did you meet Belvedere?"

"We met at Wegman's Supermarket across from the Oakdale Mall. I was just getting started back then and mostly worked out of my apartment. I would go to Wegmans to have a coffee and a break. It was not too crowded in the afternoon so I could set up shop so to speak. One day, I had a lot of papers spread out on a table there as I was getting ready to go the Co-operative Mortgage Service office on the Vestal Parkway for a house closing. A bunch of papers fell off the table as I was trying to sort them out. Jason was walking by with a sandwich and coffee on a tray and saw my predicament and put his tray on my table and helped me pick up the papers. The table could seat four people so there was plenty of room and I suggested he join me as the dining area was starting to fill up. That's how it all started. Friends at first and then the relationship developed. That was almost twelve years ago."

"I assume you knew Jason was married?"

"Not initially, he didn't wear a wedding ring. As we got to know each other, he told me about his wife and son. At that time we were just friends. Looking back, it was an odd relationship. I was single; actually I still am and he was married with a child. I told him I wouldn't be a part of breaking up a family and attempted to end the relationship but somehow it just kept going. Neither one of us had the courage to take the next step and end it."

"What did he tell you about his business life?"

"Jason was very reserved and we never talked about his business or his family. I never knew much more than that he was in property development.

"Did he ever ask for your help on any real estate or other business issues?"

"No, never. He had a lawyer in town who handled his legal issues. I think I have his contact information, I used him once on a house closing. Yeah, here it is, George Adamo. Maybe he knows something about Jason's business."

"Why did Jason fix the heating and air conditioning system? Did he actually own the building?"

Marjorie did not answer immediately. She sat quietly looking at some papers on her desk. Just as the detectives were going to repeat the question, she said, "Jason bought the building for me about six years after we got together. Later, when he found out that the heating and air conditioning needed to be replaced, he arranged for a contractor to do the work and paid for it. He laughed and said it would cover his rent."

Todd and Tony looked quickly at each other, both thinking the same thing. Is this where Belvedere had his office? They knew he had an office somewhere around town but could never find it.

"What rent?" asked Tony.

"Jason used one of the offices in the back of the building for his business. We have plenty of space. Now, I use it for storage. Property signs, posters, stuff like that. After he was killed, I put all his things in a couple of boxes and keep them in the office there. I was going to give them to his wife but she didn't know about Jason and me so I thought it best to stay out of her life."

"What's in the boxes?" asked Todd.

"Oh the usual office things. A laptop, files, pads, pens, stuff like that. I can show them to you,"

"They went back to the office and opened the two boxes. When the detectives saw the contents, Todd said, "we need to take this back to police headquarters. We'll give you a receipt for them."

The two detectives left Valley Real Estate with each carrying a cardboard file box with a Staples Office Supplies logo on the side.

"Talk about a home run!" laughed Todd.

"More like a bases loaded grand slam," replied Tony, "we need to call Lieutenant Hendricks and Al Stewart. This will make their day."

"For sure, but we're only half way there. We've found the elusive Jason Belvedere but there's a bigger story to find yet. Who killed him and what was he up to? He was playing with some bad boys in a high stakes game. I think we're looking at the tip of the iceberg. This guy has been in business for a long time and I bet there's a pattern here that repeats. Maybe not new players every time but a familiar cast, sort of like a stable. Once we get the forensics guys in Albany to take a look at this, we'll know a hell of a lot more."

While all of this was going on, Fred Doblonsky working out of Scranton, was able to run down the shooter. He ran the tags through the DMV database and got his address. His name was Armand Houghton and he lived in Stroudsburg, Pennsylvania. Checking around, he found that he had lived in Stroudsburg for a number of years in the same house, about a mile west of town in a rural area. He lived alone; no Mrs. Houghton or little kiddy Houghton's. When Fred was with the Scranton police force, he had a good reputation for being fair and never took advantage of his position. This helped him now that he was doing private investigative work; people would talk to him, especially the ones on the other side of the law. He tapped all his sources to see what he could find out about Armand but so far nobody knew of him. *This is strange* thought Fred; *he may be mobbed up but clearly not one of the known contract hit men. I can't imagine the dude is operating solo, who's paying him?*

Chapter 21

The meeting at Third Dominion bank in Miami did not get off to a good start. When Alastair and Cisco Riviera arrived at the bank, they were taken to a large conference room on the second floor where the bank had assembled a team of eight people, including a senior vice president, two lawyers and an assortment of other staff. When Cisco saw the group, he whispered to Alastair, "Hey Al, they're playing their whole defensive team today."

The men sat down and introductions were made. When Alastair was introduced, the bank team did not know how to deal with him. They expected government or state officials. But a private eye? There was silence for a bit as they tried to figure out where Alastair fit into the mix. Then one of the attorneys sitting across from Alastair spoke up. He had been referred to as outside counsel in the introductions and was a senior partner in a large Miami law firm.

"Mr. Stewart, I remember your name. Were you with the FBI in Miami about six or so years ago?"

"That's correct," replied Alastair, "I was a field agent."

"I remember well what happened to you, your wife and unborn baby. My son, was a city beat reporter for the Miami Herald back then and covered the story. It was tragic. I hope you've been able to move on from the assassination. You suffered a great loss."

"I've been able to rebuild my life thanks to great friends and family. I went back home to Binghamton, New York and started a private investigation agency."

A lot of the tension seemed to leave the room. Although Alastair's presence in the meeting was still not clear, the bank team looked at him with different eyes now. Other members of the Third Dominion team also remembered the assassination.

Cisco stood up drawing everyone's attention to him. "Gentlemen, the government does not have an issue with Third Dominion. We're not here to question your banking policies or practices. We're interested in obtaining information on one of your clients. He was murdered about two years ago in Endicott, New York which is a small town near Binghamton. The case is still open.

The room was quiet as the group considered Cisco's comments and then the bank senior vice president, Harper Milloy spoke, "Gentlemen can you give us the name of the client in question and also a few minutes to discuss this amongst our team?"

"The name is Jason Belvedere," replied Cisco, "The Binghamton Police have recently been in touch with you regarding him and you advised them that a subpoena would be required. We don't have a problem with that but the issue is the anticipated response time from the bank. We are asking for your active cooperation."

Cisco's words were not lost on the group. Don't slow-roll us. Although nothing was said directly about the timeliness of the bank's past responses, the message had been sent. Alastair and Cisco left the conference room while the bank team discussed their next steps and also looked at Jason Belvedere's relationship with the bank. A regular customer? Maybe a lot more. After about ten minutes, a secretary appeared with coffee and bite-size donuts.

Cisco laughed when she left, "I suspect these guys have a lot to talk about. H'm, maybe this is a peace offering. I wonder why we're always fed donuts. Maybe it's true, Cops love donuts!"

"I guess it comes with the territory," laughed Alastair, "I prefer bagels but don't tell anyone, I don't want to destroy the image!"

After thirty minutes, one of the attorneys asked Cisco and Alastair to join them in the room. "Sorry for the delay, we had a lot to talk about."

When they were seated, Harper Milloy, the senior vice president spoke. "Gentlemen, we certainly want to cooperate with your investigation. We'll try to answer your questions today but we may need to do further research to fully understand them. To maintain continuity, Mr. Gibbons, our lead attorney will be your contact person as we move forward." Turning to Cisco he continued, "please issue your subpoena so we have a solid justification for our discussions. You can file it on behalf of the FBI and Binghamton Police."

"Thank you for your support," said Cisco, "Can we start with Mr. Stewart asking some questions?"

Alastair, looked over the room trying to gauge the mood of the group. He did not detect any open hostility but knew some of them were not comfortable talking to the government and now a private investigator was in the mix. He needed to be careful and not press them too hard for information. *Try to establish a flow, keep things moving,* he thought.

"Mr. Belvedere's wife and son receive a monthly check from a local bank in Binghamton. The funds are transferred from Third Dominion. Do they originate here or is this an onward transfer?"

George Gibbons, the lead attorney responded, "We receive the funds from Global Caribbean Bank in the Cayman Islands. It's a direct pass through although we do levy a small administrative charge. It's a monthly transfer to us."

"Why bring your bank into the process? Can't they just transfer it directly?" asked Alastair.

"Well, I guess they could," said George, "but they don't have banking relationships with any banks in Binghamton and they know us. I really don't know, just speculating but it's not an uncommon practice."

"They may also want to stay away from New York State banking regulations too," said Cisco.

"That too," responded George, "again, it's a common banking practice."

"What was Belvedere's relationship with your bank?" asked Alastair.

Nobody was in a rush to answer. Finally, Harper Milloy, the ranking person for the bank responded, "He had three accounts with the bank, a personal one, a business one and a trust account."

"Let's deal with the personal one first," said Alastair, "how much money did he keep with the bank?"

"The balance was never less than three hundred thousand," responded Harper, "other times, significantly more."

"Why the changes in the amount of money in the account, where did it go?"

"We operate a large trust division," said Harper, "he would move money from the account to his trust fund."

"Where did the money come from that went into his personal account?"

"The money came from his business account. He apparently received payments from various corporations. I assume it was for services provided," replied Harper.

"Do you know where the corporations were registered?" asked Cisco.

'I don't have that information. However, I can tell you the money came to us from Global Caribbean Bank."

"Shell companies?" said Cisco.

"Your words, not mine," replied Harper.

"Why didn't Belvedere use his trust account with your bank to make the monthly payments to his wife and son?" asked Cisco, "Why use Global Caribbean?"

"I don't know," replied Harper, "We were operating under their instructions and had no say in the source of funds."

"There is something here that I can't get my head around," said Alastair, "How did the Caribbean Bank know when to start the trust fund payment? They started after Belvedere was killed so who turned them on? How did they know he was dead and who had the authority to start the trust fund payments. There's a layer here that we don't understand."

"Well Mr. Stewart, we know of Belvedere's relationship with Global Caribbean because of the payments coming to his account at our bank, but we had no knowledge of the extent of his business with that bank. As I said before, we didn't know Belvedere was dead and had in fact continued to send statements to New York. Somehow the Caribbean bank was given binding directions to initiate the trust fund payments, but not by us." replied Harper.

Alastair and Cisco asked for a short break so they could discuss the new found information. They had gotten a lot more than they expected. Cisco was surprised at the level of cooperation from First Dominion. *I wonder if they see this going south and want to make sure they were not a player in anything Belvedere did. Maybe they're just a banking service for Belvedere and they want to make sure they don't end up on the other side of the fence,* thought Cisco.

"How far do you think we can take this today?" asked Alastair.

"Let's take the money and run. I don't think we can get much more today. We can ask for details of his accounts and that should give us plenty to chew on," replied Cisco.

"I know I'm like a bear with a sore paw Cisco, but someone turned on Global Caribbean to start making trust fund payments after Belvedere was murdered. He could have left instructions in the event of his death but I doubt it; there's another player here," said Alastair.

The two men came back to the room as a buffet service of sandwiches, fruit and coffee was being set up.

"We're close to noon and thought we could continue over a light lunch," said Harper.

"Thank you," replied Alastair, "I have a tight connection after the meeting so this makes it a lot easier."

"What more can we do for you today, gentlemen."

"As you can imagine," said Cisco, "we'd like the details of Belvedere's accounts."

"We knew that was coming," laughed George Gibbons, the lead attorney, "We're prepared to provide the information but first we need that subpoena and also an explanation in the subpoena or a cover letter regarding the demise of Mr. Belvedere. As we said earlier, the bank would like it to be issued by the FBI here in Miami."

"We can do that," said Cisco, and I'll also have the Binghamton police send you the murder report."

As they were finishing up lunch, Alastair asked, "What will happen to the money in Belvedere's accounts?"

"That's a good question," answered Harper, "As you know we have continued to send statements to his address and have not received any notification of his death and none of the statements were returned. I don't know if the man had a will or left any instructions. Barring a will, the next of kin would normally be the beneficiary. However, given Mr. Riviera's presence today, there may be an issue of the funds being 'dirty money' and that's another issue altogether. So, short answer, I don't really know at this point."

"Just as a point of interest, what address did you use in New York for your correspondence?" asked Alastair.

One of the accountants spoke up, "It's actually Vestal, New York. Plaza Drive from what I can see here. Is it important?"

The mention of the Plaza Drive address caught Alastair's attention. Someone had to turn on Global Caribbean to start the trust fund payments to Belvedere's wife and son. *Marjorie Monette,* he thought, *I don't think you told Detective Adams everything; we need to have another conversation.*

Looking over at the accountant, he respond, "It doesn't impact the bank. The address is for an office not a home address. It has a bearing on our investigation but is not connected to Third Dominion. One last question, how much money are we talking about?"

"Well, as you know three hundred thousand is in his personal account and over twenty-two million in the business account," replied Harper.

Big bucks, thought Alastair, *who were you involved with? We may have found you Jason but this is only a starting point. How much do you have stashed at Global Caribbean?*

Cisco drove Alastair to the airport which gave them a good opportunity to discuss the next steps. The case was entering a new phase. They had found Jason Belvedere and knew who shot him. This fulfilled Alastair's mandate from Marion Belvedere. The criminal investigation into the murder and Belvedere's business life would shift to the Binghamton Police and FBI. His role in the case was not clear. If Marion Belvedere asked him to stay on the case he would do so. He felt she wanted to get to *the* bottom of it all and finally get closure. If he did continue, his role would be secondary to that of the police and FBI. *I'll be walking a fine line, he thought.* He spoke to Cisco about his role now and they agreed to keep in touch and see how it all played out.

"You're still family Al, we're not going to kick you to the curb. There's a lot of cards to be played. I don't think we've seen the last of you.

"I owe you one, Cisco," replied Alastair, "we could never have had this meeting and gotten such good results without you. I think your boss is right, they are afraid of you!" laughed Alastair.

"Banking in this part of Florida is not like up north. The banks here do a lot of business in the Caribbean and as you know it's a different game there. The Florida banks are always just one step away from a violation. It reminds me of the policy towards gays in the military when Clinton was president, 'Don't ask, don't tell'. They want to do business with the Caribbean banks because the money is so good, but it's not without risk."

"Sort of like swimming with sharks," laughed Alastair.

Chapter 22

Alastair's flight was about thirty minutes late leaving Miami. Fortunately he had a nonstop flight to Syracuse, so he didn't have to worry about catching a connection in Atlanta. While driving back to Endwell from the airport, he decided to call Lieutenant Hendricks, as there were a lot of gears turning in the investigation and the next steps would be critical. Now that Jason Belvedere's secret life had been exposed, it could mean that Alastair's role in the case was complete. After all, Marion Belvedere had asked him to uncover her husband's business life and murderer, and he had done that.

But the story was far from finished. They had found his 'office', for want of a better term, and had a trove of information to investigate, and they also found the shooter who might lead them to some big players. Furthermore, Alastair's meeting in Miami with Third Dominion opened up the relationship Belvedere had with Global Caribbean Bank in the Cayman Islands. Nobody banks in the Caribbean for convenience or a free toaster; lots to learn there.

So, the question as Alastair saw it was whether he could stay with the case or would have to close it out. Clearly the murder and financial investigation were the responsibility of the police and most likely the FBI, considering the Caribbean banking involvement. It depended on Marion Belvedere and her wishes and also what role the police and FBI would want from Endwell Investigations.

He called Lieutenant Elton Hendricks on his mobile phone as it was late in the afternoon and he might have left the office by now.

"Al, nice to hear your voice, where are you?"

"I'm driving back from the Syracuse airport, halfway home, just coming into Cortland now."

"Todd kept me up to speed while you were gone," said the lieutenant, "sounds like the case is really opening up. Office in town, the shooter and now a Caribbean connection."

"It is Elton and I think we need to talk about the next steps."

"Well you're about forty minutes away from home, so what better way to pass the time than talk about the case," laughed the lieutenant.

"Okay, but I'm not sure what play I have in the case now. Marion Belvedere asked me to find out who killed her husband and what kind of business he was in. We've found the shooter and it's pretty clear that Belvedere was playing on the other side of the fence, although the extent of his business dealings needs to be understood. My point is that I see the next steps as a law enforcement operation for you guys and I think the FBI, given the Caribbean connection. I can't make arrests and don't have the resources to adequately investigate the financial side of his dealings. I'm going to call Mrs. Belvedere when I get home and try to meet with her this week."

"Okay, but what do you want to do Al?"

"I'd like to stay with the case if I can, there's a lot more to uncover, but again where do I fit?"

"Well, from my perspective, I want you to stay with the case. Your agency broke it open. We were stuck and you guys got it moving again. You have great cards with the FBI in Miami. You're in the club there. I hope Mrs. Belvedere wants to keep you on the case, but if she's happy with what you've found and feels that you met her objectives, I still want to have access to your agency as we move forward."

"Okay Elton, thanks for that. Let me speak with Mrs. Belvedere and we'll talk again. By the way, will you be at our status meeting? It'll be my guys plus Todd and Tony."

"Yeah, Todd mentioned it the other day. Looking forward to it; lots to talk about."

"I'll have Fred Doblonsky from Scranton join on a Zoom call. He's the guy who found the shooter."

On the way home, Alastair stopped by Chantal's house to pick up Sherlock, who wasn't in any hurry to leave.

"She's a great dog Al, she sleeps by the foot of our bed and my boys love her. Sometimes, I swear I can talk to her and she understands."

"I know what you mean, I talk to her the time. Seems like I've got some real competition," laughed Alastair, "I need to 'up' my game or she'll never come back home."

When they got there, Sherlock rambled around the house remembering familiar smells while Alastair called Marion Belvedere.

"Marion, can we meet and discuss the case? There have been some significant developments."

"Did you find Jason's killer?"

"We've identified the man who killed him, but think he was working for someone else."

"Are you going to arrest him?"

"Let's not get too far ahead of ourselves. We can go over all of this when we meet. Is tomorrow a good time?"

"Sure, I have a hairdresser's appointment but that's easy to change. Where should we meet?"

"Let me come to you house."

"Should Steve join us?"

"I think it's better if we do this without him initially. I have some significant things to discuss and it may better if it's just the two of us. Certainly, you'll want to bring Steve into the picture, but for now let's not involve him. Does nine-thirty work for you?"

"Sure, I'm always up before eight, any time is fine."

The meeting was set with Marion for Tuesday and the combined meeting with the Binghamton Police was Thursday. That left Wednesday to tie it all together.

Alastair sent a text to Chantal letting her know he would be dropping off Sherlock at the office and would be back later in the morning, and also asking her to remind Randy and Gil that they all needed to meet on Wednesday.

It was a short fifteen-minute drive from his house to Marion's house. His fiancé Marty Fitzgerald always joked that everything was fifteen minutes away from everything else in this part of the State. *The joys of a small town,* thought Alastair. So the following morning, It was easier to go straight to Marion's house and not stop by the agency. He sent Chantal a text with the change of plans and headed out. As he walked up the steps, Marion met him at the front door.

"What a beautiful dog, have you had her for a long time?"

"Coming on to three years now. She's my best friend."

"We had an Airedale Terrier named Mr. Kelly, when Steve was growing up; I still think about him."

"I know what you mean, they really become part of your life. Is it okay to bring her in? She won't mind staying in the car."

"Not at all Al, love the company. I even have some treats I keep for the neighbor's dog."

They sat in the kitchen while Marion made some coffee. The kitchen was well appointed with up-to-date appliances, counter tops, and lighting. It opened up onto a deck looking over the backyard.

"I wish the weather was better, we could sit on the deck."

"The kitchen's fine, we can talk here over coffee."

Marion was clearly nervous as they sat down. She knew the information about Jason was not going to be pleasant but still hoped for the best.

"Al, I don't want you to hold back any information. I'm prepared for whatever you have to tell me. I've never been comfortable with Jason's working life; too many unanswered questions. I chose to ignore it all these years, which was a mistake."

This is going to be tough, thought Alastair, *I wish there was some way I could ease her into this. Damn, I've got to tell her that Jason had a long running affair here in town. She won't see that coming. I'll start out with the murder and go from there.*

"We got lucky and found some engineering video tapes of the Main and Grippen Street intersection. A lad was killed there some years back and the county and town decide to upgrade the intersection to make it safer. Part of the project was a traffic analysis which included video of the traffic."

"I remember that," replied Marion.

"As you know, the intersection is next to the golf course parking lot and gave us a pretty good look into it. We saw an SUV go into the lot and park next to Jason's car. Although we couldn't directly see the driver when he went over to Jason's car, we were able to confirm that the driver of the SUV murdered Jason. It was the only car that parked next to Jason and we have complete coverage while Jason was in the parking lot waiting for someone. When he left the golf course parking lot, the shooter turned right onto Main Street and stopped at the Grippen Street intersection, we were able to get a good picture of him and also his license plate number."

"And the police never found this?" asked Marion.

"No, and we wouldn't have found it either except one of our investigators had a high school friend who is the Endicott town engineer. He met with him and the upgrade work was discussed among other things. It just came out in the conversation. If Randy, that's our investigator, had not known the town engineer, this wouldn't have happened. The slang term the cops use for this is catching a break."

"So, the video data was here all the time?"

"Not quite," responded Alastair, "a company called Empire Traffic Analytics over in Horseheads did the work and the law required them to keep the tapes for five years. We were lucky, really lucky."

"My goodness, sounds like something out of a detective novel," laughed Marion, "you should write a book about this."

"Who knows, maybe I will someday."

"When you got the license plate number, you could find the name of the shooter I guess."

"Yes, we have his name and found out where he lives. However, most likely this was a contract killing and he was employed by someone else."

"Do you know who he worked for?"

"Not at this point. The shooter lives in Stroudsburg, Pennsylvania. We'll need the police from here and Stroudsburg to be involved in his capture. The Binghamton Police will have him arrested and extradited back here to face charges."

"When will this happen?"

"I'll know more later this week. We have a meeting with the police on Thursday."

"What else were you able to uncover?"

Alastair hesitated for a moment. He was about to tell her that Jason had been cheating on her for years. He wished he had discussed this with his fiancé, Marty Fitzgerald, a therapist at the Samaritan Counselor. *How do I tell her? Damn, this isn't part of the job description. I guess I'll try to ease into it,* thought Alastair.

"Marion, I have some very unpleasant information to pass on to you now. I wish there was an easy way to put this on the table."

"Al, if you're going to tell me Jason was cheating on me, I always suspected it. I never had the courage to call him out. I was afraid how it might impact our son, so I just ignored it and I guess, hoped it would go away. I need to know though, I'm tired of carrying the doubt."

"It appears that Jason was involved with a woman here in town for the better part of twelve years. Jason bought the building that she uses for her business and he kept an office there for his own work. After he was murdered, the woman took all his office records and laptop and stored them. She says she had no idea what he was up to regarding his business but I'm not so sure now. The police have taken his records and will analyze them."

"Twelve years?" replied Marion, "twelve years?"

"That's what it looks like."

"I'm having trouble getting my head around the length of the relationship. It was a second life Al, not just a one-night stand. What do you know about his business dealings or is it still too early in the investigation?"

"Well, at this point, we know that the trust fund money paid to you and Stephen comes from a Caribbean bank. The Miami bank is just a pass-through. I'm not sure where all this is headed yet but, if at all possible, I suggest not spending any of the money as it may be from illegal operations and could be recovered by the government. We just don't have enough information yet."

Marion was at a loss for words. She could not accurately express how she felt. *I've been betrayed,* she thought. *I wonder if this is like when someone is a traitor to their country. I don't really feel much anger at this point, I guess I just don't understand it yet. He was a good provider for the family, we always had everything we needed and I thought he loved me. I've been a blind fool all these years.*

Alastair could see she was trying to understand what had happened but knew it would take time. "Marion, I wish I had some solid advice for you but candidly, I don't know what to say. From my experience when I lost my wife and unborn child, I can tell you it takes time, and a solid circle of friends are important too. Why don't I leave you for now and we can pick up on this later?"

"Okay, I'm going to need a bit of alone time to think this through. But before you leave, what are the next steps?"

"We found the killer and have opened up Jason's business and personal life. From here the case will be led by the police and probably the FBI given the Caribbean banking connection. I can close out my participation if you like."

"No, I need you to stay on the case," replied Marion, "I have full confidence in the police but will need an advocate as this goes forward. I know this will only get worse regarding Jason and I'm determined to stay with it until everything is on the table. Your role may be changing now but you're integral to the next steps. Are the police okay with your continued involvement?"

"I spoke with Lieutenant Hendricks the chief of detectives and he would like me to stay with the case."

"Then, that's it, nothing's changed," replied Marion.

Chapter 23

It rained on Wednesday, as the Endwell Investigations team spent most of the morning preparing for the meeting with the Binghamton Police the following day. Although they now knew a lot about Jason Belvedere and had identified his killer, there were many unanswered questions. Alistair wanted to make sure they covered all the major points in the case when they met.

Chantal and Randy had worked on the case and Gil, although not directly involved, had a good overall understanding of the issues. Along with Sherlock the three investigators and Alastair met in the conference room at the agency at nine o'clock. Gil had arrived early and made the coffee. They didn't want any interruptions so Chantal put the office phones on voice mail.

"Guys, I want the meeting tomorrow to run from a tight agenda. There's a lot of things to talk about and if we're not careful, we'll end up fixating on a minor topic and chew up a lot of time. Let's start with the shooter. We know who he is and where he lives. Fred Doblonsky actually went to Stroudsburg and took some pictures of him and his house. The next step is for the Binghamton cops to issue an arrest warrant so that the Stroudsburg cops can extradite him to Binghamton to face the charges. We need to press this guy hard to see who orchestrated the shooting. I don't believe he was flying solo. If he doesn't want to cooperate, he carries the full load. If he does want to talk, I'm sure the FBI will be all ears."

"Do we have any play in this?" asked Chantal.

"Not really," replied Alastair, "Randy turned over his files to Detective Adams and it includes the work Fred did for us finding the guy. Once he's arrested, it's a cop show. The ball's with the Binghamton police now. As I said, they'll need to issue an arrest warrant for the shooter, a Mr. Armand Houghton, presently living in Stroudsburg. This is pretty straightforward and I don't expect any problems. The case against him is pretty solid and will hold up in court. Okay, let's move on to the next item."

"Quick question Al," said Randy, "do you think they'll cut him a deal if he talks?"

"Depends what he has to sell. It's the FBI's call. If they can connect this to any of the bad boys they're currently chasing, anything's possible. I don't think the Binghamton cops will be interested in a deal with Houghton though, they got the murderer, but the Feds are a different story."

Next on Alastair's list was Marjorie Monette who owned Valley Real Estate on Plaza Drive in Vestal. Based on Alastair's meeting with Third Dominion in Miami, he was pretty sure she was a lot more involved with Jason Belvedere than she let on to Detectives Adams and Ronaldo. Someone directed Global Caribbean to start the trust fund payments to Jason's wife and son. Someone close to Belvedere. *She's a player,* he thought, *I need to get with Detective Adams and sort out the next steps. Twelve years? Maybe more than just a romantic relationship; a partner in some capacity?*

One sticky point kept coming back to Alastair: why did she keep Belvedere's records? They should have been in the shredder a long time ago, yet she kept them at the office without any security provisions. *Sort of reminds me of our government officials and their carelessness with classified material,* he thought, *but yet you willingly handed it over to the detectives. Marjorie, we need to have, as the Japanese say, 'a frank and sincere conversation.'*

Chantal was busy composing the meeting agenda as the team discussed the case. She was projecting the developing agenda onto the large screen in the conference room. It was a great way to keep the meeting topics in front of everyone.

"The next one up is the Miami and Caribbean banks. The local cops got a lot of information from Belvedere's office at Plaza Reality and it's on the way to Albany for analysis. But I also think we'll need to bring the FBI in on this. Let's put it on the agenda and talk about it tomorrow," said Alastair, "Lieutenant Hendricks always thought this smelled like money laundering and he's probably right."

Gil had been quiet during the meeting as he didn't have any direct input into the discussion up to this point. However, when he worked the recent insurance scam involving the Burris brothers, the cops found Jason Belvedere's name on one of Adam Burris' invoices and that led them to Plaza Drive and Jason's office. He was worried that Burris would be lost in the case.

"Burris will be going to trial in a couple of months and Detective Adams agreed to speak to the DA on his behalf regarding his cooperation. Burris could have stonewalled them if he wanted to but didn't do it. I hope the cops will talk to the DA. I guess his brother Marcel doesn't figure into any of this?" said Gil.

"Good point, let's put it on the agenda and see what the cops have to say," said Alastair, "I believe Pennsylvania will handle Marcel; either the Carbondale cops or State Police. What else?"

"Well," said Randy, "we have a very large case that cuts across a lot of jurisdictions and disciplines; the FBI in Washington and Miami, the Binghamton cops and Stroudsburg cops, and us. On top of that, there is a ton of data from Belvedere's files that was sent to Albany for analysis and as you said, the FBI should look at this also. Oh yeah, I almost forgot, we still have a murder investigation to complete. We need a focal point to manage or monitor all this activity or it will just spin around and eventually disappear."

"You're right," said Alastair. "We need a steering committee made up of the FBI, Binghamton cops and us. This sort of reminds me of my days with the Bureau in Miami. Large complicated investigations; lots of moving parts. We used to have weekly status meetings and, in some cases, daily meetings. It was the best way to keep them moving. What has happened and what needs to happen was the theme. Let's put it on the agenda. Chantal, will you print this out and send a copy to Detective Adams and Fred Doblonsky; that way we all start from the same point tomorrow. Okay, I think we're in good shape, anything else?"

The meeting ended after a review of their current workload, then everyone went back to their current cases. Chantal was chasing a dead-beat husband who was hiding assets in a divorce settlement while Randy had just started looking into a missing person who disappeared four years ago and his wife claimed she saw him at the Nordstrom Rack store in Syracuse the other month. They didn't think they had much of a chance to find the guy, assuming he was actually there but agreed to take a look at it. Gil, being the new guy on the team, got the cheating spouse and was gathering evidence on a wayward husband. The agency didn't do many of these cases anymore but in this instance, the cheating husband was a judge and Alastair knew his older son from the golf league at the Enjoie Golf Course. His mother asked her son to speak to Alastair; hard to say no.

Alastair also had a meeting with a new client in the afternoon. Endwell Investigations was producing much better results than a lot of the insurance company investigators. The agency was getting more calls regarding bogus claims. Some were pretty straightforward and easy to close; others surprisingly sophisticated. The meeting today involved a fairly large claim regarding allegedly stolen jewelry. How do you lose multiple pieces of jewelry? Maybe a piece, but ten pieces and no evidence of a break-in at the house. Interesting.

Chapter 24

The rain from Wednesday had continued. So, on a soggy Thursday the Endwell team and Binghamton Police gathered in the conference room at Endwell Investigations. Sherlock greeted everyone as they arrived.

By a little in front of nine o'clock, they were all there. Detectives Ronaldo and Adams and Lieutenant Hendricks from the police along with Randy, Chantal, Gil, Alastair, and of course Sherlock from the agency. Fred Doblonsky had also checked in on Zoom. They all knew each other so the local news and sports were the first topics of conversation. Syracuse University had a new basketball coach which was of great interest to Gil and Detective Ronaldo. And the new BJ's Discount Warehouse to be located in Johnson City at the old Oakdale Mall was also of interest.

Gil had baked what he referred to as 'mini-scones' for the group.

"Gil, these are really good," said Detective Ronaldo, "How did you learn to make them?"

"My mom was an avid baker, I guess some of it rubbed off on me. She made most everything from scratch and I was the one who got the ingredients out of the pantry and refrigerator for her. It gave me a good feel for ingredients and how they can complement each other. I still use a lot of her recipes. Sort of keeps the bond between us intact; she's been gone now about four years."

"I hope everyone had the opportunity to review the meeting outline," said Alastair, "it's not cast in concrete, I just wanted to give us something to work from, we have a lot to discuss."

"We went over it yesterday," said Lieutenant Hendricks, "thanks for putting it together. You're right, lots to talk about."

"I put the murder up first," said Alastair, "so we don't tie Fred up for the entire meeting. You're welcome to ride it out with us or break off after we talk about the shooter."

"I'll hang around," replied Fred, "it's an interesting case and now that I'm retired, I miss these complex cases and love getting involved. Although I didn't see it on the agenda, I can go down to Stroudsburg and put some eyes on Houghton to make sure he doesn't do a runner on us if you like. He may get wind of an impending arrest and get scarce.

"I like it," said Lieutenant Hendricks, "by the way Fred, do you know anyone in Stroudsburg who's on the job?"

"Yeah, a guy who used to work for me when I was with the Scranton police is a Lieutenant in the detective division there. More like a group rather than division. Maybe three guys total. He's the senior guy and I think he'll be the one to arrest Houghton."

"I like the loop," said the Lieutenant, "how about giving him a heads-up on what's coming. It should help ease things along. Once we send the paperwork down, some eyes on Houghton would be a good insurance policy. Stroudsburg's a small town and I'm sure they don't do a lot of extraditions so this could easily get out."

"Okay, I'll call Dave and let him know what's coming."

"What about squeezing Houghton for the name of his employer and associates?" said Randy.

"We'll do that for sure," said Lieutenant Hendricks, "but I want to get him charged and safe in our jail here before we go after the guys behind the shooting. By the way, does he have any family?"

"From what I've seen so far, he lives alone, no wife or kids. I don't know about siblings or extended family," said Fred, "does it matter?"

"Always good to know," said the Lieutenant, "if he starts giving up names, he'll be at risk and maybe his family, if he has one. We need to understand the full scope of any potential problem. We'll pull in the FBI when we arrest him, they'll talk to him about his employer."

"Yeah, we had a similar conversation about this earlier," said Randy, "do you think they'll cut him a deal?"

"Probably," said the Lieutenant, "assuming he has something solid to offer, but he also has to come clean about his role and past history. All I know at this point is we, well you guys really, caught the killer and we're going to prosecute him. It's between Houghton and the FBI as to what else falls out regarding his employer, past activity, and possible deals."

"Do you want anything more from us regarding Houghton?" asked Alastair.

"No you're good, Fred has the bet covered with the Stroudsburg cops and will be keeping eyes on our boy. We're in the hunt," replied the Lieutenant.

The team then moved on to Marjorie Monette, the owner of Valley Real Estate. From what Alastair had uncovered in Miami when he and Cisco met with Third Dominion Bank, it was clear that someone had given Global Caribbean Bank instructions to start making trust fund payments to Jason's wife and son. Given her long-term relationship with Jason, she had to be the prime suspect.

"I think she slow rolled us," said Detective Adams, "Tony and I thought we had gotten it all but clearly another conversation needs to take place."

"I have the feeling she is pretty naïve about Belvedere's business. Sort of an unwitting participant," said Tony.

"Yeah, but I bet there's probably a boatload of money in that Caribbean bank and the lovely Marjorie may have access to it. Those sobs and tears may have been a show." said Todd.

Tony laughed, "you mean that pretty face hustled us?"

"Not you hard charging detectives," laughed Randy, "maybe us slow private agency types though."

"How do you guys want to handle this?" asked the Lieutenant.

"Tony and I will go back for a second meeting. We'll put Al's findings on the table and see where we can take it."

"Where are we with the computer and files you guys recovered from your first meeting?" asked Alastair.

"Everything's in Albany now, they've had it for a week or so. I've not heard back yet, but I know we're a priority task for them. I'll track down the guy who's leading the analysis and check the status. As always, getting into the computer will be a challenge and I bet most of the good stuff is there," said Tony.

"When you guys meet with Marjorie, take a hard look at the office Belvedere used. Desk, filing cabinets, stuff like that. Sometimes computer passwords are hidden on them somewhere. You guys know the game, turn it all inside out," said the Lieutenant.

"I'll also check with Belvedere's wife, and see if she knows anything about how he handled passwords," said Alastair.

Although the cops referred to Marjorie Monette as a 'person of interest', she was much more important than that to the investigation. Alastair felt she was more like the key to opening the door. A lot of the case progress would depend on her. *I wish I could be part of the next meeting with her,* thought Alastair, *but it's a cop show now.*

For them all, the elephant in the room now was the FBI. The case was much more than a murder and a long-time girlfriend. To get to the bottom of this they needed to fully understand the game Belvedere was playing. Although they had a good idea of what he was up to with his development deals, they had no proof. Based on their limited knowledge at this point, Alastair thought a lot of Belvedere's projects were funded with mob money and that meant money laundering. Always the same game, take the dirty money and invest it in legitimate projects. However, they needed to analyze his files and more importantly, get into his computer to prove anything.

"So," said Todd, "how do we bring in the Feds and not give it all up? I always worry about some hard charger in Washington thinking he can do it all."

"Maybe not as bad as we think," replied the Lieutenant, "Al has good cards with their field office in Miami and we can call Agent Dye in Washington. He was the lead agent when we had that money laundering case here a few years back with that CPA over on Sunrise Terrace and also with that chop-shop case here and in Scranton. We're not on each other's Christmas Card list but we do keep in touch. He can get us to the right people. I'll call him when Houghton's locked up in our jail."

"I can have the same conversation in Miami also," said Alastair, "I agree it's best to wait until we have Houghton in jail here before we call them in."

"I guess the next event, for want of a better word, is the extradition of Armand Houghton and we'll get right on it," said Detective Adams, "I'll keep Fred in the loop and keep you all posted. In the meantime, Tony and I will call on Marjorie Monette. I'm sure there's another chapter there."

"I'll give Marion Belvedere a call tonight and see what she knows about Jason's approach to passwords."

"I guess we've handed out all the homework assignments," laughed Lieutenant Hendricks, "I'll give the Chief a heads up on what we're doing when we get back to the office. Between the FBI and Albany, we're going to have a lot of interest in this case. Anything else we need to talk about?"

"I have something", said Gil, "I worked an insurance fraud case awhile back and the guy we were looking at, Adam Burris, was helpful. He actually led us to Jason Belvedere. He's guilty as hell, but asked for a good word to be passed to the DA about his cooperation. He's was an idiot trying to scam the insurance company and his brother Marcel tried the same game in Carbondale, Pennsylvania, but he did lead us to the real estate office in Vestal where Jason Belvedere had an office."

'I know," replied Lieutenant Hendricks, "Todd and Tony briefed me. I'll speak to the DA this week. No promises, but you can tell Mr. Burris that the message was received and passed on to the DA and he makes the decision."

"Okay," said Gil, "that's all we can do."

"By the way Gil, you did a really good job on that case, nice work," said Lieutenant Hendricks, "you gave us a tight case, it'll be a slam dunk."

That evening Alastair called Marion Belvedere.

"Marion, I'm sorry to call you in the evening but it was a long day here."

"That's okay Al, I'm waiting for my son to pick me up. We're going out to dinner at Bud's in Apalachin."

"I know the place, they make a pretty good martini," replied Alastair, "Can I stop by your place tomorrow? I'd like to look around your home office and talk about computer passwords."

"Sure, I'm here all morning, any time after eight is good, and bring Sherlock."

Chapter 25

Alastair arrived at Marion Belvedere's house around nine o'clock. Sherlock was with him and bounded up the stairs to the front door and let out a bark which seemed to say, "we're here!" When Marion opened the door, she had a treat for Sherlock.

"You'll spoil her and she'll never come home with me!"

"I'd keep her if I thought I could get away with it," laughed Marion, "come on in and tell me how I can help. I have some coffee ready."

They sat in the kitchen with the sun coming through the sliding doors to the deck. It was opened slightly to let in the cool morning air. Sherlock stayed by Marion's side, clearly looking for more treats.

"As you know, we recovered a computer and files from Jason's office in town. We don't have the password and that makes getting into it very hard and maybe not even possible. I'd like to look around your home office and see if he may have kept the password there. If he did, it could be anywhere so I'll need to spend a couple of hours looking around."

"I moved a few things around in the office but nothing has been thrown out. I'm not aware of any password listings or a directory but that doesn't mean much, with all the other secrets he kept from me, who knows what's in there."

With a second cup of coffee in hand, Alastair went into the office and sat at Jason's desk. He looked around the room to try and get a sense of the place. There were some prints on two of the walls. Outdoor scenes, nothing special, maybe a cut above what you'd find in a descent hotel. There was a low rectangular book case along one of the walls that had two windows but there wasn't much in the bookcase in terms of documents, just some books and travel mementos. Two four drawer vertical filing cabinets were along the opposite wall. He started the search by looking behind the pictures and then moved on to the bookcase. He sifted through the pages of the books looking for anything that could be a password: no joy. He also looked at the travel mementos with the same results.

I'll look at the desk next, he thought, *It's where I'd hide something.* He took the three drawers out of the desk and emptied them onto the coffee table in the corner of the office. He carefully went through the contents and looked at the sides, bottom and back of the drawers. He emptied a coffee cup full of pens but found nothing and looked at the scratch pad on top of the desk but found nothing there also.

After that he went through the filing cabinets. Surprisingly, there was not much in them as Jason did most of his home office work on the computer. The police had taken the home computer and were looking through it. So far, It was just activity pertaining to the house but maybe there's something hidden there. Two and a half hours later he had nothing to show for his efforts. He sat at the desk and wondered, *have I missed something? What haven't I look at? What am I missing? If he has the password here, it's well hidden.*

He decided he had taken the search as far as he could and joined Marion who was sitting on the back deck with Sherlock by her side.

"Did you find anything? You were in there a long time."

"No luck, I'm afraid, it may not be there or I just can't find it."

"What are you going to do now?"

"I don't know. Maybe it's over in his office in town, we're going to take a hard look over there also. Did Jason ever talk about passwords?"

"Not really, but he always tried to keep them simple in terms of the number he used. He had the same password for the home computer, tablet, bank accounts and credit cards. He was a bit anal about it, frankly."

Damn, thought Alastair, *could this approach be in play with the computer that was is his office at Plaza Reality?*

What was the password you used here?"

"It was made up of all our initials and some numbers. I still use it. Old habits die hard I guess. It was JBMBSB142536jbmbsb!. As you can see it was the initials of all our first and last names in upper and lower-case letters, a number sequence and finished with an exclamation point. We've had it for years, he never changed it. Do you think he used the same password on that other computer?"

"I don't know," said Alastair, "but we'll run it down."

"All of this makes me so angry," said Marion, "I try to put it out of my mind and then something like this computer password thing brings it all back. Sometimes I feel as if I've been mugged. Whatever feelings I had for him are long gone. I have to be careful or I'll end up filled with bitterness and hate."

"I guess you're walking a fine line and it won't get any better in the near term. The cops will be making an arrest soon and the media will be all over it. You and Steve have to be ready for another round of heavy media coverage. The cops will try to keep a lid on it but it could go viral."

"I'll talk to Steve and let him know what's coming."

When Alastair and Sherlock left, he sat in his car outside of Marion's house and called Detective Adams. "Todd, looks like Belvedere used the initials from the families first and last names along with a number sequence and ended with an exclamation point. He used it on all the digital stuff in the house and didn't change it over the years. The password is JBMBSB142536jbmbsb!. Don't bother writing it down, I'll text it over to you when we finish. Ask the guys in Albany to run it and If it doesn't work, ask them to try

JBMM142536jbmm!, he may have used Marjorie Monette instead of his family. I'll text you both of them."

"Nice find Al," said Todd, "maybe we can get lucky. I'll call Albany as soon as I get your text. Hey, you may be in for the 'crime stopper' of the month award if this works!"

"Oh joy, another opportunity for fame," laughed Alastair, "private eye and wonder dog solve major crime!"

"By the way, Tony and I are going to see Marjorie Monette this afternoon. Judging from her tone when I called her, she seems a bit concerned that we're coming back. I was careful not to spook her but she knows something's up. I'll keep you posted. Hang on, Lieutenant Hendricks just poked his head in and asked that you call him when you get back to your office."

When Alastair got back to the office, nobody was there. He knew Randy was working on the missing person case and would be up in Syracuse at the Nordstrom Rack store looking at security tapes. The odds were slim that he would find anything as all he had were some photos from eight years ago. But he did have the date, time, and location of the possible sighting at the Mall, so maybe he'd find something. Worth a look. Chantal had left a note advising that she was with Gil who was looking into a deadbeat husband. Sherlock wandered around the empty office looking for her buddies. Alastair got a lime-flavored water drink from the small refrigerator in the printer room and called Lieutenant Hendricks. "Elton, what's up?"

"Just wanted to let you know I spoke with Fred's colleague at the Stroudsburg Police. Name is Dave McPherson. Seems like a good guy. I told him we'll be faxing them the arrest warrant and extradition request this afternoon. He said they'd process the paper quickly and arrest Houghton tomorrow morning. Would you call Fred and see if he can get down there and keep an eye on the place. Tonight and tomorrow should cover it."

"Good news, I'll get right on it. How long before you have him in jail here?"

"They'll have to book him in Stroudsburg and then we can come and get him. I'll have Todd and Tony drive down and bring him back. He should be here in a couple of days. We'll see what we can get out of him and then call in the FBI."

"We should know where we stand with the computer password by then. Todd contacted Albany and asked them to run a couple of passwords."

"Yeah, he spoke to me about it. What do you think our chances are?" asked Elton.

"Belvedere was a creature of habit," replied Alastair, "I think we're on a good track. I'd love to have the computer opened up when we call the FBI. You know, a nice complete package, computer, files, and Houghton."

"Rami called last night, he's on semester break next week and wants to play golf. You up for it?"

"Only if your son will spot me four strokes a side," Laughed Alastair, "the kid always thumps me! I'm good any day next week, let me know."

When they finished the call, Alastair called Fred to let him know about keeping eyes on Armand Houghton for the next few days. The pace of the investigation was picking up. If they could get the password for Belvedere's computer and extradite Houghton, they would be at the point of finally opening up the case.

Chapter 26

When Todd and Tony met with Marjorie Monette, she was clearly on edge, more like on guard. She sat at her desk trying to put forth a casual manner but was constantly rearranging things on the desk to calm her nerves. Although she had cooperated with the detectives when they first met by turning over Belvedere's computer and files, they now felt she hadn't told them everything. Someone had turned on the Global Caribbean Bank to start the trust fund payments to Marion and her son Steve, and Marjorie was the hands-down favorite.

Todd decided to take a different approach to the questioning. Instead of asking her a series of questions, he thought he would try to keep her off-balance and get her to think they knew more than they did.

"Marjorie, we need you to tell us the rest of the story," said Todd.

"What do you mean? I told you all I know."

"We know you haven't. This is a murder investigation, not some shoplifting charge. If you impede this investigation, you can be charged with obstructing justice. This isn't going away. It's decision time, you need to decide which side of the investigation you're going to land on."

Marjorie was starting to cry and the detectives were concerned that they may have pushed her too hard. Todd regretted the approach now. It was more like bullying. He felt he could have handled it better.

"I didn't hold anything back, I thought I told you everything. I'm not a crook. I don't understand what's going on now. Do you think I was in some kind of business arrangement with Jason?"

"Just tell us what you know. We're not here to arrest you, but you have specific knowledge that is important to the case and we need your help."

Marjorie sat quietly at her desk and appeared deep in thought, probably weighing her options. Finally, she looked up and said, "Jason told me that there was a trust fund that would pay his wife and son a monthly amount of money. I don't know how much, but it was to start after he died."

"We are aware of that; did you communicate with the bank to get the payout started?" asked Todd.

"No, No, he had an attorney in The Cayman Islands who handled it. I received a letter from him confirming that the trust fund payments had started. As I said, Jason mentioned a trust fund for his family but he never went into any detail. He was very secretive about his business dealings and family."

"Okay," said Tony, "but who told the lawyer Jason was dead and how did he find you?"

"I don't know," replied Marjorie, "when I got the letter, I called the lawyer and asked him why he was sending this to me and did I need to take any action. He told me that Jason had given him instructions that I was a correspondent on his activities in case of his death. He told me there could be other actions and he would notify me as required. This was the first I heard of the payments starting. As I said, I don't even know how much money is involved or how it's paid. He never discussed his banking activities with me and I never knew what banks he dealt with."

She continued, "I have no idea how he found out Jason was dead. As I said before I didn't know the guy existed until I got his letter.

Maybe he had some software program that monitors obituaries here. I really don't know. I kept the letter he sent me; do you want a copy?"

"Yes please," said Todd. "Are you receiving any money from Jason's estate?"

"Certainly not!" replied Marjorie, "I would have told you."

The two detectives looked at each other both thinking the same thing. *How the hell did we miss this when we first spoke to her? Were we asleep? We didn't ask the right questions and dig deeper.*

"This goes without saying," said Todd, "but if you hear from this lawyer again, we get the first call."

"I understand, I just want to be left alone. I never knew any of this was coming. I don't want any involvement in his personal affairs. He never told me anything about this. I feel like I'm being used."

"You're the judge of your personal life and that's your business. We don't have any issues with you; just keep us informed of any further contact with the lawyer, said Todd."

When they got back to the office, Lieutenant Hendricks was on the phone with Alastair. He waved the two detectives into his office and put the call on speakerphone to continue the conversation.

"They arrested Houghton yesterday morning. No issues, they nabbed him going to his mailbox. He never knew it was coming. Thank Fred for keeping an eye on him ahead of the arrest. It may be another day or two before we can bring him here though; he lawyered up and his attorney is contesting the extradition. Dave McPherson, from the Stroudsburg police isn't worried, thinks it's just a smoke screen," said the Lieutenant.

"Hey, on the way back here, I got a call from my guy in Albany who's handling Belvedere's computer; they got into it, thanks to you Al. You're definitely the favorite for the 'Crime Stopper of the Month' award now," laughed Todd.

"Did your guy say which password worked?"

"Yeah the second one, it had the initials MM in it," replied Tony. "Great intuition Al, I don't think they would have been able to crack it without your help."

"Can you have them send us a copy of the computer files?" asked Alastair. I've worked with a guy in town here, named Brad Petronella. He isn't an accountant but he's a great detail guy who's familiar with this kind of stuff. I think we need to have a grip on this when we call in the FBI. Brad should be able to get that for us."

"We're set up to handle large amounts of data between departments and agencies. Todd, have them send a copy to us and Brad can come over to the station and review it. I don't want to send the information out of the department, it's too sensitive. I remember his name; I think he did some work for us in the past."

"Okay, I'll call Brad and see what his availability looks like."

"How did you and Tony make out with the real estate lady?" asked the Lieutenant.

"Well, we sure didn't get it all the first time. Turns out Belvedere had an arrangement with an attorney in The Caymans to activate the trust fund payments to his wife and son in the event of his death. Belvedere had a long-time relationship with Marjorie Monette, the owner at Valley Real Estate in town, and had listed her as the correspondent in any actions after his death. She knew nothing about it and only found out about it when she received a letter from the lawyer. She has no active role in the management of the trust fund."

"Why did he list her as a correspondent and why didn't he tell her about it" asked Tony, "what was his game?"

"I guess he wanted someone up here aware of what he was doing, but it doesn't make any sense not to tell her. She really has no play in any of the arrangements he made with the bank in the Caribbean. Did the lawyer tell her there would be more activity at some point?" said Alastair.

"That's what she said," replied Todd, "I still think there's a boat load of money there and it will be moved at some point."

"What are you thinking Todd?" said the Lieutenant, "some kind of payout?"

"I think he may settle the account at some point and everyone gets a piece; wife Marion, son Steve, and longtime girlfriend Marjorie."

"We need to find out what instructions Jason left with that lawyer in the Caymans, but he's not going to talk to us. We can't tell him it's an open murder investigation, we already have the bad guy," said Todd. "He'll claim lawyer-client privilege and tell us to go away; we need some leverage."

"Let's find out more about the lawyer," said Alastair. "We have his address from the letter Marjorie gave you guys: let me give it to Cisco Riviera at the FBI field office in Miami. In the end, it's going to be a Gov show dealing in the Caymans, especially if it's money laundering and the mob. Once you guys finish interrogating Houghton, we'll be bringing in the FBI and we revert to a support role."

"I agree, Al," said Lieutenant Hendricks, "but after the revelations from Ms. Monette, I have the feeling that Belvedere's lawyer here in town didn't tell us everything either. It's the old duck and dodge game, if you don't ask the right question, you don't get the answer. Let's shake that tree again. What was the guy's name?"

"Ah, let me think," said Todd. "Was it Alamo? No, it was Adamo, yeah that's it, George Adamo. Isn't that it Al? Let's bring him in, that way he'll know we mean business. Al spoke to him initially; now if we bring him in, we should get his attention. Hell, Belvedere is long gone, what's left to hide?"

Chapter 27

Alastair called Brad Petronella and found him at Wegman's Supermarket in Johnson City finishing up some shopping. "You're a brave man Brad, every time I go to Wegman's, I spend three times the money I had planned and end up buying all kinds of stuff. It's a dangerous place!" he said, laughing.

"I know what you mean, my wife gives me a list and I can only buy what's on it. It's a great place to shop, they really know how to merchandise groceries. I have lunch over there sometimes, nice eating area, great selection. Anyway, I'm sure you didn't call so we can compare shopping habits; what can I do for you?"

"Do you remember the guy who was murdered in the parking lot of the EnJoie golf course about a year and a half ago? His name was Jason Belvedere."

"A bit, yeah, it was all over the media for a few weeks."

"We were retained by his widow to take a look at the case as it had gone cold. The cops did a good job of investigating the murder but hit the wall. It happens. We got lucky and found some video of a traffic analysis at an intersection next to the golf course. It gave us a good look into the parking lot and we were able to find the shooter. He was arrested in Stroudsburg the other day and will be brought back to Binghamton to face charges. The guy that was murdered led a double life. He was a so-called property developer who operated well outside of the envelope. We were able to recover his files and computer and sent them to Albany for analysis. Lucky for us we sorted out the password and they were able to get into the computer. We have a copy of the files and computer contents coming from

Albany and want you to take a look at it all. The cops will make them available to you at the station."

"What are you looking for?"

"Hell, at this point, anything, and everything. We want to get a feeling for what the guy was up to."

"Lieutenant Hendricks, the Chief of Detectives, thinks he was using mob money to finance his projects and that usually means money laundering. We don't know anything about the mob players yet."

"What do you think? Local and State bad boys?" asked Brad.

"Maybe, and most likely Florida too. He did banking in Miami and in the Cayman Islands. So, as you can see, we want to get a bit smarter regarding the adventures of Mr. Belvedere."

"I have time these days. I still do mediations at the Resolution Center downtown and also Lemon Law arbitrations. But I can easily fit this in."

"Great, I'll give your mobile number to Detective Adams and he'll call you when the files are available. Should be in a couple of days."

While Alastair was at the dog park with Sherlock later in the day, he got a call from Lieutenant Hendricks.

"Hey Al, wanted to let you know that Todd and Tony are going to Stroudsburg tomorrow to collect Houghton. They're leaving early and will have Houghton back here later in the day. Once we book him into jail, we'll question him. Should be the day after tomorrow."

"Great, I guess Houghton's attorney couldn't stop the extradition."

"Not a chance. A lot of noise and bluster but that's all."

"I'd love to sit in on the interrogation but it's not for us civilians."

"Well, there is a one-way mirror in the room and you could look in. You've been integral to the case; I think it makes good sense. You have a better feel for the guy based on your investigation. Sort of like going to the movies looking through the one-way mirror, or a victory lap, don't you think?"

"Victory lap Elton; I hope we can take it further with this guy. I bet he knows a lot."

"He's not going to tell us anything willingly but maybe we can put a scare into him, and make it easier for the FBI when they interview him. In the end, they'll be offering the deal if it comes to that."

Todd called Brad early the next day before he left for Stroudsburg. "We have the files ready for you, it's set up in a conference room next to Lieutenant Hendricks office. Tony, my partner, and I will be out of the office, we're going to Stroudsburg to pick up a guy. We'll be back later in the afternoon; I'll stop by and introduce myself."

"I know your name from Lieutenant Hendricks but I don't think our paths have crossed," replied Brad, "I have time to spend most of the day working on the files, stop by if you can."

It was about a two-hour drive to Stroudsburg from Binghamton. Down I-81 to I-380 and then I-80. There was a bit of a delay going through Scranton but other than that, smooth sailing. They had checked out a police SUV from the motor pool as they wanted to have a secure back seat area for their guest. *All the comforts of home*, thought Tony.

The detectives decided to have an early lunch and then go over to the police station. They wanted to drive straight back to Binghamton with maybe a pit stop if necessary. If they had to stop for food for Houghton, they'd used a fast-food drive-thru and keep him in the car. They didn't know much about Houghton in terms of aggressiveness and demeanor. *Keep it simple, thought Tony.*

They found the Stroudsburg Police Station a lot smaller than the Binghamton station. It was a fairly new building located in East

Stroudsburg. After they checked in with the desk sergeant, they were taken to Dave McPherson's office.

"I've got all the paperwork here but let's sign it in front of Houghton, I want him to understand that he's being formally handed over to you guys. I'm not sure he really understands what's happening. Probably, his lawyer filled his head with a bunch of stupid information. I think he believes he's going to be charged in Binghamton and released on bail. I'll have him brought to the interrogation room down the hall. Let's send him a message."

The two detectives were surprised when Armand Houghton was brought into the interview room. He was a skinny guy; maybe five foot eight if you checked his height with his shoes on. Fred Dublonsky had commented that Houghton was a 'short ass' but they didn't pick up on it at the time.

You always think of a killer as big and bad, thought Tony, *yet here is this guy who looks lost. His jail scrubs certainly don't do much for him either, way too big.* Tony had never been on a case where they had to pick up a suspect and take him back to Binghamton, so the interaction between Todd and Dave was very interesting. Although Houghton was in the room, they never spoke to him or referred to him by name nor acknowledge his presence in any way. It's as if he wasn't there. Papers were signed, and that sealed the deal so to say.

Eventually, Todd looked over at Houghton and for the first time spoke to him. "We're driving straight back to Binghamton so if you need to make a pit stop, now's the time. Once we hit the road we're going straight through."

Dave took Houghton to the men's room and then they were off. Houghton was in handcuffs which were shackled to an eye-bolt in the floor of the SUV. Not a word was spoken to him on the ride back to Binghamton. He was checked into the County jail on upper Front Street, and a court appearance date was scheduled to allow him to enter a plea.

When Todd got back to the station, he poked his head into Lieutenant Hendrick's office. "Signed, sealed, and delivered, Elton."

"Any problems?"

"No, he just sat there. I think he's pretty scared, he has no idea what evidence we have against him. The Stroudsburg cops weren't talking to him during the hand-over and we sure didn't on the way back. Dave McPherson got a search warrant for his house and car, and said we can join the search if we want to."

"McPherson seems like a pretty heads-up guy, let's stay out of their backyard. Fred Doblonsky can call him and check-in, that should be enough. By the way, Brad Petronella has been here since nine o'clock. I think we should call him 'digger', he's relentless!"

"I'm going to check in with him, we've never met."

Tony was already in the conference room when Todd arrived. "Brad, this is my partner, Todd, I don't think you guys have met."

"Nice to put a name with a face," said Brad, "your boss has mentioned you a couple of times."

"I hope he had good things to say about me, I've returned all the stolen money," laughed Todd.

"I think you're safe for another couple of weeks," replied Brad, "you've certainly given me a pile of data to look through."

"I know it's early days, but what do you think?"

"At this point, I'm trying to put this stuff in a logical order so I can make better sense of it, but it looks like Belvedere funded his projects in two ways, bank loans and private capital."

"You mean investors?" said Tony.

"For want of a better term, that's right," replied Brad, "but it looks like the funds flowed through companies, not individuals."

"How many from each source?" asked Todd.

I don't have a hard number yet, but I can tell you that most of his projects used private funds. I don't know why he even used banks; it seems as if he had ready access to private capital. Has anyone spoken to the local lawyer who put these investment companies together? I can see his hand in almost all of the private capital deals."

"Al Stewart did when he first started his investigation."

"I think he's worth another look. He rolled out and closed up a lot of companies for Belvedere over the years, so he should know what was going on, or he was as dumb as a bag of rocks. He may not have been part of the projects but clearly he had to be close to it."

"I've spoken to Al about him, we're going to bring him in for a chat."

"Let me dig some more before you bring him in, I think I can give you some interesting questions to ask the guy."

Chapter 28

Armand Houghton was taken to court to hear and respond to the charges against him. As expected, he pleaded Not Guilty. Tony was in court to watch the proceedings and was surprised to see that Houghton had a criminal defense lawyer from New York City representing him. He didn't know the attorney or his law firm; but clearly the guy was not a public defender. Todd made a note of the attorney's name and law firm and would check him out when he returned to the office.

Houghton's attorney, Roderick Benjamin argued forcefully for bail for his client but the judge would not grant it. The assistant district attorney countered that the charge was first degree murder and Houghton was a flight risk. It was mostly posturing by Benjamin, who knew bail would not be on the table. So, Houghton was denied bail and sent back to jail to await trial.

When Tony returned to the office, he spoke to Todd about the court session. "It was all pretty straight forward, except Houghton had a heavy hitter from the City in his corner. Someone is bank-rolling Houghton; the guy was impressive. I have his name and his law firm."

"Okay, let's see what we have in the database and, we can ask Elton to talk to his buddies at the NYPD to see what they know about the guy. He's up in Albany today; I'll send him a text."

The two detectives did an internet search on Benjamin and found his law firm, Mitchel, Cameron, and Clay, who mostly handled criminal defense cases. "I bet they charge more than one hundred dollars an hour," laughed Todd.

"Probably more like six or eight times that plus travel and subsistence," replied Tony.

"Let's see what Elton can find out from the NYPD, I'm sure they know about these guys."

Lieutenant Hendricks replied later in the day that Benjamin and his firm did a lot of criminal defense work around the East coast but did not work for the mob and had a good reputation. The NYPD was surprised to hear that they were representing Houghton.

When the cops interrogated Houghton, he was brought to police headquarters. They could have used a conference room at the jail, but the cops wanted to make an impression and set the tone. This time he was represented by another lawyer from Mitchel, Cameron, and Clay. Maybe Roderick Benjamin was out chasing bigger game. The cops left Houghton and his attorney alone in the room for twenty minutes before they came in. Alastair was on the other side of the one-way mirror. Lieutenant Hendricks and Todd handled the interrogation while Tony sat in, but was not an active participant.

Lieutenant Hendricks started the conversation. "Mr. Houghton, can I call you Armand?"

"I don't care."

"Okay, forget the civilities, let's cut to the chase; we know you killed Jason Belvedere; we have it on tape."

"I don't believe you. You're telling me a golf course parking lot had video surveillance? Come on Lieutenant," said Phil Colbert, who was the attorney present, "what is that place, a high crime area?"

"No, not at all, it's a nice residential area," replied Todd, "this is upstate New York, counselor."

"And I didn't say there was surveillance in the parking lot," said the Lieutenant.

"What are you talking about? If you have some surveillance footage, let's see it." said Phil.

Todd had set up a monitor and DVD recorder ahead of the meeting. It was on a cart in the corner of the room and had not been noticed by Colbert or Houghton. Todd rolled the cart over to the end of the table and looked over at Lieutenant Hendricks, who nodded for him to play the DVD. At this point, Colbert was on edge He didn't expect this. The DVD was about forty minutes long. The cops wanted to show the whole time when Belvedere was in the lot waiting. It was important to show that nobody was in contact with him before Houghton arrived, so the cops ran the recording from thirty minutes before Houghton entered the lot. To begin with, nothing happened, but after thirty minutes things moved quickly. Houghton enters the lot, parks next to Belvedere's car on the driver's side. He gets out of the car, walks over to Belvedere and after a brief conversation, shoots him. After that he quickly walks back to his car and leaves. Although they were not able to see him actually shoot Belvedere because of the trees, they could see him leave his car and go over to Belvedere's car. It was clear that nobody else was in play.

"That's it? That's all you have" asked Phil Colbert. I don't see my client shooting anyone. Like that old lady used to say in the Wendy's ad, 'Where's the beef?'"

"Do you see that car parked two spaces over on the driver's side of Belvedere's car?"

"Sure, so what?" said Colbert.

"Well. keep an eye on it," said Todd, "About five minutes later a guy goes to the car and then notices Belvedere. He goes over to check on him and finds him dead. Guess what? That's me. So the only person who was near Belvedere was your client. We have Belvedere coming into the lot and me finding him dead. Nobody, but nobody, went near the car except Houghton."

"Our DA is happy with the case and is ready to go to trial," said the Lieutenant, "Oh, another thing, before we started, I got a call from the Stroudsburg cops who executed a search warrant on your house, Mr. Houghton, and found three pistols hidden in the wall space between your laundry room and furnace. I'll bet you a paycheck that one of the guns was used to kill Belvedere. Looks like you didn't use throw-aways. We're going to run ballistics tests on all three; I think we'll find some other murders where those guns were used."

The room was silent as Houghton and Colbert considered the minefield they had walked into.

"I'd like some time with my client please," said the attorney.

"Certainly, we'll leave a uniform outside, let us know when you want us back," said the Lieutenant.

When they got back to the office, Tony said, "When did you get the call from the Stroudsburg cops?"

"Actually, a text," replied the Lieutenant got it just as I was leaving my office, from Dave McPherson. So, let these guys talk and see where they want to take it."

Thirty minutes later, Phil Colbert asked the uniform outside the room to ask the detectives to come back. For a few minutes, nobody spoke, each waiting for the other side to start the conversation.

Finally, Colbert said, "what do you have to offer for our cooperation?"

"You got this ass-backwards, counselor. We have a solid case on the murder and are prepared to fight it out in court. On top of that, we have three pistols from Houghton's place. I'm betting your boy never disposed of his weapons after a hit. Who knows where this will take us; the FBI keeps meticulous ballistics records. So, stand by for a surprise party. The real question is: what do you have to offer us?. You're the seller and we're the buyer. Don't try to flip the table."

Houghton was visibly scared and was starting to rock back and forth in his chair. It seemed like a coping mechanism for stress.

"So, let us know what you want to do. We're happy to convict Houghton for the murder of Jason Belvedere and let the FBI do whatever they want with him. If you've got something to sell, I'll put you with the FBI."

"What do you and the FBI want from my client?"

"To ask that question is to know the answer." said the Lieutenant, "We want to know who Houghton was working for and why he whacked Belvedere. Also, maybe he has some interesting adventures to tell the FBI about his past activities. The ball's in your court, counselor, keep in touch."

The cops left Colbert and Houghton in the room to talk about their next moves. When they finished, Colbert would head back to New York City and Houghton to the jail on upper Front Street.

"This is bullshit," said Houghton, "I'm a dead man. If I talk to the FBI and give up anything, they'll kill me, I won't last a day in prison. Even if I don't talk; they'll still kill me. You know they never take any chances. And you, he said looking at Phil Colbert, I don't even know who you are. You'll probably go back and tell them everything that went on today. Yet one more reason for them to kill me. Shit, I'm toast."

"Mr. Houghton, we have no vested interest in your employers, whoever they are. The only reason we are representing you is because one of our senior partners told us we had to do it. This whole thing stinks in my opinion. The partner is rumored to have heavy gambling debts and may have been pressured to take your case. I don't know the people who are in back of this and, I don't want to know."

"What should I do?"

"As your attorney, I advise you to meet with the FBI. As I said, I know nothing about your employers and furthermore whether or not the FBI is interested in them. In my opinion the case against you is strong. We can argue that the evidence is circumstantial as there is no direct evidence showing you actually killing Belvedere, but the cops have a solid story before and after the shooting and I think it will hold up in court. I don't think you can beat the charges.

Your only chance is to cut a deal with the FBI. If you have enough to sell, they might put you in protective custody and relocate you somewhere far away from here. Short of that you can roll the dice."

"Am I safe in jail here?"

"I don't know, talk to the cops, and let them know what you're thinking. Maybe they can keep you away from the general prison population if you decide to cooperate. You need to understand that if you do go down this road, you'll be flying solo. Your meetings with the FBI will just be you and them. We can counsel you ahead of the meeting, but we won't be sitting at the table when you talk about your employers and past activity."

As they were finishing the conversation, a uniform came into the room to let Houghton know it was time to go back to the jail.

"Give me a call when you make a decision," said Colbert.

The next day, Houghton called Detective Adams. "I want to cooperate, but I'm worried that once they find out about it, they'll kill me. I want to be moved to a safe place in the jail."

"The Broome County Sheriff runs the jail, we'll call him."

Chapter 29

Brad Petronella had been hard at work since last week and assembled a good picture of Belvedere's business operations. The basic model was easy to understand. He used private capital to fund his projects. Separate companies were formed for each development project. Belvedere used his Binghamton lawyer George Adamo to form the companies. Once a project was completed it was sold on to an investment or management company in the US within two years. Then the initial project development company was dissolved --—gone. And that completed the cycle; the money was laundered.

When a project development company was formed, it was registered in Delaware and money was invested in the company from the subsidiary company in the islands. Never any names of investors as it was company to company transfers. Clearly money was moved from accounts in the islands to the newly registered company, but who were the players?

Brad was able to find ten projects that all used the same model. There were also two other companies funded by loans from US banks. There was no off-shore money in the two companies. It was not clear why he did this when the Cayman Islands seemed to offer a limitless source of capital. Brad suspected it had something to do with tax filings with the Internal Revenue Service.

" Elton, I've taken this about as far as I can. We need to have the forensic accountants look at this. Ideally folks who know about money laundering."

"Sounds like we're ready to bring in the FBI," said the Lieutenant, "but before we go there I want to take a closer look Belvedere's lawyer, he had to know what was going on. Someone had to register those companies in the Cayman Islands and I bet it was his local lawyer who handled it from this end. I'll have Todd bring him in. Meeting here will get his attention."

When Todd got hold of George Adamo, he went immediately to a defensive posture.

"I already met with an investigator about Jason Belvedere, I don't have anything more to say. I'm sorry but I can't help you."

"Mr. Adamo, this is a murder investigation. You can meet with us voluntarily or we'll issue a subpoena. It's your call, sir."

"Well, what do you want to talk about?"

"I'm not going to go over it in detail over the phone, but we're interested in the incorporation of his development companies and have additional questions."

"Why don't you talk with Mr. Stewart, I told him everything I know."

"We're going in circles Sir and you need to make a decision; are you willing to meet with us or do I get a subpoena?"

"Alright, when do you want to meet?"

"I'm in court tomorrow morning but anytime in the afternoon is okay. You can pick the time; whatever works for you."

The next day at two in the afternoon, George Adamo met with Lieutenant Hendricks and Detective Adams in one of the interrogation rooms at police headquarters. The rooms were sparsely furnished. Grey walls with no pictures, simple metal table and chairs and a large one-way mirror on one of the walls. Adamo was nervous and looked at the mirror wondering who was on the other side. The cops left him alone in the room for fifteen minutes and observed him through the one-way mirror.

"He looks nervous," said Todd, "this is all new to him. I doubt if he ever handled any criminal cases."

"I think you're right," replied the Lieutenant, "this is unfamiliar territory for him. Let's give him a few more minutes to think about it all. Let's also have Tony sit in here and observe the interrogation."

When the detectives went into the interrogation room, Lieutenant Hendricks carried two large folders. They had nothing to do with Adamo or Jason Belvedere, but he wanted him to think they had a lot of evidence. The ploy worked as Adamo stared at the large folders wondering what was happening.

"Mr. Adamo," said the Lieutenant, "why don't you tell us about the work you did for Jason Belvedere, all of it this time."

"I already told everything to Mr. Stewart. I set up corporations for Mr. Belvedere and when the projects were finished, dissolved the companies."

"Yes you did," said Todd, "and these companies were also registered in the Cayman Islands."

"I don't know anything about that," replied Adamo, clearly on edge now.

"Look, you're not telling us everything. These companies did not magically appear in the registry in the Cayman Islands. You had a hand in it. "

"I didn't have any role in registering the companies."

"You may not have filed the actual registration but you played a role in it getting the documentation to a party in the islands who did register the companies. Now, here's how this is going to unfold. We don't have the resources to conduct a full investigation of the Cayman Islands side of Belvedere's activities, so you can stonewall us and maybe even get away with it. But we're not going to let that happen. This is a money laundering operation and you know it sir. We'll soon be meeting with the FBI and they'll take over the investigation. Trust me, it will be thorough and everything will come out."

At this point, George Adamo was visibly shaken. This wasn't just the local cops running an investigation, it was going to get much bigger. *Oh God, why did I ever get involved with that guy. I knew he was up to no good but thought I could stay out of it. Now he's dead and the FBI is being called in. What a mess. What am I going to do?*

Adamo did not immediately respond. Todd reached into a small folder he had brought into the meeting and took out the copy of the letter from the Cayman Islands attorney sent to Marjorie Monette advising that trust fund payments were being made to Belvedere's wife and son.

"Recognize the name and address?" he said as he slid the letter over to Adamo.

"Yeah, that's the law firm I dealt with. Once the development company was formed and registered here, I sent the documentation to him and I guess he registered it in the Cayman Island."

"You guess?" said Todd, "maybe you can be more specific."

"Okay, I suspected Belvedere was up to no good but did not press him on it. This was his business and I was only sending on corporation documents. It was his show."

"Did he ever discuss any of this with you; mention any names or associates?"

"No, his was the only name on the incorporation documents I handled. I asked him once why use the Cayman Islands and he sort of laughed and said tax advantages. I always thought he was up to no good but I didn't feel I was part of it. I was just moving paper for him."

"What about when a project was finished?" asked Elton.

"He would tell me to dissolve the company and let the lawyer in the Caymans know. This happened after the project was sold on to a company here in the US. That was all my involvement with Belvedere. I never dealt with any financial transactions with him.'

'Why did he use a separate company for each project? Could he have just used the same company over and over?" asked Todd.

"I guess he could but I think he wanted keep everything separate. Once the onward sale was completed, he dissolved everything associated with it. I've told you all I know; now, can I go?"

"We're done for today," replied Lieutenant Hendricks, "but the FBI may want to speak with you and you may have an issue with the Broome County Bar Association. They may not be happy with you. Do you have anything else to tell us? Now's the time."

Adamo didn't say anything but the detectives felt there was more to the story.

Chapter 30

When Armand Houghton was arrested in Stroudsburg, Pennsylvania and extradited to Binghamton, the media were all over the story. It was a big event and covered in depth. They wrote about the murder of Jason Belvedere, the investigation going cold, then brought back on track after Endwell Investigations took it on. There were no accusations of incompetence on the part of the police; In fact, the police spoke highly of Alastair and his team for opening up the case. Alastair never liked publicity of any kind and always kept a low profile, but before the media finished, his FBI career and loss of his wife and unborn baby were also part of the story. There was no way to avoid something like this, you had to let it run its course. Over the weeks it did die down but was still painful to him.

He spoke to Marty Fitzgerald about it. They planned to marry at the end of the year and Alastair was worried about the impact on her. She dealt with similar issues as a therapist at The Samaritan Counseling Center in Endwell and was a welcome resource for Alastair.

"I've come to terms with it over the years," said Alastair, "but I hate to relive it through the news. I feel like I'm on display and an object of pity."

"Well, you are Al no doubt about it. You're going to have to put on your flak jacket and get through it. Give it some more time, these things are short-lived and will soon finish."

"Most folks have been pretty good about it, but I can see it in their expressions. 'You're the guy who was shot in Miami and lost your wife and baby'. "

"Just don't talk about it with them and it will die out quickly. Don't fuel the discussion."

"I'm pretty much doing that, but I don't like the notoriety and publicity for the agency. We need to stay under the radar; our clients expect it."

"Give it another week and I bet the media will be feeding in a different pasture."

The last few days, Alastair had noticed a black Lincoln Town Car parked in the small strip mall across from the agency. It was an older Lincoln, maybe ten years or so but looked to be in great shape. He also saw it on a couple of evenings driving by his house after he came home from work. He got the plate number and called Lieutenant Hendricks.

"Elton, I think there's been a car following me. I've seen it across the street from my office and also driving by my house. Can you run the plates for me.?"

"Sure, has anyone been in contact with you? E-mails, phone calls?"

"No, nothing. I'm not positive they're following me, but I've seen the car a few more times than I like."

"Let me call the desk sergeant at the station, he can run it down. New York plates?"

"Yeah, here's the numbers."

"I'll call you back in five minutes."

When the Lieutenant called back, his voice was animated. "Al, this is interesting, the car is registered to Alfredo Bertolli. Goes by Fredo; do you know the name?"

"I think I've heard of him, fill me in."

"He's a local bad boy who's reputed to be in the mafia or at least involved with them. We've never had him to the station, but he's on our radar along with his associates."

"What's he want with me? I've never even spoken to him. I wonder if it's connected to Jason Belvedere?"

"That would be my guess," replied Elton, "Either they set up the hit on Belvedere or know something about it."

"Where are you with Armand Houghton? Any developments since the interrogation?"

"Not yet. As you know, we left it that if he doesn't cooperate with us and the FBI, he'll carry the full load which is murder one. I'm waiting for his attorney to come back to me with their decision. Candidly, we don't have anything to offer him, it's the FBI's call and that will depend on what he has to sell."

"So, when is this going to happen, the FBI I mean?"

"I'll call the FBI shortly, but ahead of that, I want to get us all together early next week and review everything before I make the call. You have field office contacts in Miami and I've worked with an agent in Washington. He's sort of a big fish now. We worked two cases in the past. I trust the guy."

"What's his name?' asked Alastair.

"Louis Dye; do you know him?"

"I briefed him a couple of times when I was in the Miami office. He has a good reputation; must be pretty senior now."

"I don't know where he is in the pecking order, but he still takes my phone calls. What about meeting next Monday morning? Bring Randy, Chantal, and Gil. We need to have everyone on the same page when we take the next steps."

"We should be good; I'll check with them in the morning. No news is good news."

When he finished the call, he decided to take Sherlock over to the dog park to meet up with her buddies. It was late on a sunny afternoon and most of the recent high temperatures had passed. Everyone in the office was out catching crooks, as Randy liked to say so Alastair decided to take advantage of the free time. The park was always busy this time of day so Sherlock easily found some familiar canine acquaintances. Lots of wagging tails!

Alastair sat on one of the wooden benches surrounding the park and started to check the market closing prices and various newsfeeds on his phone. He usually let Sherlock run free in the park. She knew the area and never wandered off. Some of the other owners followed their dogs around and it seemed as if the dogs were taking them for a walk. As he was looking around the park to check on Sherlock he noticed a black Lincoln Town Car in the parking lot. He couldn't see the plates but felt sure it was the same car that had been following him. He couldn't see if anyone was in the car as the sun reflecting off the windshield limited the view inside. *Why the interest in me, thought Alastair? I've never dealt with Fredo Bertolli before.*

As he was thinking about this, a man came along and sat on the bench next to him. He had very expensive loafers and his shirt and pants were a cut above the usual style in Binghamton. Before the man could say anything, Alastair spoke to him.

"Okay my friend, what your game plan?"

Before he could answer, Alastair said, "Keep your hands where I can see them."

"I'm not here to shoot you pal, relax."

"Oh, that makes me feel much better; happy days are here again. What do you want?"

"Mr. Bertolli would like to speak with you."

"So, you follow me around for four days. What are you worried about? I'm not going anywhere; you can easily call the office and sort out a time to meet."

" Mr. Bertolli doesn't know you and is a very cautious man. He's sitting in his car over there, let's go and meet with him."

"I'm not getting into a car with the two of you. Tell your boss, I'll listen to what he has to say, but you stay here until we finish. If he doesn't like the arrangement, we can set a time at my office."

Bertolli's driver, who was also his bodyguard, went back to the car and returned after a few minutes.

"That's okay with him. I'll wait here."

When Alastair got to the Lincoln, the rear door on the car opened and a short, lean man looked out at him.

"Please sit in the back with me Mr. Stewart; it's easier to talk sitting side by side."

Alastair judged Fredo Bertolli to be in his early seventies and in good physical shape. His hair was grey and he had dark eyes. Maybe he was five foot eight, but not more than that.

"This is your meeting Mr. Bertolli, what can I do for you?"

"I've been asked to pass a message to you regarding the incident in Miami when you were with the FBI."

"Let's not mince words," said Alastair, "It was an assassination. I lost my wife and baby and damn neared died myself! What can you possibly tell me about that?"

"My associates in the City want me to pass on to you that the shooter was not contracted to kill you. He was supposed to shoot at the car, not kill you or anyone with you."

"I tracked down the shooter in a hospice in Teaneck, New Jersey," said Alastair, "He had lung cancer and in his final days. I was able to speak with him and let him know I'd found him. His name was Rocco Lanza. Usually, when someone screws up a hit, he doesn't last very long. They take him out: Lanza was an old man, maybe in his late seventies."

"He was a 'made man' and that saved him. They never used him again and cut him loose from the family. He was pretty much a bag-man after that doing odd jobs. No responsibilities and no future."

"Why are you telling me this? It serves no purpose. My wife and child are gone and now your associate says, I'm sorry? I'd ask you for the name of your associate but I know that's not going to happen, it would open him up to a murder charge."

"My associate lives by his own rules. All I can tell you is that when he saw your name in the press a while back he asked me to get hold of you and pass on this information. I never knew Lanza, but he was a fool for letting this get out of control."

This was little consolation to Alastair; his wife and baby were dead regardless of the intent of the shooter. There's a bigger game going on here he thought. *I wonder if Belvedere was involved with the mob in the City on his development deals?*

There was no way forward with the conversation. Bertolli would never admit to any involvement. The name of the person behind the shooter might come from Armand Houghton; if he decided to cooperate. However, Alastair didn't want to leave without taking a shot.

"So where does Jason Belvedere fit into all of this?"

Bertolli was quiet for a few moments, clearly deciding on how to respond. Finally he looked over at Alastair and said, "I never knew the guy or ever did business with him. He was never in play with me."

"Nobody comes into your territory for a hit without you being advised. Come on Mr. Bertolli, I know the game."

Clearly angry now, Bertolli responded. "I was advised that there was a hit coming in my territory but had no names, no dates, or the place it was going to happen. Take it or leave it Mr. Stewart, I don't care."

"Okay Mr. Bertolli, finding out that the shooting in Miami was not intended to be a hit is of little consolation but I do appreciate finally knowing what was behind it."

Alastair got out of the car and went back to the bench where Bertolli's man was standing. Sherlock saw him and came bounding over. She wiggled in between the two men, tail wagging.

"Nice dog, Mr. Stewart."

"That she is; I'll see you around."

After Bertolli left the dog park, Alastair sat quietly thinking about what had just transpired. Sherlock came over and sat near him, knowing that they would be leaving soon. *Nothing ever happens with these guys without a reason* he thought, *somehow Belvedere's in this mix, but for the life of me, I can't connect the dots. Also, telling me about Emi and the baby doesn't get you a 'get out of jail free card'.*

Chapter 31

When Alastair got home, he called Lieutenant Hendricks. "Elton, sorry to call after work but I didn't want to sit on this. I just spent an hour with Fredo Bertolli over at the dog park here."

"Really, is he a dog person?"

"Hardly, but he did have a bodyguard," laughed Alastair.

"What's going on? Did he threaten you or try to push you around?"

"Nothing like that. We sat in the back of his Lincoln and he told me that the assassination attempt on my wife and me in Miami was a mistake. The shooter, a guy named Rocco Lanza was only supposed to scare us, not try to kill anyone."

"How did he know this?"

"One of the crime families in the City asked him to pass the information to me. He wouldn't give up the name of the guy as it would open up a murder charge. Bertolli said the guy in the city saw my name in the papers when you extradited Belvedere to Binghamton. Bertolli was just the messenger."

"Why now, and frankly, why did he even tell you this?"

"I don't know. Maybe he's getting out of the business and wants to tie up loose ends, or maybe he's connected to the Belvedere case and is looking for some reciprocity. If Houghton will talk to us, we may be able to get closer to it."

"So it wasn't supposed to be a hit in Miami?"

"Nope, apparently, just shoot up the car and scare me, hoping I would back off on the investigation."

"Well Al, I hope you get some closure on this. It won't bring your wife and baby back, but maybe all the chapters have been read now and you can close the book or at least put it on the shelf."

"I guess, but these things are never neat. So, it was a mistake. It doesn't make anything better: in fact, it highlights the stupidity of the whole thing. But at least I know Emi and the baby were not targets. Oh, while I have you on the phone, we're good for meeting next Monday, I'll have a full crew."

"What are you doing this weekend? I'm going to do some ribs and you can bring the beer, if you like."

"I'd love to, but my sister's boys are home for the weekend and she's cooking up a storm."

"No problem, catch you next time around."

Friday was a quiet day at the office. Gil and Randy were still out on cases, so Chantal worked in the reception area covering the phones, and Sherlock was with her, always on the lookout for a treat or a pat on the head. Alastair had two appointments in the afternoon with new clients; other than that, not a lot was happening. He went out to the reception area and joined Chantal and Sherlock.

"Al, have you seen Houghton since the cops brought him back?" asked Chantal

"Sort of; I've not spoken to him but I observed his interrogation through a one-way mirror. He's pretty scared and is worried that he may get killed in the jail here, and more likely in a Federal Prison if he's convicted. Even if he doesn't talk, I don't think the bad boys will take a chance on him. It'll be a life sentence and anything can happen along the way. He'll always be at risk."

"Sounds like a dead man walking," said Chantal.

"Yeah, for sure. If he has something to sell, the FBI could put him in witness protection, but he needs something big to catch their attention. I'm not sure how big a contract player he was with the mob. In any case he's going to have to hang a lot of guys out to dry, and also come clean on his own past activities."

"TBD," replied Chantal, "to be determined."

"This will morph into an FBI case once we have our meeting next week and call them in. I think we're frying some very big fish but it's early innings."

Chantal didn't bring up Alastair's new found notoriety from the recent extradition of Houghton to Binghamton. What more could be added to the saga?; let it go. For the remainder of the morning, they talked about current and upcoming cases and then went over to Pete's Legacy Diner on the old Vestal Road for lunch.

"Sherlock can guard the office while we're out," laughed Alastair.

Chapter 32

On Monday, Alastair, Chantal, Gil, and Randy from Endwell Investigations, along with Elton, Todd, and Tony from the Binghamton Police met in the conference room next to Lieutenant Hendrick's office. Todd had arrived early so the coffee was ready and an agenda was projected on the big screen.

Rather than support the image of us cops eating big donuts, we have Danish pastries as well as bagels, and for anyone still in that hard-core group, a few donuts," laughed Tony.

"Great stuff," said Randy, "you should cater office meetings, I bet you could build a nice side business."

"Well you guys are always such good hosts when we meet at your place, we wanted to show you we had style too," replied Todd.

After a round of small talk about local happenings, Todd opened the meeting.

Looking at the agenda on the screen, he said, "The order is pretty much as it came to me. Give it a look and see if I missed anything. It's not very long and I keep thinking I might have come up short."

The room was quiet for a few minutes while the group looked over the agenda. Nobody had any additions, so they decided to run with it. The agenda consisted of the names of people involved in the case and the next steps. Although not listed on the agenda, the elephant in the room was what would happen to their roles once the FBI was involved. Would they lose all control and be cut out of the investigation? Anticipating this, Lieutenant Hendricks brought the subject up.

"I think we're all wondering about the same thing. What happens when we bring in the FBI. Will we get pushed aside? I've been down this road twice with these guys and haven't been shut out. They have more resources than we do, so it's a given that they'll take the leadership role. I've no problem bringing them into the game. As I said earlier, they have a lot of resources and can do things we can't. Also, Al is from their Miami office and they should be a major player. I think we're solid with these guys and it'll work."

From there, they went to the first name on the list, Marjorie Monette. Todd started, "We've interviewed her twice now and I think Tony and I have gotten close to all she has to offer. Admittedly, she didn't volunteer all the information at first, so we had to go back a second time and have a pointed conversation. She claims she never knew about Belvedere's Caribbean connections or that she was listed as a correspondent with the bank there. My sense is that as his longtime partner in an affair, she never asked any questions. She willingly gave up Belvedere's office at her agency and also the letter from the attorney in the Cayman Islands' so I don't think she was his partner in the business, but we think she still knows more than she's telling us. My gut feel is that once she saw the letter from the Cayman Island attorney regarding the trust fund for Belvedere's wife and son, she figured she might also be in line for something, and was trying to keep that away from us and I also think she knew about her correspondent relationship with the bank. Maybe she didn't know anything about his business dealings but the letter from the attorney she gave us was not a total surprise to her.

Lieutenant Hendricks and Alastair sat quietly and let the exchange between the investigators and detectives unfold. They were careful not to dominate the meeting. They let the team set the pace.

"So, you don't have it all?" asked Gil.

"Not yet," replied Todd, "but when we bring the FBI in, we should have another go at her. As I said, I'm sure the Caribbean side was not a total surprise to her. Also, we still don't know how the Caribbean bank found out about Belvedere's murder."

"We never found any letters or communications between Belvedere and Marjorie so whatever was going on was probably either a verbal understanding, or there's other files we've not seen," said Tony, "I bet there are other files."

"For her to be registered with the Global Caribbean Bank as a correspondent, wouldn't they want some kind of identification and verification from her? I can't believe it was simply Belvedere telling the bank to copy her on all correspondence in the event of his death. Surely, they must have sent her some kind of documentation to be filled out and probably notarized in the States? I'm sure they have a law firm in the States that does this for them." said Chantal, "I think there's a lot of money in those Caribbean accounts and it looks like to me Miss Marjorie is the keeper of the vault. I'll bet you Gil's next paycheck she has a file dealing with this."

"Why my paycheck?" laughed Gil.

"Good call Chantal," said the Lieutenant, "Todd, when you write a summary memo for the FBI, make sure we cover this. Maybe more layers of the onion to peel back."

Next up was Belvedere's local attorney, George Adamo. As with Marjorie, they felt that they didn't have the full story yet. Over an extended period of time, Adamo had rolled out and rolled up a number of investment companies for Belvedere, and both Alastair and Lieutenant Hendricks felt he knew more than he had disclosed so far.

"There must have been conversations between them about some of the players who invested in Belvedere's companies. Sure, they invested through the shell companies but I have to believe Belvedere and Adamo must have talked about it; individual names and places to some degree. Adamo could not operate with a completely hands-off approach," said Alastair.

"What do you want to do about him?" asked Todd.

"I'd like to see you guys and the FBI make a run on him."

"Tag team," laughed Todd.

"Yeah, something like that," replied Alastair, "there's more information to be mined."

"Okay," said Lieutenant Hendricks, "we'll take it as an action item to bring him in when the FBI comes on board."

The next name on the list was Marion Belvedere. "I know she's not involved in her husband's business, but I put her name up there because I think we need to keep a communication channel open with her. This case will get a lot of attention once the FBI shows up," said Todd, "My thought is that we need to keep her in the loop as best we can. Maybe nothing more than phone calls now and then, but we don't want to shut her out. Al, I think you're the point man for this."

"Yeah, I agree. I own this one. I'll need to coordinate with you guys in terms of what we tell her as this unfolds. Most of it will be close-held, so it won't be an open book disclosure with her for sure."

"What is she doing with the trust fund payments?" asked Randy, "If it's laundered money, can she keep it?"

"I told her to keep it in a separate account and not spend any of it. If it's 'tainted', she may not be able to keep it. Same thing for her son Steve, he's also getting trust fund payments. We won't know how this will play out until the forensic accountants finish their analysis and that's a long way off."

"Al, did Belvedere do all his banking with the Caribbean bank?" asked Gil.

"Looks like Florida and the Caymans. Best we know at this point, based on Brad Petronella's look at Belvedere's files, is that all his project companies banked through Third Dominion in Miami. Most of his projects were funded through investments by shell companies in the Cayman Islands but there were some, maybe two, that were funded by US banks.

"That's odd," said Randy, "His projects never went south of Washington, DC, and yet his banker was in Miami."

"I think it's tied into Global Caribbean Bank in the Cayman Islands. Belvedere may have wanted a bank in Miami that knows its way around the territory. It's going to take a lot of effort by the accountants to unwrap this," said Lieutenant Hendricks.

"And yet the trust fund payments come from the Caymans?" said Chantal.

"Yep, if they had come from Third Dominion in Miami, there could be a case for some of the money not being laundered, as two of the projects were funded by US banks and did not involve Global Caribbean. My guess is everything out of the Caymans was laundered," replied Lieutenant Hendricks.

"So it's all dirty money?" said Gil.

"Looks that way," replied Alastair.

"I think that's all the people on the agenda," said Todd, "did I miss anybody?"

"What about Armand Houghton?" asked Chantal.

"Yikes, I knew someone was missing, sorry."

"Wow, we all missed it when we reviewed the agenda," said Alastair. "So much for our hard charging investigation team," he laughed. "Okay, let's talk about him."

"He's safe in the County Jail," said Tony, "We have him isolated; he has little or no contact with the other prisoners."

"I got a call from his attorney yesterday advising that Houghton wants to cooperate in the investigation. It's verbal at this point and I'm waiting for a letter confirming it. Assuming they're not playing games, we can put him in with the FBI. He has to have something to sell and I know his attorney understands this. I'm guessing Houghton has spoken to him in some detail and they decided to take the next steps. Maybe the Feds will like what he has. In the meantime, we keep him in County Jail until he meets with the FBI. After that they'll take him over if they buy his jams and jellies."

"What happens if the FBI doesn't like the package?" asked Gil.

"Not good for him," said Todd, "We'll try him for the murder of Belvedere and he's off to prison. They can try to place him in a safer prison but with a life term, he has a long road ahead of him. Long odds for survival."

"Okay, we own the action on this," said the Lieutenant, "I'll cover it with Agent Dye."

"I think we've covered all the players," said Alastair, "let's move on to how we bring in the FBI. I'm assuming that their office in Miami will be the main field office with support from their Binghamton office as required. Elton, do you guys know anyone in the FBI Binghamton office?"

"I sort of do," laughed Todd, "my volleyball league plays a combined team from Vestal and Apalachin, and Ted Murray plays for them; he's an agent in the field office here."

"How good is that?" laughed Randy. "Hell, it's a start – the joys of a small town."

"So, we'll be the point man for the Binghamton office," said Lieutenant Hendricks, "Al, I guess you own the Miami office?"

"Sure, my main point of contact there is Cisco Riviera. I also met the agent in charge, Gordon Marella; he's a good guy. Elton, I assume you'll make the initial contact with the agency in Washington?"

"Yes, I'll call Agent Louis Dye. As I mentioned earlier, we've worked a couple of cases together. He may not be the guy who'll run with this case but he'll put us with the right talent. When we were chasing that chop-shop operation around here and northern Pennsylvania, he put us with the right folks. I'll make the initial call to the FBI to get us started and then they'll call the Binghamton and Miami offices to let them know what's in play. I assume the bureau in Washington will bring them on board. I'll contact Agent Dye this afternoon."

"Damn," said Todd, "We need to add the Forensic accountants in the Attorney General's office in Albany. They're looking into Belvedere's files. They need to be plugged into the FBI."

"Thanks," said the Lieutenant, "I walked right by it. I'll make it part of the call with Agent Dye."

The team had completed the review of the agenda and had a good game plan for the next steps. Todd and Tony had reserved the small meeting room at the Park Diner on Conklin Avenue across the Susquehanna River from the police station, and the team headed over for lunch. For Todd and Lieutenant Hendricks, this always meant breakfast for lunch. Great sausages!

Alastair felt comfortable with their progress. They were entering a new level in the investigation and events would move quickly now.

Chapter 33

Special Agent Louis Dye was on travel when Lieutenant Hendricks called his office after the meeting. The following morning he returned the call.

"Elton, nice to hear from you; it's been a while. How's the crime business up your way?"

"Always a growth business Lou, a bit like the kid's game 'Whack-a-Mole'," replied Elton, "take out one bad boy and another one pops up."

"What can I do for the Binghamton police?

"This is a bit of a rambling story, so bear with me. Over a year ago, a guy was murdered in the parking lot of a golf course in Endicott, a town next to Binghamton."

"Was it the Enjoie Golf Course? I've seen it on TV. They're a stop on the PGA Senior Tour aren't they?"

"Yeah, that's the place. I play in a league there. So far, the course record is safe," laughed Elton. "It's a nice course, well maintained by the grounds crew and the players."

"Tell me about the hit," said Agent Dye.

"Professional, two twenty-two caliber bullets behind the left ear. No witnesses. Two of my detectives put in a lot of time on the case but kept hitting the wall. We were close to a year into it with no breaks. We kept the file open but weren't making any progress. Then the victim's wife contacted a private detective who runs an agency over in Endwell, another town close by. She wanted to get some closure on his death. You may know the investigator; his name is Alastair Stewart, he used to be a field agent in your Miami office."

"Oh yeah, I do. In fact I met him a couple of times when a case took me to Miami. I remember he had a family tragedy while on the job. I think he lost his wife and child."

"That's right, he came back here and started a private investigation firm. He's been very successful. Our paths have crossed on a couple of cases, solid guy."

"Was he able to break open the case?"

"He sure did. One of his investigators knew the Endicott Town Engineer. They were high school mates. He met with him to discuss security videos that might be around the golf course area. You know, small businesses, a nearby church, etc. We had already looked into this but didn't find anything. However, the engineer mentioned that the town had modified the intersection next to the golf course after an accident where a young lad was hit by a car and killed. As a result, the town installed traffic lights and crossing lanes. Part of the project was a traffic analysis of the intersection from all directions. The town didn't have the tools or talent to do this so they hired a company from Horseheads, New York to do the work. What Randy, that's Alastair's investigator, found out was that a major part of the data was gathered by video surveillance of the intersection. The murder took place while the intersection was being analyzed,"

"I think I can see where this is headed," said Agent Dye.

"The company who did the work, Empire Traffic Analytics had to keep the videos for five years; it's a State law. The videos gave us a great look into the parking lot. Although they didn't show the guy actually firing the shots, we were able to establish that a car pulled into the lot, beside the victim, and the person driving the car was the shooter. We were actually at the golf course playing golf that day and one of my detectives, Todd Adams, discovered the body shortly after the murder. The video shows the shooter leaving his car and walking over to the victim's car, and also shows that nobody else was near the victim's car before or after the killing. Later when the shooter went through the intersection with the cameras, we got his picture and vehicle plate number. He lives in Stroudsburg, Pennsylvania. The cops there arrested him and he's now in our jail awaiting trial. The case is solid. The Stroudsburg cops also searched his home and found three guns; one of which we matched to the shooting."

"So, case closed. Slam dunk," said Agent Dye.

"Well, we got the shooter, but we think this is the tip of the iceberg. The guy that was killed, Jason Belvedere, lived a double life. His wife and son knew nothing about his business dealings. He was a property developer, mostly large office buildings. We think he was laundering money for the mob for over ten years. Most of his projects were financed through offshore shell companies in the Cayman Islands. He also did a few developments with some US banks but the bulk of his projects were with companies registered in the Caymans. This wasn't just a one-off deal. As I said, he played this game for over ten years. Break this open and you can probably put some long-entrenched mob folks out of business."

"I wonder if we'll be able to get to their money?" asked Agent Dye.

"I don't really know. Belvedere has accounts in Miami and the Caymans. I guess it's his cut of the action. Best we know, the shell companies sold off the properties to genuine US companies, and then the shell companies were dissolved. So, the money has been laundered and is gone."

"Maybe not gone," replied Agent Dye, "we still may have some cards to play to get to the money."

"How so?" asked Elton.

"Well the US companies who bought the properties should have done a due diligence analysis, not only on the property being purchased, but also on the sellers, and the shell companies. It's getting harder to hide these days. We'll need to let our forensic accountants look into it. I'd love to shut the mob down and also anyone doing business with them."

"Maybe this is the dirty money that we hear about all the time?" said Elton.

"Could be, ill-gotten gains is another way to look at it," replied Agent Dye.

"The shooter, Armand Houghton, wants to cut a deal. He knows he's toast and wants to get into witness protection. He's worried he'll never last in jail and will be killed by the mob; they don't like loose ends. I don't know what he has to sell; we told him that's between him and the FBI. We also have Belvedere's local attorney who incorporated and dissolved the shell companies, and then there's his long-time girlfriend, who's a lot closer to this than she let on. Turns out Jason Belvedere kept an office at his girlfriend's real estate business. We recovered his files and laptop there."

"Were you able to get into the laptop?"

"Yeah, we've taken a look at it to try to get a feeling for the scope of his dealings and then sent the files and laptop to the forensic accountants in Albany."

"Have you heard back from them yet?"

"I know they're looking at it now but haven't finished. These guys are a small office and are always loaded with work. I've not pressed them for results yet; we've been busy with Houghton."

"I'll need to talk to some people here who deal with these kinds of crimes. There's a couple of places this could land."

"The detective who found Belvedere in the parking lot has written a good summary of the investigation, let me send you a soft copy; it'll make it a lot easier to explain as you discuss it at the Bureau. We had a washup with Al Stewart's guys the other day to pull it all together. I can also send down a copy of the hard drive and files we recovered."

"Great, that makes my life a lot easier. As this is being reviewed, I want one of our agents here who deals with major crime to interview Houghton and see what he has to sell. I'll have an agent from our Binghamton Field Office join him. Let's find out if Mr. Houghton is a player."

"Do you need anything more from me?"

"Not at this point, you've given us a lot to chew on. I'll be back to you shortly. I think we're going to need to form a team as this moves forward. You guys, Al Stewart's agency, the Bureau, and the Miami Field Office; they know the Caymans. Not everyone will be involved every day but we need to stay connected. Oh, before I forget, send me the name of Houghton's attorney; we'll want to speak with him too."

Chapter 34

The day after the meeting on the Belvedere case, Randy went over to Vestal to brief a client on the progress of her 'missing husband' case, which had an unusual twist. After the relationship became toxic, she filed for divorce and was awarded support payments by the court. When these failed to arrive, it became clear that her husband had 'done a runner'. However she now claimed to have seen him at the Nordstrom store in Syracuse, and Endwell Investigations had been tasked with the job of finding him.

Randy knew the head of security at the Mall where the Nordstrom store was located, from an earlier case involving stolen merchandise. He met with him to review the security video from the day in question. He had some pictures of Michael James, the soon to be ex-husband, and was able to identify him on the security footage. A further search of county records had yielded two persons named Micheal James, living in the Syracuse area. So, the next step would be to stake out the addresses and see if he could find a match. Short of that she could turn the file over to the police and let them finish the case.

Not a chance; she wanted his head on a platter! He wasn't going to get away. First, establish a positive identification, and then she would go to the police with a complete package. No chance for him to slip away again.

Randy proposed to go up to Syracuse and stake out both places for a few days. It would be routine and he expected to close it out quickly. Alastair was always careful to make sure the clients knew about costs for their work as the case progressed. He didn't want to drop a large fee on them at the end, and then have to try and justify the expenses. So Randy reviewed the next steps with her to make sure she was onboard with the scope and cost.

On the way back to the agency he drove down Murray Hill Road from the upper Stair Tract in Vestal, and stopped at the intersection with the Vestal Parkway. He was in the left-hand turn lane on Murry Hill Road waiting for the green light. Before the light turned a BMW came around the corner turning right from the Parkway going way too fast and swerved into Randy's lane. He crashed into his car, hitting the left front end and fender. Randy's air bags and the BMW's inflated. Randy could not open his door so he crawled over to the passenger side to get out. Traffic was tied up now, and getting onto the Parkway and Murray Hill Road was not possible. As happens these days; people had their phones out and were more concerned in recording the accident than seeing if anyone was hurt. *What is this, a movie?* he thought. *Is this my Andy Warhol fifteen minutes of fame?*

When Randy got to the front of his car, the driver of the BMW came up to him yelling and swearing. "You dumb ass, you blocked me and I couldn't make the turn. You caused this and I'm going to sue your sorry ass!"

"Easy partner," said Randy, "I was stopped behind the stop line. You had plenty of room; if you would've slowed down and kept the Beemer under control, this wouldn't have happened. Don't lay this on me."

Randy called 911 and asked for the Vestal Police and EMS. The driver of the BMW had blood on his head and shirt. He had been wearing glasses and they were probably impacted by the airbags. As he was finishing the call, the BMW driver came up close to Randy. "You're in trouble you dumb shit, I'm calling my lawyer."

"You can call the Pope if you want. Don't threaten me, let's just sort this out. Nobody's seriously hurt."

The driver of the BMW came yet closer to Randy and pushed him back aggressively into his car. "Dial it back," Randy said, "there's no need for this, the cops will be here in a minute; relax."

"Relax my ass, you smashed my car." With that, he pushed Randy back again into his car and then took a swing at him. Randy ducked under the swing and came back with a straight right-hand punch to the BMW guy's face. He connected flush on his nose and an explosion of blood followed. *Oh shit thought Randy, why did I do that? Now we have an assault issue. Damn it, stupid move on my part.*

Randy had a clean towel in his gym bag in the car and gave it to the guy to stop the bleeding and help clean up the mess. "I'm filing charges you asshole, you're going to jail. Do you know who I am?"

"I'm not sure but I'd guess you're the village idiot."

"Screw you!"

The BMW driver appeared to be getting ready to take another swing at Randy who stepped back away from him. "If you come at me again, I'll knock you to the ground. Stay by your car until the cops come."

The police had just arrived along with two tow trucks and took control of the situation. As the police were looking over the scene, a young girl approached one of the officers and said, "I have all of this on video." Pointing to the BMW driver, she said "He was speeding and crashed into the Jeep. Then he attacked the driver. The other guy defended himself. You can download it from my phone." The officer gave her a business card with the police station email address and asked her to send it to Lieutenant Johnson, the duty officer that day.

An EMS ambulance had arrived and was looking after the BMW driver. Fortunately, no broken nose or other injuries. Another police car had arrived and they put the BMW driver in one of the cars and Randy in the other.

"Okay, said the police officer, "let's go to the station and we can take your statements." When they arrived at the police station, the desk sergeant made copies of their vehicle registrations, driver licenses, and insurance cards. They were taken to a small conference room and met by Lieutenant Johnson who had finished reviewing the young girl's phone video. Before he could say anything, the BMW driver spoke in a loud voice. "I was viciously attacked and I want to file charges against this guy. He damn near broke my nose. He should be arrested. I want to call my lawyer."

"Sure you can call him anytime, but first, let's all take a look at this camera video." The Lieutenant put a thumb drive into his laptop and projected the video onto a screen. It was surprisingly clear and even had audio. When he finished running the video, he ran it again just to make sure both men understood what had happened. When he finished, he looked at Raymond Miller, the driver of the BMW. "Mr. Miller, we are going to issue you a traffic citation for speeding and not keeping your car under control. I believe the video backs up the officer's evaluation of the accident scene and also the witness statements he obtained. You can contest this and take it to court; that's your decision. Raymond Miller was quiet at this point, obviously seeing that he had little if any grounds to contest the accident. Randy was still angry at himself for taking a swing at the guy. He could have just stepped aside and let the man rant and yell. Hitting back was stupid, it only complicated matters.

"As for your altercation, I'm not inclined to charge either one of you. I think there's enough bad judgment to go around. You can certainly sue each other until the cows come home, but I want you to consider an alternate approach to this. I recommend that you participate in a mediation process and see if you can come to an understanding of what you both did and find a way forward."

The room was quiet as Randy and Raymond considered the offer on the table.

"How do we do this," asked Randy, "how does it work?"

"It's pretty straight forward," replied Lieutenant Johnson, "it's an informal process where the two of you meet along with two mediators and discuss your altercation. It's not a court process, you make the decisions and determine the outcome. The mediators' role is to facilitate the conversation."

"Do I need a lawyer with me?" asked Raymond.

"No, but you can have one with you if you want, providing Mr. Morris agrees. It's not a court proceeding."

"I don't care if he has a lawyer with him," said Randy, "I'll be by myself."

"But, what if we don't reach an agreement?" asked Raymond.

"Then you go to your other options, sue each other. You're not giving anything up by trying to mediate the dispute."

By this time, emotions had cooled and more sensible thinking was starting to surface.

Again the room was quiet, then Randy spoke. "Okay, I'll try this."

The Lieutenant looked over at Raymond Miller. "What are your thoughts sir?"

"Okay, I'll try it too."

"I'll call ACCORD in Binghamton and set this up. They provide mediation services in cases like this. I suggest you take a week to let all the emotions cool down before you meet. Take a few minutes now and call your insurance companies and make arrangements about your cars and rentals if you need them. We'll drop you off at a car rental agency if you want."

Randy finally got back to the office, thoroughly exhausted after his misadventure. Chantal was in the reception area working on some research for a new case. When she saw him she exclaimed. "What happened to you? Your clothes are a mess and you have scratches on your face. Were you in an accident?"

"That and more," he replied, "I got into an accident at the bottom of Murray Hill Road and the Vestal Parkway. The other guy took a swing at me. I hit back and we both ended up at the Vestal Police Station."

"Were you charged with assault?"

"No, the Lieutenant wants us to go to a mediation session at a place called ACCORD and sort it out. The guy who hit me got a ticket; he was at fault. I never should have swung back at the guy. So dumb."

"Hey, Brad Petronella does mediations there, give him a call and find out more about it. Maybe he can be the mediator?"

"I'll call him, thanks. Is Al around? I need to update him on the Syracuse case."

"He's out, but will be back around three; Sherlock's with him. Go back and lie down on the couch in his office, you look awful."

When Alastair returned, Randy was still asleep on the couch. He didn't want to disturb him so he worked in the reception area with Chantal, who told him about Randy's adventure. "Poor guy," said Alastair, "it's hard to keep your emotions in check in a situation like that. I'd struggle with it too. Sounds like Lieutenant Johnson over in Vestal is a cool head. Mediation is a better call then peeing on each other's shoes in court."

As they were talking, Randy came into the reception area looking a lot better.

"Hey killer," laughed Alastair, "what's new?"

"Oh, Chantal told you. I lost my cool."

"Been there too," said Alastair, "it's embarrassing. I think you have a good way forward with mediation, good luck. So, tell me about Syracuse."

"She wants me to stake out the two addresses we found. Once we identify the guy, she'll go to the cops. I can go back to Syracuse on Monday and Tuesday next week."

"Sounds good," said Alastair, "Find a motel up there so you don't have to run back and forth."

Chapter 35

Early the following week, Lieutenant Hendricks got a call from Agent Dye at the FBI Bureau in Washington. "Elton, we have a meeting this afternoon to sort out how we staff this. My boss wants me to stay with the case based on my past history with you guys. The main reason for the call is I want to set up a meeting with Armand Houghton; ideally at your place as we want to minimize the chance of anyone finding out about our interest in him. I'll have Agent Gary Filton come up to Binghamton to run the interview. He works in major crimes and knows a lot about the crime families. If Houghton has anything to sell, he'll know how to value it. We'll also have one of the Binghamton Field Office agents join the meeting. Can we do this next Monday?"

"I'm sure we can; we'll get right on it. We'll contact the jail and Houghton's attorney. Glad to hear you'll be a player as this moves forward. Do you want any of my guys sitting in on the interrogation? Ha, I think I know the answer!"

"It's best to keep this close-held, the fewer people involved, the better. The major crime guys here are very interested in this case. Going after a long running mob game is really important to them. We don't know what we might be opening up at this point and we don't want to put anyone at risk, so we need to limit the players. When you call the jail to have Houghton brought over to the station, tell them it's a District Attorney issue dealing with the upcoming trial; don't mention us."

"I understand. We'll use the conference room next to my office, it's out of the traffic flow here. How will Houghton's lawyer handle this?"

"Most likely he'll brief him ahead of the meeting as to how this will roll out, what to expect, stuff like that, and then leave him on his own. Houghton will be flying solo."

"What about Belvedere's lawyer and girlfriend? Do you want Agent Filton to talk to them while he's in town?"

"No, maybe a different group will deal with that side of the case. We know where they are and can get to them quickly when we roll out our team."

Agent Dye was worried about keeping a lid on Houghton's intention to cooperate. Their Field Office in Binghamton had received a letter from Mitchel, Cameron and Clay advising that Houghton wanted to cooperate in their investigation. Most likely, either Phil Colbert or the senior partner, Roderick Benjamin, had communicated this to the people paying for Houghton's defense. Given this, he had to assume that the cat was out of the bag and the bad boys knew what was happening. He felt that Houghton was relatively safe at this point, as the Broome County jail was not large compared to a big city jail and he was isolated from the general population. Safe for now, but if Houghton didn't have anything to offer the FBI, all bets were off. He would be put back into the general population during the trial and after that, uncharted waters.

He reviewed his concern with Lieutenant Hendricks.

"I agree, Lou. He's safe for now but if you guys don't like what he has to offer, it'll be a risky situation for him, especially as he tried to cut a deal for himself. "

"Well, all we can do is move quickly and see what he has to offer. If all he has is a list of past hits he did for these guys, we are probably not interested. Your case is solid, damn near bullet proof; so I don't see him going back on the street. You've nailed him."

After the call, Lieutenant Hendricks called Todd Adams and Tony Ronaldo to his office to update them on the next steps.

"I had a call from Louis Dye this morning. The FBI is sorting out their team this week and he'll be staying with the case. His boss wants him to be the focal point for the FBI team and us cops. He's a solid player; glad to have him with us."

"So, what are the next steps. Do we standby?" Asked Tony.

"Not quite, things are moving; the FBI is sending an agent here next week to interview Houghton. Their field office in town will support him. I need you guys to call the jail and arrange for Houghton to be brought here for a meeting on Monday morning in our conference room. The FBI doesn't want to take a chance that anyone will see their interest in the guy. If anyone at the jail asks, tell them it's about Houghton's upcoming trial. Do not mention the FBI."

"I assume we're not part of the meeting," said Todd.

"Right, they want to keep this close-held. It will just be the FBI guy from Washington and the field office agent. If Houghton has something special, they need to keep it under wraps."

"Will he have an attorney?" asked Tony.

"He'll be here but not part of the meeting. He'll brief Houghton ahead of the interview and then leave the room. I need you to call Phil Colbert at Mitchel, Cameron, and Clay. They're in the city. I don't know what arrangements Houghton has with them, other than he represented him earlier. If they're no longer with him, I'll get a public defender to brief Houghton. I don't want him going into the meeting without some legal guidance. It's likely Houghton's on his own now after telling the FBI he wants to cooperate."

After the meeting Lieutenant Hendricks called Alastair Stewart to update him on Houghton's upcoming meeting with the FBI. "Al, the FBI is sending an agent from Washington with knows a lot about the crime families to debrief Houghton. The guy's name is Gary Filton, do you know him?"

"Yeah, I do. I've not worked directly with him but have seen him in the Miami office a few times while I was there. I think he's spent most of his time with the Bureau dealing with crime families."

"So, he could write a book?" laughed Elton.

"A book and probably a lot more. If he's coming, I think the FBI is really tuned into this. We'll never know what comes out of the meeting, but that's the way it should be. It's a classic 'need to know' situation."

As all of this was going on, Randy was on his way to Syracuse to finish up the case involving the disappearing husband. On the drive up, he called Brad Petronella to ask about his upcoming mediation session. Lieutenant Johnson from the Vestal Police had called to let him know that it was scheduled for next Monday morning.

"Brad, do I have to do anything to prepare for this or bring any documentation with me?"

"Not really, just take a few minutes and review what happened. Chantal called me to see if I might be one of the mediators and briefed me on your adventure; exciting times."

"I guess that's one way to look at it. I never should have punched the guy. I lost my cool."

"Don't be too hard on yourself, it happens in situations like that. I think the Vestal police did you guys a favor proposing a mediation session. It gives you a chance to sort it all out and not depend on the courts for a resolution."

"Can you be one of the mediators?"

"No, I know you and that might impact my objectivity. We don't take sides and always remain neutral. Don't worry, they have a good group of mediators there, you'll be in good hands. The important thing is to not let your emotions get in the way. There's two things in play here, the accident and the altercation. The accident is off the table. The other guy was given a traffic violation citation so there isn't anything to talk about. The insurance companies have it now. Stay focused on the altercation. That's why you're there."

"But what if the other guy brings up the accident?"

"I'm sure the mediators will pick up on it and bring the meeting back into focus. If you are asked to comment on the accident, just reply in a calm, measured voice that the police have addressed it and now the insurance companies are dealing with the cars. Don't get emotional, it won't help."

"Okay, I understand. I'll let you know how it comes out."

"Don't worry, you're headed in the right direction."

Randy had just passed the Syracuse University sports Dome on I-81 and was headed to Mattydale, a suburb, north of Syracuse near the airport. It was midday and he thought he might see Michael James around the house or coming back from work, assuming he had a job. *Okay, he laughed to himself, do I have my stake-out kit? Travel mug of coffee, sandwiches, snacks, binoculars, music CDs, and my camera.* He looked over at his gear on the front passenger seat and decided he was good-to-go. *Maybe I'll get lucky and find it's the first guy,* he thought.

When Randy got to James's house, he drove past it to get the lay of the land as they say in the movies. It was a small house, maybe three bedrooms, on a good size lot. The driveway was on the left side of the house leading to an attached garage. He parked next to a vacant lot a few houses down the street that provided a good view of the driveway and garage. Being next to a vacant lot was a good location as it would attract less attention than parking in front of a house..

Nothing, happened during the afternoon. Randy had played both of his Willie Nelson CDs a couple of times and was surfing on the radio hoping to find something of interest. *If I don't see this guy by eight o'clock, I'm going to call it a day and get back here early in the morning,* he thought, *Stake outs are sure a cat and mouse game.* Then just before seven o'clock, a blue Hyundai Sante Fe SUV pulled into the driveway and Randy got a good look at the guy using his binoculars. *Well hello, Michael James,* he thought, *so nice to meet you.* However, James was not alone; he was with a woman who appeared to be much younger than him. Using his camera and a telephoto lens, he managed to get good pictures of both of them. *Thank you very much Mr. James and good-looking lady friend, I can head back to Binghamton now and sleep in my own bed tonight! I got everything I need from here.* Before getting on to I-81 he pulled over and sent Alastair a brief text. 'Got him, headed back, let's talk tomorrow.'

Chapter 36

It took three phone calls to Mitchel, Cameron, and Clay to connect with Phil Colbert.

"I apologize for not getting back sooner, Detective Adams, I have a big case that will go to the jury in a few days, so busy times for me. What can I do for you"

"I'm calling about Armand Houghton; he'll be interviewed by the FBI next Monday and I wanted to give you a heads-up in case Mr. Houghton has not been in contact with you."

"We don't represent him anymore. We were told to drop Houghton about three days after I got back from Binghamton. I don't know if he has any representation at this point."

"Can we talk off the record?"

"Sure I'll try to help you but I may not be in a position to answer all your questions."

"I understand. My sense is that once the people supporting Mr. Houghton found out he was considering or had decided to cooperate with the Government, they walked away. Can you confirm this?"

There was a long pause. Clearly, Phil was thinking about how he was going to answer the question. About the time Todd thought the call had been dropped, Phil responded. "I can tell you that when I returned from Binghamton, I met with Roderick Benjamin, the senior partner who assigned me to Mr. Houghton. I advised him that Houghton was going to cooperate with the FBI, and had directed me to send a letter to them to that effect. Shortly after, we terminated our representation with Mr. Houghton."

"Can you tell me who was bank-rolling Houghton's defense?"

"I don't know and am not inclined to try and find out. Roderick was the point man for this, I was just support and frankly, I'm happy to be away from it."

"Thanks, Mr. Colbert, I know you're walking a fine line with this. We'll get Houghton a public defender; we want to make sure he understands the game when he meets with the FBI."

"It's very important that the public defender makes it crystal clear to Houghton that he must tell the truth and not hide anything. If the FBI thinks he's not telling the whole story, they'll cut him loose. This is a make-or-break meeting for him; he only gets one kick at the can."

When Todd finished the call, he and Tony Ronaldo met with Lieutenant Hendricks. "Guess what Elton? Mitchel, Cameron, and Clay cut Houghton loose."

"Well that's a surprise," laughed the Lieutenant. "I guess I'd better call the DA and have a public defender assigned, at least for the FBI meeting. If he's available, I'm going to ask for Roger Jackman. He's the best litigator over there. I don't know if anyone in that office has any experience in dealing with the FBI but Roger will sort it out."

"The guy's good," said Tony. "He grilled me in court last month on a simple hit and run and damn near got the case tossed."

"I remember," replied Elton. "We were sloppy in our preparation for court and paid the price. I'll make a call today and see if he's available."

The following Monday at eight-thirty, Armand Houghton and Roger Jackman sat across the table from each other in the conference room next to Lieutenant Hendricks' office. Agent Gary Filton from the FBI Bureau in Washington and Agent Henry Abbot from the Binghamton Field office were in an office one floor down. They didn't want to risk Houghton seeing them ahead of the meeting;

they wanted to keep him guessing. When Jackman finished, they would come up to the conference room.

"Do you understand how this is going to work today?" asked Roger.

"Sure, I'm going to tell them what I know."

"Not quite that simple. They're going to ask you a lot of questions about your work for the mob. Not just the hit on Belvedere. They want to know who you killed over the years, as well as any other work you did for them. You cannot lie to the FBI. You need them much more than they need you. Don't forget; it's their show. You only have one shot at this; do you understand what I've said?"

Houghton was nervous now and tried to tell Roger what he had to offer; he cut him off quickly. "That's between you and the Feds. I can't value any of your information and frankly, don't want to know what you have to offer. Just remember what I said. Don't try to play these guys, it won't work."

Roger left Houghton in the conference room and a uniform stepped in to babysit him while he went to Lieutenant Hendricks's office to let him know he was finished.

"I briefed him on the interrogation and he understands the game. Whether or not he'll be able to deliver is another question. I think he thought the FBI would welcome him with open arms."

"Well, it'll all come down to what he has to offer," said the Lieutenant.

"Amen," replied Roger, "the ball's in his court now."

When Agents Filton and Abott walked into the conference room, Houghton stood up. He was not sure what to do; shake hands or just remain standing. Although the agents did not introduce themselves, it was clear that they were FBI.

"Relax Mr. Houghton," said Agent Filton, "sit down please. I'm sure you've been advised by counsel, but let me restate our position.

We expect you to be totally honest and answer all our questions. If we feel you're not forthcoming or are lying, this interview will be stopped and you go back to jail. I'm not trying to intimidate you, but it's essential that you understand the rules of engagement. Also, you can stop the interview at any time. You are under no obligation to complete this."

"I understand. Mr. Jackman, the public defender, was very clear about this."

"Let's start at the beginning. Who were the families you worked for?"

"Mainly two over the years. Napolitano from the city and Bolsonari in Miami. They are connected at various levels depending on the deal in play. Sometimes, just the soldiers, and other times, the big boys."

"How many years have you worked for them?"

"About ten years; started when I got out of the Army."

"What did you do in the Army?"

"I was a sniper."

"You were only in for one tour; how did you get to be a sniper so quickly? It usually takes experience to be considered."

"Not all the time. I was always able to slow my breathing way down and had good hand eye coordination. My marksmanship scores were very high in basic training. They picked up on it and sent me to sniper school."

"Why did you get out; seems like you were on a good track?"

"They were good to me but I didn't like the Army, it was too regimented. I just didn't fit and was never comfortable with the military structure."

"How many people did you murder for the mob?"

It was a direct question and Houghton was not ready for it. He had never thought of them as murders, but only 'hits', using the slang term from the streets for the deaths. In the Army, they used the word 'kills'. Coming right out and using the word murder, made Houghton think about what he'd done over the years.

"Maybe four or five."

"Not good enough. One more time, how many people did you murder?"

Houghton was silent for a bit wondering if he had just lost the game. "I whacked five people."

"You mean you murdered five people; don't try to sugarcoat this."

'Yes, yes, okay, I murdered five people, starting back in 2009."

Agent Abbot pushed a pad and pen over to Houghton and said, "Names and dates."

It took Houghton a bit of time to list the names and dates. The agents sat quietly looking over their interview notes. When he finished, the agents looked it over and were satisfied.

"Okay, let's move on," said Agent Filton, "What else did you do for these guys?"

"The bulk of my work for them was moving stuff, like large envelopes and money."

"Money?" said Agent Filton.

"Yeah, I'd pick up cardboard filing boxes like the ones you can buy at Staples or Office Depot, and they were full of money."

"Why did they trust you to do this?"

"On one of my early runs for the Napolitano family, I was jumped at a truck stop in South Carolina. I had gassed up, and was on my way out headed to Miami. A car cut me off and two guys with guns tried to get into my car. I shot one in the chest and hit the other in the thigh. There was a war going on back then between two of the families. I was new to these guys and didn't know much about any of it. I think that sort of got my ticket punched, and they trusted me after that."

"How did you start working for them?" asked Agent Abbot.

"I had a friend in the Army from Brooklyn. We were pretty close. We were getting out at the same time and he asked me if I would make deliveries for some people. I didn't know it was mob connected at the time. It was an easy way to make some really good money. From there it grew."

"So, the first name on the list is your first murder for them?" asked Agent Abbot.

"It may have been those guys in South Carolina. I didn't include them in the list. The guy I hit in the chest went down quickly and the guy I hit in the thigh was bleeding badly. I don't think either one made it. I didn't hang around to see how they were doing. I found out later that the attack was mob related and then started connecting the dots. Other than South Carolina, my first murder was in 2009 around two years after I started with them. It's on the list there."

"Did you ever know what you were carrying?"

"No and I didn't ask; for some runs it was money, I knew that from the large file boxes, and other times it was paperwork of some kind."

"Okay, I get it, but what are you bringing to the table?" asked Agent Abbot.

"I kept a diary of every run I made for these guys over the years and there were lots of them. It's mainly the two families but not always the same members in the families. I even have a notation on each run identifying it as money or paper. I have it all, the names, dates, origins, and destinations for over ten years. It ties the two families and other mobsters together."

"Where are the diaries?"

"Hidden in Stroudsburg."

"I'll need to see them, Mr. Houghton; I can't just accept them on your say so," said Agent Filton.

"What guarantee do I have that you won't just take them and forget about me? I need some assurance that you won't just take the diaries and cut me loose."

"We have a good history of relocating people. I like what you're telling us, but until we review and assess the diaries, I cannot commit to anything at this point. You're going to have to roll the dice and take a chance."

Houghton was quiet for some time, weighing his options. *Christ, do I have any option but to trust these guys? They could easily take the diaries and forget about me, then I get whacked. Damn, I really don't have much of a choice. Let the diaries rot in Stroudsburg or try to sell them to the FBI for a relocation deal. If I end up back in jail, I'm a dead man. As Filton says, I've got to roll the dice.*

"Okay, I'll tell you how to get them. You'll need someone to go to my house. In the closet of the master bedroom, there's a two-foot square access port in the ceiling that opens to the attic, which is covered in a layer of insulation that's twelve inches deep. Stand on a step ladder and look directly west. About three feet out, there are six large brown envelopes containing the books, buried in the insulation. Numbered and dated. I did a lot of courier work for these guys over the years. It's all there in detail."

"Why did you keep the diaries?" asked Agent Abbot.

"Insurance, I guess. You never know. With a name like Houghton, I'm never going to be in their club, so I wanted some protection in case things went south on me."

"I guess they did and here you are," said Agent Filton.

That finished the meeting; assessing the diaries was the next step. Agent Filton met with Lieutenant Hendricks to update him on the meeting.

"Who did you guys work with in Stroudsburg when you extradited Houghton to Binghamton?"

"Detective Dave McPherson; you can trust him," said Lieutenant Hendricks.

"I need him to go to Houghton's house to retrieve some diaries, and have someone bring them to Washington for analysis."

"I'll call him now. From what I know of Dave, he'll get them and probably deliver them himself. Do you think they're significant?"

"I liked what I heard; but the proof is in the pudding, or the reading in this case. Can the County Jail keep Houghton isolated from the general population for another week or so?"

"I'm sure they can."

Later that afternoon, Dave McPherson retrieved the diaries from the attic of Houghton's house. The next day, he drove to Washington and handed them over to Agent Dye who had assembled a team of four agents to assess them.

"You've given us quite a bundle to review. I can see my guys producing a large spreadsheet with names, places, and dates. Thanks for bringing them down personally. With a bit of luck we may have quite a road map here," said Agent Dye.

"Good hunting," said Dave, "if we can help, let us know. I've got his house locked down and can get back in anytime."

Chapter 37

While Houghton was being interviewed by the FBI at police headquarters, Randy was at ACCORD, a few blocks over on State Street, along with Raymond Miller, the driver of the BMW, to take part in a mediation session. Brad Petronella had scheduled the meeting but did not participate in the process as he knew Randy, and it was essential that the mediators were impartial. ACCORD had assigned a member of staff and a volunteer mediator for the session. Clearly, a strong team.

Randy and Raymond sat across from each other in one of the meeting rooms. Neither man said much except to acknowledge the other's presence. However, from the body language, it appeared that most of the hostility from the accident was gone. Lieutenant Johnson of the Vestal Police Department had made a wise decision in not scheduling the mediation immediately after the accident and altercation. Cooler heads were definitely in the room now.

After the mediators introduced themselves, they reviewed the process with the two men, explaining that it was not court directed and that the mediators were there to help them reach a conclusion that would satisfy both of them. Randy and Raymond would be making all the decisions. The next step was to jointly sign an agreement consenting to the mediation. After that, the two mediators said nothing more, but waited for one of the men to initiate the conversation. This was a technique used to start the mediation, designed to make them own the process.

After a few minutes of awkward silence, Randy said, "I shouldn't have taken a swing at you. I know you were pissed off that your car was smashed up."

Raymond responded by claiming yet again, it was Randy's fault. The mediators had expected this and refocused the meeting away from the accident which had already been addressed by the police. "We're not here to talk about that today. A traffic citation has already been issued by the police regarding the accident; you can contest it in court if you want," replied Kayla, the staff mediator. That put the mediation on track again and over the next hour or so, the men were able to engage in a civil conversation and understand their behavior. It was a good outcome, especially for Raymond Miller who was able to accept responsibility for his actions and admit he was at fault by initiating the altercation.

As they finished and were preparing to leave the room, Julie, the volunteer mediator, spoke up. "May I make a request, gentlemen?"

"Sure," said Raymond, "fire away."

"I'd love you to shake hands," replied Julie.

"That's it? said Randy. "Happy to do it."

With that, the mediation was concluded and both men left with a better understanding of the past events——and themselves. Randy called Brad on his way back to Endwell Investigations.

"Thanks for the help on this, we got everything sorted, and I kind of like the guy I punched," he laughed, "he's not a bad guy."

"Great to hear. You have to be willing to listen to the other party and it looks as if both of you stepped up. Good show!"

The remainder of the week was quiet for both the Binghamton Police and Endwell Investigations regarding the Jason Belvedere case. The FBI was busy analyzing Houghton's diary, and the forensic accountants in Albany continued looking into Belvedere's companies. Agent Dye called Lieutenant Hendricks to let him know it would be two to three weeks before they'd be in a position to summarize the findings. He suggested a meeting at the Binghamton Police Department when they were ready.

"I don't want to drag everyone down to Washington for a meeting; Binghamton is a reasonable mid-point, "said Agent Dye, "I'm sure you cops can fit us all in."

"Sure, no problem, just don't forget to bring the doughnuts," laughed the Lieutenant.

Over at Endwell Investigations, Alastair, Randy, Gil, and Chantal discussed the Belvedere case after the Friday washup dealing with the accounts and caseload, both of which were manageable for a change. They sat in the comfortable chairs around the coffee table in Alastair's office with Sherlock, the office ambassador, as Chantal referred to the dog, always a participant in the meetings especially now, after finding Mrs. Gilday's cat Barney in the woods a few months back.

"Al, what do you think is happening on the Belvedere case?" asked Gil.

"I don't really know. The guys in Albany and Washington have a lot of information to digest. Houghton's diaries are with the FBI and Belvedere's files are in Albany and Washington; they should be telling, but we need to hear from the Gov guys."

"What's going to happen to Houghton?' asked Chantal, "is he still in the County jail?"

"For now, but I expect the FBI to reach a decision on a move soon. They should have finished an initial valuation of the diaries by now. If they like what they see, they'll start the process of moving him."

"How does it work?" asked Randy.

"There's a special group that handles this; if they decide to relocate him, all we'll ever know is that he's not in the Broome County Jail anymore."

"What happens if they decide they're not going to offer him a deal?" asked Gil.

"Well, he stays in our jail, goes to trial, and if he's found guilty, he'll be sent to prison. Not a good outcome for him; he's a marked man for trying to cooperate with the FBI."

"What do you hear from the forensic accountants in Albany?" asked Chantal.

"Not much, I spoke with Lieutenant Hendricks the other day and he mentioned that it was a high priority program now and they've been talking to the FBI. I also heard from Agent Dye and they're busy reading Houghton's diaries. So, lots of gears turning."

"All good news Al," said Chantal, "but I get the feeling you're not comfortable with something about this case."

Alastair was quiet, composing his thoughts. "I worry that we may have two very good pieces of evidence which we may not be able to tie together. Maybe we don't have to, but they would make for a more compelling case if we can. Here's the thing, at this point, we don't know if the families in the diaries are same ones involved in Belvedere's companies. Although we know a lot about the deliveries Houghton made, we don't actually know what was in the envelopes and boxes. Hell, it could be Girl Scout cookies or Boy's Life magazines."

Alastair continued, "I think the diaries by themselves are not conclusive. They don't prove anything other than material was being moved between the families. Although we believe that the money Houghton brought to Miami ended up in the Caymans, we have to tie it to Belvedere's companies. Then it's compelling. On the other hand, Belvedere's companies can probably stand by themselves. The diaries may be the glue that ties the families together, but we don't know enough at this point. We'll have a big 'show and tell' with the FBI and Albany forensic accountants in a couple of weeks and that should tell us where we're headed."

"They could be frying some big fish," said Gil.

'I agree," replied Alastair, "and don't discount the diaries yet, they may be the roadmap and glue."

The talk shifted to current events around town and their families. This was a bonding affirmation for the agency. You can't schedule it, but when it happens, it's special. *We're a family,* thought Alastair. *You guys are so much a part of my life. You'll never know. Thank you all.*

Over the weekend, Alastair got a call from Lieutenant Hendricks. "Houghton has been moved."

"Relocated?"

"Yeah, they took him around noon on Friday."

"So, I guess his diaries are worth something after all."

"I agree, we'll get more information on them when we all meet in a couple of weeks."

"I wonder where they placed Houghton?"

"Somewhere on planet earth!" laughed the Lieutenant, "so, what does your weekend look like?"

"Meeting up with Marty for dinner; one of her boys is home on leave from the Air Force. He has a mate in Syracuse so we're headed up there for dinner."

"Is she really going to marry you?" laughed the Lieutenant.

"Sure, I'm a great catch. I pay my credit card off every month and I come with a dog. We finally set a date for later in the year. Don't forget, you said you'd be best man."

"Happy to do it my friend. I'm already working on my speech; it will be brilliant and inciteful."

"Elton, I'm starting to get worried now. Do I get a draft to review?"

"Hell no! I want to keep you guessing."

Chapter 38

Lieutenant Hendricks got a call from Agent Dye in Washington.

"Elton, we'll be ready to go by the end of this week, how about meeting next Monday at your place?"

"Sure. How do you want to staff the meeting."

"There will be three of us; me, Agent Filton from Washington, and Agent Abbot from the field office in town. I suggest you have your two detectives join us for the meeting. We'll also have two guys from Albany: one, was the lead forensic accounting analyst and the other deals in major crimes. I've worked with them in the past."

"What about Al Stewart?"

"For sure, he should be there, and bring one of his investigators. Oh yeah, we'll need a secure line with our Field Office in Miami. We're going to need them as we look into the Caymans. I'm not sure how they'll staff it yet other than Cisco Riviera. Al worked with him on this earlier."

"Okay, I'll have our IT guys get in touch with the Miami Field office and make sure we have compatible secure video systems. I don't see a problem there, we'll make sure it all fits," said the Lieutenant.

"Sounds good, let's talk on Wednesday to make sure we're headed in the right direction," replied Agent Dye.

"Quick question, seems like you liked the diaries. I heard Houghton's gone."

"We did, it's not a home run but a solid triple; a lot of good stuff."

After they finished, Elton called Alastair to let him know about the meeting and to ask him to bring one of his investigators with him. Both Randy and Gil were working cases in the field, so Chantal was the logical choice. She was doing some research on an upcoming case and could break away.

"You know Elton, I forgot how complicated these investigations are. Not as simple as chasing a bad guy, catching him, and putting him in jail. I expect we'll be working on this six or eight months from now. This could be a big case, cutting across a lot of families. I feel like I'm back in the FBI again."

"Looks that way. The last time we went down this road with the FBI, it took months to close it out, and then there were all the trials. It's a tangled web and doesn't unravel easily, but it's worth it."

Alastair left the office around five o'clock to take Sherlock to the dog park. She spent much of her time in the office, 'hanging out' as Gil liked to say, and didn't get as much exercise as Alastair wanted. He was in the habit of taking Sherlock for a walk each morning, but felt she needed something more vigorous, so an hour at the dog park running around with all her buddies was a nice way to end the day. As he was driving out of the office parking lot, he noticed a familiar car parked in the small strip mall across the street from the office. A black ten-year-old Lincoln Town Car.

Fredo Bertolli thought Alastair, *what does he want now? Just call the damn office. Why all the secrecy? I wonder if he knows much about the Belvedere investigation? Maybe he's even a player?*

When Alastair got to the dog park, he sat on a bench near the parking lot. Sherlock bounded off into the enclosed area looking for her friends. Bertolli's car was parked nearby. His driver/bodyguard got out and sat down next to Alastair.

"What do you want?"

"Mr. Bertolli would like to speak with you."

"Well, here I am. No more cloak and dagger meetings in his car. It's a nice day to be outside."

His driver was not happy with Alastair's response but there wasn't much he could do about it. He went back to the car to speak with Fredo, who shortly after, got out of his car and walked over to Alastair.

"Mr. Stewart, I'm not trying to play games with you. I'm a cautious man; I'm sure you understand."

"What do you want?"

"Let me be up front with you. I know the FBI is launching a big investigation into that guy who was whacked at the Enjoie golf course. Your agency did some work on the case and may still be involved. I'm not here to discuss any of that. For what it's worth, I've never had any play in any of that business."

"Okay, so what do you want from me?"

"It's my younger sister's son Pauly. His father died about six months ago and the boy is getting out of control. He's very angry about the loss of his father, who died of pancreatic cancer just three weeks after the diagnosis. Pauly was devastated and now is headed for trouble. I've seen it so often before."

"Isn't this a job for a therapist? I can recommend a very good one here in town."

"At some point, yes, but for now, I need to understand what he's up to. My sister is very worried because Pauly won't talk to anyone in the family. His grades are dropping and he has new friends. You can see where this is headed."

"Are any of these 'friends' connected to your activities?"

"Hell no. I've taken steps to make sure that never happens. I grew up on the other side of the fence and was determined that kind of life would not be an option for any of the children."

"Where do they live?"

"In Norwich. Pauly is a junior in high school."

"I need to make some calls; I'll get back to you. How can I contact you?"

"Here's my cellphone number."

Alastair and Fredo sat for a bit, neither man talking. Then his driver blinked the high beams on the car and Fredo got up, said "Thanks for your time Mr. Stewart" and left.

Must be a call or an appointment, thought Alastair, *he's a busy guy.*

The next day, Alastair called Lieutenant Hendricks and also Agent Dye in Washington with the same question. Should he take on the case given all that was going on with the Belveder investigation. He wasn't sure if Fredo Bertolli was 'a person of interest' to the police.

"Al, the guy's not on our radar," replied Lieutenant Hendricks. "We know about him but have not had much to do with him for a number of years. I think he's sort of retiring or getting out of the business."

When Agent Dye called back, his information was much the same.

"We don't see his name on any of the evidence we have at this point. I can't say he's clean, but he's not of interest yet. Personally, I wouldn't get involved with these guys at any level. My experience is that it always turns to shit at some point."

"That's my thinking too. I'd like to help the kid but it's a slippery slope with these guys. There has to be a defined line between us. I'm going to call Bertolli and shut it down."

When he called Fredo Bertolli, the phone was answered by an unfamiliar voice, clearly not Bertolli. *He sure is a cautious dude,* thought Alastair, *lots of layers.*

After Bertolli picked up, Alastair said "Fredo, I'm not in a position to take on your case. No sense going into any of the details, I think you understand. However, let me offer some advice. I know a therapist here in town who is excellent. She raised her two boys after her husband died and both have thrived. Even though you may not know everything Pauly is up to at this point, don't delay starting therapy."

"Well Mr. Stewart, this is not what I expected but I'll have to live with your decision. Can you give me the name of the therapist and I'll call my sister. Maybe this is the best way forward now."

"Call me Al, I think we've danced around the candle enough now."

"Okay, Al it is. I don't know much about therapy; we usually dealt with things in a more straightforward manner in my line of work. Would you do this if it was your family?"

"In a heartbeat. She sorted me out when I came back from Florida."

When they finished the call, he sat for a bit thinking about what had happened and how it might play out in the future. Clearly Endwell Investigations could not do business directly with Fredo Bertolli, but a relationship had been established between them and he felt that there would be more cards to be played in the future.

Chapter 39

On Monday, everyone arrived early to the meeting at police headquarters in anticipation of major developments. The Belvedere case was at the point where a way forward could now be established. They had a lot of questions and hoped that the briefing would provide some answers, and more importantly, a solid case strategy.

Special Agent Louis Dye chaired the meeting. An agenda was projected on the large screen in the conference room and was the center of attention as they entered the conference room. A soft copy of the agenda had been sent to Cisco Riviera who was standing by on a video link at the Miami Field Office. Coffee, bottled water, and pastries were on a table in the back of the room. After a few minutes of chatter among the group, Agent Dye walked to the front of the room and called the meeting to order.

"Okay, let's get started, we have a lot of material to discuss today and we also have to set a game plan for the next steps. If I've missed anything, let me know. I think all the local guys know each other, but we have two new faces from the AG's office in Albany. Warren Hackler deals with organized crime, and Dick Strong is their lead forensic accounting analyst. Also with us today on a Zoom call from our field office in Miami is Special Agent in charge, Gorden Marella and Agent Cisco Riviera who looks after the financial side of their investigations. New faces for all of you except for Al Stewart who met with the Miami Field Office earlier in the case. As this goes forward, there will be a lot of activity going on in parallel. To keep this under control, Agent Filton will be the focal point for all your findings and he'll make sure we're all up to speed and on the same page. We'll set up a secure site that we can access so we don't have to play telephone tag."

Special Agent Dye continued, "The first item on the agenda won't break the case open, and may seem trivial, but we need to take another look at the two individuals who were close to Belvedere; that's his lawyer George Adamo, and his longtime girlfriend, Marjorie Monette. The Binghamton cops believe they have more to tell us. Agent Abbot from our Binghamton office will issue subpoenas and bring them in for an interview at our office. I want them to know we're taking this seriously. I don't want to just call them and ask them to come in for a chat, I want them to be issued a subpoena. It should get their attention; they'll be served tomorrow."

Chantal leaned over and whispered to Alastair, "Damn, these guys are playing for keeps."

"They'll be loaded for bear; the cops and the AG's office gave them all their files. Stand by for a boarding party," replied Alastair.

"Let's move on to Armand Houghton. By now, most of you know that he's been placed in the witness protection program and is no longer in the Broome County Jail. His diaries provided about a ten-year detailed account of papers and money moving between the New York and Miami families. We don't know what papers were in any of the envelopes, but we know that the file boxes contained money. We'll get back to that later when we hear from Dick Strong."

Everyone in the room was thinking the same thing at this point. *'I wonder where they placed Houghton?'* Chantal looked over at Alastair who smiled and shrugged his shoulders.

Agent Dye picked up on the curious looks going around the room and laughed. "Don't look at me folks, I don't have any idea where they placed him."

The next item on the agenda was Third Dominion Bank in Miami and Global Caribbean Bank in the Cayman Islands. "George, I'll need you and Cisco to run with this. My opinion is that Third

Dominion didn't have any play in handling the money that Houghton brought to Miami by the mob. I think it was moved directly to the Caymans and specifically, to Global Caribbean Bank. What we do know is that Third Dominion was their transfer agent for the trust fund payments to Belvedere's widow and son. They've been doing business with Global Caribbean for a long time; we suspect they know a hell of a lot more than they're telling us."

"You're right," said George Marella, "it's always the same game, if you don't ask the right question, you don't get the right answer. Always a cat and mouse game; they never volunteer information."

"We may be able to squeeze them a bit," said Cisco, "They have a large subsidiary that manages condominiums. As you know, there have been some bad accidents recently in Florida with condominiums collapsing. I don't know if their management company has been involved in any of the condominium structural problems, and if they were managing any of the buildings that collapsed, but If they were involved, the inquiry will have a life of its own. However, they never want any media attention and may be inclined to be more cooperative with us if we can limit the media interest in our meetings with them. It's possible our investigation could take off dramatically at some point and get a lot of media coverage.

"What about Global Caribbean?" asked Warren Hackler, "Do you have a way in there?"

"Always a challenge," laughed Cisco, "The International banking regulations are slowly changing in our favor, but it's still a struggle. The banking privacy laws are very strict in the Caymans, so you can't call them up and ask for names, accounts, and related items. But they are cooperating regarding money laundering. I know it sounds odd but that's where we are today. We have to show the bank what's happening and how it's happening and If we can do this, then they'll cooperate. We have to make our case."

The room was quiet for a bit as everyone digested the information.

"So, if we can show them that the money Houghton delivered to Miami ended up in their bank, then they'll talk to us?" asked Detective Adams.

"Pretty much like that," replied Cisco, "but we can't just run in with our hair on fire, that's for sure. We need to build a trail."

"No slam dunk then" said Detective Ronaldo, "seems like a long road ahead."

"Don't despair," laughed Agent Dye, "Don't forget, we're the good guys and we always win!"

After the laughter in the room died down, Cisco continued. "I have some contacts in the Caymans who have been very helpful in providing us with 'guidance' for want of a better word. Let's keep pushing."

"The question now is how do we build the money trail. It always comes down to money in this business," said Agent Dye, "One of my old bosses used to say, 'Follow the money, it'll get you there.'"

After an hour, the group took a small break so everyone could catch up on their emails and missed phone calls. Alastair and Lieutenant Hendricks moved off to the side of the group.

"What do you think Elton?"

"I agree with Lou; it'll all come down to the money trail. These guys are laundering money and we don't know yet how they're doing it. It didn't end in Miami; they had to move it on to the Caymans and wash it."

"It's sort of funny how these cases evolve," said Alastair, "We got lucky when Randy's mate in Endicott put us on to the traffic analysis videos and we were able to ID the shooter. Look at where we are now. You can't write this stuff."

When the meeting resumed, Dick Strong, the forensic analyst from the AG's office was the next presenter. If it can be said that there is a body type or style for a forensic accountant, Dick seemed to fit the profile: balding and thick glasses. Detective Ronaldo smiled thinking that he would be a good candidate to be in a movie dealing with these crimes. Good type casting!

"Good morning, always nice to be back in Binghamton," said Dick, "I graduated from Binghamton University back when it was State University New York (SUNY} Binghamton. I always loved the local food. I'll be bringing home a big bag of speidies from Lupo's, that's a local shop here. For our guests from Miami, speidies are pieces of meat, usually chicken or lamb marinated in a savory sauce. They're actually Italian in origin. I was sorry to see that Sharkey's bar and grille has closed since my college days; they had great steamed clams and speidies.

However, so much for the culinary tour. Let me review how Belvedere played the game. When he formed a company to support a project, a large cash infusion was put into the company to support the project. Actually, it was not usually just a one-time infusion. Most times it was two or three infusions of capital as the project developed."

The spreadsheet Dick had projected showed ten companies and the dates when they received cash infusions. It was an extensive list. By itself, it didn't mean much. So money was flowing into these companies, and used for project costs; it seemed like a normal business practice.

"Check out all the money that was moved into the development companies over the years," said Agent Dye, "This was a systematic and ongoing program and processed a large chunk of change, close to six hundred million dollars."

Dick Strong continued. "We obtained the information from his computer. He kept very good records, so it was fairly easy to understand. Fortunately, he didn't use code words or secret names. His local lawyer put these companies together and dissolved them when the project was finished. Within two years of completing the project, it would be sold on to a management company or venture capital firm, usually US based."

"Did these guys know what they were buying?" asked Alastair.

"I've asked myself the same question," replied Dick, "Clearly, they had to perform a due diligence evaluation in purchasing the mall, building, or whatever, but the question is, did they bother to look past the actual acquisition and check out the seller, which is the development company who owned the property. My opinion is they never looked past the property being purchased. Sure they looked at things like liens, mortgage debt, pending lawsuits, building codes, stuff like that, but not much deeper. Maybe they had their suspicions but it didn't get in the way of an attractive purchase."

Next, Dick turned his attention to Houghton's diaries. "Now, I'm going to show you a spreadsheet with the dates when we believe money was moved to Miami by Houghton."

This spreadsheet, like the previous one was interesting but didn't show anything conclusive by itself. However, when he projected the two spreadsheets side by side with the dates aligned, a picture emerged.

"I'll be damned," said Lieutenant Hendricks, "There's a correlation."

"Oh yes, not day for day, but look at the timing. Within thirty days of Houghton bringing money to Miami, there's a cash infusion into the current US company. Sometimes he makes a second run pretty close to the first one. I'm not sure why that is but maybe it was an insurance move. If something happens, they only lose part of the money, but I don't really know, just speculating," replied Dick, "In any case, it looks like the trail is from New York to Miami and then on to the Caymans."

"Is there any way they could just use the company that's incorporated in the US?" asked Chantal, "I think I know the answer, but let me ask the question."

"It's a valid question, but no way they could do it. They couldn't pass the scrutiny of the US banks or IRS," replied Agent Dye.

"Cisco and I need to dig into this," said Gordon Marella, "We know the money ends up in the Caymans but not much more than that How does it get back to the U.S.?"

"I have a couple of ideas," said Cisco, "Let me talk to some folks in the Caymans, and do some digging."

"I have one last piece of data," said Dick Strong, "This is a list of names we compiled of people who were involved in the transfers for the first two companies which were financed by U.S. banks. We also found both New York City and Miami investors. Regarding New York, we think some of the names are major players, but others most likely foot soldiers. All I have for the other corporations are the names of shell companies."

"Interesting, we'll run down the Miami names," replied Gordon Marella, "we know a lot of these guys."

After another short break, Agent Dye brought the meeting to a close. "We've covered a lot of ground this morning; let me try and capture all the action items. We'll have the meeting agenda and action items on a secure site by tomorrow, along with a copy of Houghton's diary. We'll also upload Dick Strong's presentation. I think that's all the visual material we used today. Agent Abbot will serve subpoenas to George Adamo and Marjorie Monette. I'd like to see them interviewed this week if possible. I think it's a good idea for Detectives Adams and Ronaldo to participate in the interviews. A strong law enforcement presence will make them sit up. Finally, Gordon and Cisco in our Miami office will be digging into Global Caribbean Bank to understand how the bad guys laundered the money. Once we have that piece, we can put the screws on the bank to cooperate. Along with that, some candid conversations with Third Dominion Bank in Miami may shed a bit more light. Let's meet on a secure video platform at the end of next week, and see where we are."

"Do you need anything from me at this point?" asked Alastair.

"You get a free ride for now, my friend," said Special Agent Dye, "and also a hearty thanks for the great job you did in opening up this case. If it hadn't been for you and your investigators, we wouldn't be having this meeting."

The comments were followed by a spontaneous round of applause.

Job well done!

Chapter 40

When Agent Abbot served the subpoenas to Marjorie Monette, Belvedere's longtime girlfriend, and George Adamo, his attorney, he advised them to have an attorney present at their interviews. The FBI didn't want any push-back on their testimony if they were charged and ended up on trial.

Marjorie was first to meet with the FBI along with her attorney, a local guy. This was new territory for him as he mostly dealt with real estate law. Along with Agents Filton and Abbot from the FBI, detectives Adams and Ronaldo from the Binghamton Police were also there. Marjorie was clearly worried, and her attorney was sailing in uncharted waters.

"Let's not beat her up," said Detective Adams. "Our last meeting was pretty emotional and we don't want to go there again."

"You're right, let's keep her in play. If she breaks down, the meeting's over," said Agent Abbot.

When Marjorie and her attorney came into the room, Agent Filton introduced himself and Agent Abbot and opened the conversation. "Ms. Monette, we're not here to arrest you. There are a number of open items regarding Mr. Belvedere and we need your help to sort them out."

"I told the detectives everything I know," replied Marjorie, "I don't know what more I can add."

"Well, let's talk about it," said Agent Abbot. "Did you know Jason Belvedere had banking interests in the Cayman Islands?"

"He never told me as much, but I sometimes heard him on the phone talking to someone I thought was outside the country. He never discussed his business with me. I asked him about his dealings a few times over the years but he always changed the subject. As I told the detectives, he was very secretive. He always locked his office when he was not using it. The cleaning lady was only allowed in his office when he was there."

"Did he ever have visitors?" asked Agent Filton.

"A number of them over the years. I think they were mostly from New York City and Albany. I once heard one of them mention a restaurant in Albany. They would arrive in big SUVs. They never spoke with me other than to say hello, and that was almost an afterthought. They dressed well but were a rough bunch, you could feel the tension when they were around. They always made Jason nervous."

"Did you ever hear any names?"

"Oh no," replied Marjorie, "and I never asked."

"Why did he list you as a correspondent in the matter of the trust funds for his wife and son? What was expected of you?" asked Agent Filton. "Were you receiving any compensation?"

"The first I heard of it was when I got the letter from a lawyer in the Cayman Islands. As I said earlier, I called him and asked him what this was all about. He told me that the trust payments were progressing and I didn't have to take any action at this point. He mentioned that Jason had other banking interests there and he would be in touch with me if required. I never heard back from him."

"Bank accounts?"

"He didn't say, but that would be my guess."

"Marjorie, did Jason ever mention a will?"

"He mentioned it once and said we would all be looked after," she replied, "I think he meant his wife, son and me."

Marjorie's lawyer said nothing, just sat there following the conversation back and forth between the FBI and Marjorie. He had no feel for the substance of the conversation, but was satisfied that she was not being bullied by the FBI or police.

Clearly, no surprises or major revelations, but more facts did emerge from the interview. Jason had more than one bank account in the Caymans, and he had a will. Agent Abbot called Cisco Riviera at the Maimi office to let him know that Jason almost certainly had multiple accounts.

"I'm not surprised," said Cisco, "most of these guys have money squirrelled away in different hiding places."

"I wonder if he was skimming the accounts?" said Agent Abbott.

"Is the Pope Catholic?" laughed Cisco. "I'm sure he had sticky fingers. As long as he didn't get too greedy, he could get away with it and over a number of years it could amount to a lot of money. This information will help us when we talk to Global Caribbean Bank in the Caymans. Those guys never volunteer anything so we need to go in with all our ducks in a row. They typically won't tell us much more than we already know, so we have to stay ahead of them."

The FBI and Binghamton police were satisfied that they had gotten a full story from Marjorie Monette. Next up on Wednesday was Geroge Adamo, Belvedere's lawyer and they were ready for him. The FBI and cops were convinced that Adamo knew much more than he was telling them. He'd been Belvedere's attorney for almost ten years, incorporating and dissolving companies. No way he could keep a blind eye to what was happening. Also, Belvedere had a will somewhere and Adamo was the logical choice for writing it and being the executor. Belvedere's wife Marion had said she knew nothing about a will. She supposed he had one but didn't know any more than that.

The FBI decided they would be more aggressive with Adamo who was trying to straddle the fence. Helpful to a point, but not much more. When George Adamo arrived, he was accompanied by a criminal defense lawyer from Syracuse. Garrison Schmidt, always called Garry, and well known to the Binghamton cops as a formidable presence in court. He was around six foot three or maybe a bit more. Along with his courtroom skills, you had to contend with his size and deep penetrating voice. He was never still and would move around the courtroom like a cat as he cross-examined witnesses. He wasn't belligerent or rude, just a significant presence in the court. Juries loved him, prosecutors respected him; he was that good.

When they arrived in the interview room, the FBI and Binghamton cops were already there with a large group of folders neatly stacked one on top of the other. This was not lost on Garry. Introductions were made and they all sat down. Neither Garry nor George spoke; they were waiting for the FBI to play the first card. It was a logical strategy on Garry's part. He didn't know for sure if his client had made a full disclosure to him nor did he know what evidence the Government had at this point. Henry Abbott the FBI local agent started the conversation.

"Mr. Schmidt, I believe our paths have crossed. We tried a RICO case in Federal Court in Syracuse a few years back and you represented one of the defendants. I think his name was Overton."

"Yeah, Cal Overton; it was a messy case and you sent him to a Federal prison in Colorado. I think he's doing twenty years."

"Correct, we sent him there to cut his communication chain with his associates on the East Coast. He was a bad actor, and kept trying to sell us useless information and get a plea deal, but we had all of the evidence we needed to convict. He wouldn't give up any of the big boys, so there he is in sunny Colorado. Over four years now."

"So, what do you need from us today?" asked Garry.

Agent Filton joined the conversation. "Your client has been doing legal work for Jason Belvedere for close to ten years. I'm not sure how well you've read into Jason Belvedere's business dealings, so let me provide some background. For want of a better word, the man was a property developer who operated on the east coast as far south as Virginia. For each project he handled, he'd open a company that provided funds for the project. When it was completed, and ultimately sold, he dissolved the company. Sounds pretty good, don't you think?"

Garry looked over at George Adamo but could not make eye contact. He kept his eyes on the table, knowing what was coming.

Agent Filton continued. "Of the ten companies we know about, the first two were funded by venture capital funds and other investors. There was nothing unusual in the make-up of the funding companies or operation, and all the investors were identified. Both of these ventures were successful, and profits were distributed about two years after completion when the project was sold. It's the other companies we want to talk about. We are of the opinion that they were used as money laundering vehicles. Mr. Adamo, you were the attorney who formed and dissolved these companies; we believe you were not fully forthcoming in your interview with Detectives Adams and Ronaldo. I'm not saying you lied to us, but your information was limited and based on what we know now, incomplete. George was clearly in full alert mode now and responded quickly, "I told you guys all I know. I was just the paper side of the operation; I didn't handle any money."

Garry Schmidt looked at George and said in a firm voice, "Stop talking and let the man finish." George was not ready for such a stern rebuke; it caught him by surprise.

Interesting, thought Detective Ronaldo, *seems George has not been totally up-front with his attorney. Garry's not happy.*

Agent Filton continued. "Mr. Adamo, you don't have to answer our questions, and you can walk out of this meeting at any time. However, I want to make it clear to you that if we find that you've been withholding information from us, we will prosecute you to the fullest extent of the law. You can roll the dice or cooperate; it all comes down to that. It's your call sir."

"I need some time with my client," said Garry.

"You can use this room if you like. It's wired for both video and audio but we'll turn it off, or you can go to Millie's dinner just around the corner. The morning crowd is gone so you should have a quiet place to talk."

"We'll stay here," replied Garry, "can we have some coffee?"

"Sure, coming right up. Call us when you're ready to start again."

While the two men were talking about the next steps, the FBI and Binghamton cops met in Agent Filton's sparsely furnished office. He noticed the detectives looking around and laughed. "Gov offices guys, you need to be in Washington to get the good digs."

"What do you think?" asked Detective Adams.

"Well," said Agent Abbot, "I'm thinking the well is a hell of a lot deeper than Adamo let on to Garry. He was really pissed off at him. I think they're having a 'come to Jesus' meeting now. If he doesn't come clean with Garry, he'll cut him loose. I think he's playing the same game with Garry that he tried on us. You know the song; 'I was only the poor lawyer and didn't really know what Belvedere was up to.'"

"Do you think Adamo understands how serious this is?" asked Detective Ronaldo

"He will when Garry finishes with him," replied Agent Abbot.

Adamo and Schmidt had started their meeting around ten thirty and it was now close to twelve. Agent Filton knocked on the meeting room door and stuck his head in.

"Gentlemen, it's close to twelve. Do you want to break for lunch or I can bring some sandwiches in. We're going around the corner to Millie's and I can bring something back."

"Maybe a couple of toasted bacon, lettuce and tomato sandwiches, some chips, and colas if you wouldn't mind. We need to carry on here. I want to finish this today as I'm due in court in Syracuse tomorrow. Can we continue into the evening if we have to?"

"I don't see why we can't," said Agent Filton, "I'm around the corner at the Doubletree and the rest of the guys are local. We'll make it work."

The FBI and cops went to lunch at Millies and returned a little in front of one with sandwiches, chips, and drinks for Garry and Adamo. Garry asked for thirty minutes to wrap up with Adamo and have some lunch. "We'll be ready to go by one thirty."

Chapter 41

When they reconvened, Garry opened the meeting. "I've explained to Mr. Adamo the risks and ramifications of providing or not providing answers to your questions. He has elected to answer your questions."

"Thank you."

"Mr. Adamo, you're not a suspect at this point but you are a person of interest. We believe you have information that is important to our investigation. I'm sure your attorney has explained this to you. Let's start at the beginning of your relationship with Jason Belvedere. How did the two of you come together?"

"He just showed up at my office one day about ten years ago. I assumed he had heard about me from one of my clients. He said he was a property developer and wanted to form and register a development company for an upcoming project. Money would be deposited in the development company by investors to support the project. Then, once the project is completed, and ultimately sold on, the company would be dissolved."

"You said register," replied Detective Adams, "do you mean in New York?"

"Actually Delaware. His choice, not mine."

"Does it make a difference?" asked Agent Abbot.

"I don't think so, as the companies were only alive for three or four years. There could have been some tax issues. I'm not sure."

"Who handled his accounting?"

"He did, he was a CPA. He did it all."

Agent Filton and Abbot looked at each other both thinking the same thing. Shit, *why didn't we pick up on that? We have all his records from his computer and office.* It wasn't a deal breaker but clearly the FBI and cops should have seen this, as it was right in front of them. This meant that the only person with access to the company books was Belvedere.

Damn, thought Detective Adams, *always something that falls through the cracks. We need to put this on the agenda for our coordination meeting this Friday. Didn't Al Stewart say something about Belvedere's background after he met with his wife? I think he did and I never thought much about it. I'll check back with him.*

"How much did Belvedere pay you for your services?" asked Agent Filton.

"I was under a retainer; it was one hundred twenty-five thousand a year."

"That's it?" said Detective Adams. "All those years of faithful service and it never changed, that was a great deal for him."

Adamo was playing games again, not fully answering the questions. Just enough information to keep the conversation going. Garry was not happy.

Adamo looked at his attorney, who looked ready to pack up. He had placed his briefcase on the table and appeared to be getting ready to put his notes into it. Then he stopped, put his hands on top of his briefcase and stared at Adamo. No words were spoken between the two men but the message clearly had been sent. 'Stop playing games or I'm out of here.' Agent Abott was about to say something, but Garry ever so slightly raised his right hand a few inches off his briefcase. Signal received; let Adamo make the next move. The room was quiet for a few minutes then Adamo spoke. The emotion in his voice caught everyone by surprise. George Adamo was not in tears but close to it. His voice was close to breaking.

"I'm not a crook, you have to believe me. I was stupid. I never asked the hard questions and never looked too closely at the work I was doing. I should have been more diligent. I'm a fool for not walking away from him. When he first came to me, it was easy money, and at that time all above board. I wasn't his partner and I tried to stay outside of his dealings. I don't know where the money was coming from other than the first two development companies, which were funded by venture capitalists and private investors in the US. We dissolved both of them about three years after completion of the projects. One was sold to an insurance company and the other to a major home builder."

"Why didn't you walk away from him when the makeup of the companies changed?"

Adamo looked over to Garry before answering, almost as if he was looking for assurance or support. He was about to cross the Rubicon and was afraid, but he knew he had no choice. Rolling the dice on a trial was a long shot. Garry didn't say anything but nodded to George to continue his story.

" When the third development company was formed, it was much like the first two and we registered it in Delaware as before. Except this time, Belvedere didn't have any active investors lined up. That was odd, as he was ready to go with the first two. It turned out he did have investors but they were silent or not visible. I asked Belvedere what further action was required, but he was non-committal. I thought my involvement was finished at that time, and worked on my other cases. Then I got a letter from a law firm in the Caymans asking for details about the new company. I called Belvedere and he told me to provide the information. It turned out that he was also registering a subsidiary in the Cayman Islands."

"Did that cause you any concern?" asked Detective Adams.

"It was a change from the other projects, but I didn't think it was strange for Belvedere to be going off shore. Frankly, I was naive about it and thought maybe the next program was outside the country and he needed to do this to raise capital. I had no cause for concern at the time. The first two projects had gone smoothly, and I got a generous bonus from Belvedere when we dissolved those two companies."

"How big a bonus?" asked Detective Ronaldo.

"Two hundred fifty thousand dollars for each company," replied Adamo.

Nobody said anything but they all had the same thought. Belvedere was roping him in. Easy money for not a lot of work and Adamo didn't ask any questions. The mold was cast for the next development companies.

Agent Filton thought, *I need to speak with Cisco in the Miami office. I'm not well read into business law in the Caymans regarding the incorporation of companies. Can you just register these companies or do you need a local Cayman level of ownership? How do they play the game there?*

"I'm not clear on what Belvedere was doing at this point. Were these new companies incorporated in the Caymans?" asked Agent Filton.

"No, not at all," replied Adamo. They were registered as subsidiaries of the US companies incorporated in Delaware. Sort of like a branch office I think."

Agent Filton wanted to take a break so the team could discuss this latest information, but he did not want to stop Adamo. Once the doors open, don't close them. He was pretty sure now how Belvedere played the game. Once he spoke to Cisco in Miami and his boss, Special Agent Dye in Washington, they should be able to lock it down. For now, keep Adamo talking.

"It appears that money flowed from the subsidiary company in the Caymans to the US company to be used in the development projects. Do I understand that correctly?"

"Yes, I was the secretary of the US corporations and would see quarterly reports from the CPA firm who handled the accounts."

"And that was actually Belvedere," said Agent Abbot.

"That's right, Wedgewood Accounting Services, LLC. That was Belvedere's firm and best I know he was the only employee. The funds into the US companies were always intra-company transfers from the Caymans."

"Were there any names provided?"

"No, just development companies with names like Blue Waters, Development Partners, Sunrise Acquisitions, odd names like that."

"Did it ever occur to you that Belvedere might be laundering money?"

"Yes it did, but I also thought it might be people with tax haven money who are investing and have some mechanism to avoid taxes. I knew it was not above board but I was only processing paper, so I kept on doing the work. I never discussed any of it in detail with Belvedere, I guess I was afraid of what I might hear. He continued to pay me a retainer and a bonus as the companies were dissolved. Sometimes the bonus money was three hundred and fifty thousand dollars."

Again, the room was silent, everyone mulling over his testimony. Adamo was quietly sitting looking down at his hands on the table. He looked as if he had just gone fifteen rounds with Muhammed Ali. His shirt collar was damp with sweat. Not the best day for him, but a least he had made the decision to cooperate."

"Tell us about Belvedere's will," said Agent Abbot, "I assume you wrote it"

"Yes. I wrote the will and I'm the executor. It's pretty straight forward. Marjorie Monette will a receive a monthly trust fund payment and also a lump sum payment of one million dollars. The remainder of the estate is divided between the mother and son."

"How much?" asked Agent Abbot.

"I don't know for sure; the will stipulates that it is not to be settled until three years after his death. He has a series of accounts in the Caymans and the bulk of the estate is there. I won't have access to the accounts until we probate the will. I think it will be a lot of money."

Again the room was quiet, everyone thinking about the size of the estate.

After a few minutes, Detective Ronaldo looked over at Adamo and said, "What haven't you told us yet?"

It caught everyone by surprise. *Good play kid,* thought Adamo's lawyer Garry, *I would have asked the same question.* It really caught Adamo by surprise. He thought he'd finished. He sat there, his mind racing. *When will these guys give up? I'm so tired and want to get this over with.*

Adamo looked up and made eye contact with Detective Ronaldo and said, "I think he was skimming the accounts."

"How do you know?" asked Agent Filton.

"I don't know for sure, but on a couple of occasions when he paid me a bonus he said, 'Some for you and some for me'. I think he may have listed my bonus as twice as much and kept half for himself or just taken a piece of the company. More importantly, I could never tell if the money that flowed into the US company was the correct amount as I only saw the final figure, but I always thought he was skimming the accounts. Those were big numbers. Easy to do, as he was both the head man and the accounting arm too."

"One final question," said Agent Filton, "how did the Global Caribbean know Belvedere was dead and to start the trust fund payments. Someone had to tell them."

'I had instructions from Belvedere to let the attorney in the Caymans know if he died. Belvedere had some kind of arrangement with him to advise the bank. I sent the man a letter and copy of the death certificate"

"Did Ms. Monette know anything about this?"

"I don't think so. Belvedere never shared much information."

By this time it was past seven in the evening. Everyone was tired and the team felt they had taken this as far as they could. They had a Zoom status meeting on Friday and would tie up the loose ends then. On the way out, Garry spoke to Agent Filton off the record.

"What do you think you'll do with my man?" asked Garry.

"We're frying bigger fish here. I don't see much percentage in taking Adamo to trial; he cooperated with us. My call will probably be to let the Broome County Bar Association deal with it if they chose to do so. Adamo got caught up in something much bigger than he understood. He's lucky he listened to you today counselor, if he had tried to slow-roll us again, it would have been a different ball game. Thanks."

After everyone left, Detective Adams called Alastair Stewart to discuss Belvedere's role as a CPA. He was pretty sure Alastair had passed this on to him and he had had dropped it.

"Al, did you tell me that Belvedere was a CPA?"

"Yeah, I got that from his wife when I first met her. I think his company was called Wedgewood Accounting or something like that; I can look it up. Is it important?"

"Sure it is, Belvedere ran all the books for the companies——by himself."

"Ouch, the fox has taken up residence in the hen house!" laughed Alastair.

"It explains a lot; I should have picked it up."

"Don't beat yourself up Todd, lots of moving parts in this case. Call Dick Strong in Albany, the forensic accounting guy. Review it with him and see if there's anything else."

Chapter 42

On Friday, all hands were on deck and ready to go. The FBI in Washington, Binghamton, and Miami, along with Endwell Investigations, and the Binghamton Police made for a full house. They knew they were getting close to something big and you could feel the excitement in the room. The FBI would pull the plug in the near future. They had the chance to close down a long running money laundering operation that was significantly more than just a run of the mill drug money deal.

Special Agent Dye from the FBI Bureau in Washington was the meeting host. "Good morning everyone, We've lots to talk about today so let's get going. I want to start by asking Gary Filton to summarize the interviews with Marjorie Monette and George Adamo earlier in the week."

"Good morning, and thank you for coming. The Binghamton Police, Agent Abott, and I met with both of them at our office in Binghamton. Marjorie Monette gave us two interesting pieces of information. Belvedere had multiple accounts in the Caymans and also he had a will. We were able to expand on this when we met with George Adamo later in the week. Ms. Monette was not directly involved in any of Belvedere's adventures, although she was listed by him as a correspondent on the administration of his trust fund and probably the will when it's probated. Other than to make sure we're copied on any future correspondence from the attorney in the Caymans, I think we're finished with her. Questions?"

"I assume she will not be charged," said Alastair.

"Yeah, she's not a major player, just someone caught up in a bad situation."

"Did she know George Adamo?" asked Lieutenant Hendricks.

"Only by name," replied Agent Abbot, "I don't think they've ever met. Belvedere never met with Adamo at the Plaza Realty offices."

"Okay," Gary Filton continued, "When we met with George Adamo, he was distinctly evasive to begin with, but once his exposure was fully explained to him, he opened up. His attorney made sure he understood the seriousness of the interview. By the time we finished, he was singing like a Christmas Tree full of canaries. I'll try to summarize some of the main points he told us. Apparently Belvedere just walked into George's office out of the blue, and asked him to set up and register a development company for an upcoming project he had in mind. We don't know how he found him; maybe a referral or the yellow pages," laughed Agent Filton. Building costs would be met from deposits made by various investors, and when complete, the project would be sold on to a property management company. The development company could then be wound down and the profits distributed to the original investors.

The first two projects were perfectly straightforward, with investments coming from individuals, pension funds, insurance companies, banks, and the like. For the third project, Belvedere told George to set up and register the company, in Delaware as before, and he said he now had different sources of finance available to provide funds as the project progressed.

George admitted that he thought this was a bit strange, but as Belvedere was paying him $125,000 a year plus hefty bonuses, he asked no questions: the less he knew, the better. A little later, Belvedere asked him to cooperate with a lawyer in the Caymans to set up a subsidiary of the US company there, which would effectively act as a branch office."

George Adamo's testimony was compelling and provided a way forward for the team. They knew now they had to meet with the banking authorities in the Caymans, to break the case open and get the names of the people behind the shadow investment companies which were funneling money into the subsidiary companies that Belvedere had registered. Who were the players in Blue Waters, Development Partners, Sunrise Acquisitions? The large amounts of money moving through the subsidiaries raised a red flag which the Cayman Islands government could not ignore.

The team could now see how the funds deposited in Belvedere's subsidiary companies in the Cayman Island and then transferred to the US company by an intra-company transfer. It was clean and quiet. That's how the money was laundered. A steady flow, and over time, a substantial amount of money. Armand Houghton, the hit man who killed Belvedere, had taken the money to Miami but had no involvement after that. So how the money got to the Caymans was still an open question but most likely, sent down by boat. It was the easiest way and had the least risk. The FBI felt that they didn't have to show how the money arrived in the Caymans so, could ignore the problem for the time being. The large amount of money invested in the subsidiary companies raised a large red flag and they felt the banking authorities could not ignore it. Adamo handled all the corporation work for Belvedere. He opened and dissolved corporations for him for about ten years, and was not involved in any of the money transfers. Belvedere was a CPA in his own right and handled all the book-keeping for the corporations.

"No outside auditors?" asked Alastair.

"None," said Dick Strong, the forensic accountant from Albany, "He managed the books and made the required filings. The best we can see was that he was never audited."

"Yikes, he flew under the radar for years," said Lieutenant Hendricks.

"The first two corporations he set up were funded by known entities in the States. The remaining eight were funded from offshore sources and that's how the money was laundered," said Agent Filton. "Adamo knew or at least suspected it was not above board but chose to ignore it. He was well compensated over the years. We don't think he knew anything directly about the money laundering but he sure didn't ask the hard questions."

"Do you plan to charge him?" asked Alastair.

"We're still looking at it. I think in the end, we'll turn his file over to the Broome County Bar Association and let them make the call. Adamo was close to the edge of the pool but he didn't jump in." replied Special Agent Dye."

Agent Filton continued, "As I mentioned earlier, Ms. Monette told us that Belvedere had a will, and Adamo said he wrote it and is also the executor. The will stipulates that it is not to be probated until three years after his death, which means late next year. We don't know the makeup of his accounts so there isn't any way at this point to assess the size of his estate. There's probably a lot of dirty money which will be recovered by the Government."

"What are the next step?" asked Lieutenant Hendricks.

"We'll have to meet with the Cayman banking authorities and get access to Belvedere's accounts, and more importantly, put names with the shadow investment companies. Once we have that in place, we can build our case. So, we're sort of punting this to the Miami office for the next steps," said Special Agent Dye.

Gordon Marella, the agent in charge in Miami, and Cisco Riviera, the financial lead, were the point men for the next stage. They would arrange the meetings in the Caymans with the banking authorities.

"I'd like to have Dick Strong with us for these meetings," said Agent Marella. "He did the initial analysis of Belvedere's records and has the best handle on this. We also want to meet with Belvedere's attorney in the Caymans. We have an 'associate' who knows his way around the islands. I'd like him to meet with the attorney ahead of us, to make sure he knows this is serious business. We don't just want to show up off the street. I think when he knows that he'll be meeting with the FBI and AG's office from New York, we'll get his attention. Most of these guys operate on the fringes and don't want anyone looking over their business, and as Belvedere's dead, he shouldn't have an issue talking with us now."

"Any questions," asked Special Agent Dye.

"Before we go to the Caymans, we need to look closer at Belvedere's last project," said Dick Strong, "Something went wrong. It stopped six months before Belvedere was killed. Certainly never completed. From what I could find out, there was a lawsuit suit against the development involving significant environmental issues. I think the site location was being challenged."

"Maybe that's why he was killed," said Detective Adams.

"Let me run with this," said Alastair, "I may be able to ask some questions."

"Okay," said Special Agent Dye, "We need to give Gordon and Cisco some time to set up the Cayman Islands meeting, and also some time for Alastair to look into Belvedere's murder. It's sort of funny but we really don't know why he was killed, although it's starting to point in one direction. Dick, would you send us a note on how much money was invested before the project was stopped? I assume the money was not recoverable?"

"Sure, I'll put it on the portal today. Let me look closer but I think all the money was frozen."

"Thank you all for the great work and support. If we can shut this down, we should be a lock for new cars and Hawaiian vacations this year," replied Special Agent Dye to a room full of laughter.

Chapter 43

When the all-hands meeting finished, Alastair, Chantal, Gil, and Randy, sat around the table in the conference room at Endwell Investigations discussing the meeting. Sherlock came into the room and lay down near Alastair.

"Look what you did Randy," laughed Chantal, "you found some traffic analysis tapes and blew the case wide open."

"We were lucky," said Randy, "If I didn't have my mate from high school who was the Endicott town engineer, we would still be scratching our heads. I'm always amazed on what can open up an investigation."

"Al, do you think the Gov can close this out?" asked Gil.

"Yeah, I do. The banks in the Caribbean are very secretive but they couldn't survive a scandal like this. The Cayman Islands government will put a lot of pressure on them. Ten years of laundering a boat load of money? It's in their best interest to cooperate, they cannot afford to ignore this. They won't be happy but it's a question of survival in the end. I think the FBI will get what they need to build their case."

"Who are you going to talk to regarding why Belvedere was killed?" asked Chantal, "sounds like an end run."

"It's a convoluted story. A local bad boy, Fredo Bertolli contacted me to pass on a message about my wife and baby's death in Miami. It was from the mob in Miami. At that point I had found and confronted the killer so it was mostly history. He came back to me again regarding his grandson who was headed in the wrong direction. He lost his father suddenly and was very angry. Bertolli wanted me to check up on the kid and find out what he was up to. I declined the offer as I didn't want us to get close to these guys. When you deal with them it never ends well. However, I did recommend Marty Fitzerald at the Samaritan Counseling Center meet with the kid. She did and they have made good progress. My thinking is to contact Fredo and cash a check."

"Does he know why Belvedere was killed?" asked Gil.

"Probably not in any detail, but he can find out. I'm going to call him."

The meeting drifted off topic as their curiosity was satisfied so topics of the day came into play. Chantal brought everyone up to date on the latest adventures of her boys and the Buffalo Bills were struggling and that required a detailed analysis from Randy and Gil.

Alastair called Bertolli; his bodyguard answered the phone. A meeting was set for the next day at the dog park. Sherlock's favorite pastime. When Al got to the dog park the next day around four in the afternoon, he saw Bertolli's car in the parking area. *H'm that's a bit odd, I'm fifteen minutes early, wonder how long he's been waiting. Wonder what's in play?*

Bertolli's bodyguard came over and sat next to Alastair.

"Did we get our times mixed up?"

"No, not at all, I had to take the boss to the dentist nearby and it was easier to come here and wait. He likes it here, maybe he'll get a dog and give me some rest!"

"I'd go over to the car to meet Fredo, but when Sherlock sees me move, she'll try to follow me. Is he Okay with meeting here like the last time?"

"I think so, it's a nice day, let me go speak with him."

When they came back, Fredo sat next to Alastair and his bodyguard stood off to the side next to a tree about fifty feet away. *Always on duty,* thought Alastair.

"Al, I was surprised you called me. Your therapist friend has made great progress with Pauly. He's turned the corner. Thank you for recommending her."

"She's very good, she certainly helped me when I came here from Miami."

"What can I do for you Al, I'm sure we're not here to discuss therapists."

"I want to try and close out the case I worked on regarding Jason Belvedere. You know they arrested the shooter. I really don't know why Jason Belvedere was killed. I have some ideas but cannot prove anything. This is mainly to satisfy my curiosity."

"I had no play in the hit; I told you that before."

"Understand Fredo, I'm not on any hunt to attach blame. The case is out of my hands now."

"What do you think happened? You're a smart guy."

"One, or maybe two things. His last development project was halted abruptly. Apparently there were serious environmental issues. It was never restarted. Somebody lost a lot of investment money. The other thing is I suspect Belvedere was skimming the investment accounts."

"Look Al, I can't make any enquiries it would open me up and others to scrutiny by the Gov. If they think I have any information, the FBI will be all over me. I'm not going there. However, let me just say that my understanding is that your suspicions are correct. Let's leave it there."

"Understood, I won't take it any further."

"Pauly, my grandson says that his therapist is getting married soon."

"Yeah, some deadbeat private eye over in Endwell," laughed Alastair.

"You're a lucky man," replied Fredo.

The two men sat on the bench and watched the activity at the dog park for a bit. Sherlock came over to them a couple of time to make sure all was well and then went over to Fredo's bodyguard. After a bit, Fredo signaled to his driver and they were off. *In another life, I could really like that guy* thought Alastair, *but at this point, we need to keep the boundary lines crisp.*

"Come on Sherlock, I want to go home and catch the news."

Chapter 44

Two weeks later, Dick Strong from the AG's office in Albany and Alastair met with Gorden Marella and Cisco Riviera at the FBI Field Office in Miami. They wanted to make sure they had a solid game plan for the meeting in the Caymans. Alastair was there as he had been involved from the beginning and knew the whole history of the case. This was an exciting time for Dick Strong, as travel in forensic analysis was never extensive. Maybe some short trips around New York State, but not much more. Now he was going to the Cayman Islands!

Cisco started the conversation. "Our contact in the Caymans spoke to Belvedere's lawyer there, and thinks he'll be cooperative. He knows what we're after and didn't push back. I've prepared a power point presentation that details the money laundering trail, and also shows it graphically. It's a compelling story and I don't think the banking authorities can stiff us. We want the names behind the shadow companies. Once we have that, we can build our case and then I think we'll be going after players in Miami and New York City, based on what you got from Armand Houghton when you arrested him."

"What about Third Dominion here in Miami?" asked Alastair.

"Belvedere had money parked there also. Once they find out that Global Caribbean and the Cayman government authorities are cooperating, they'll roll over and sing."

Dick Strong chimed in: "I know this isn't part of the trip, but I dug a bit deeper and now know what happened on the last project Belvedere was working on. "He jumped the gun and launched the project without the EPA approvals and codes in place. Really got jammed up. He was headed to court. It was pretty serious; it involved draining wetlands among other things. Never a good idea."

"So, anybody with money in that project would lose it?" asked Gordon.

"That's right, the money is frozen until the case is litigated. The project was dead on arrival. Whatever funds there are will probably be used to settle the law suit from the EPA."

"How much money had been invested?" asked Alastair.

"A little over eighteen million," replied Dick.

"Whoa, serious money," laughed Cisco, "I bet the investors wouldn't have liked him for that, and wanted their money back."

"And most likely, Belvedere was also skimming the accounts," added Alastair.

"I guess his performance did not meet their high standards," laughed Cisco.

The flight time from Miami to the Caymans was about an hour and forty minutes. They arrived about four in the afternoon and settled into the Grand Cayman Marriott. The weather was not too hot or humid this time of year so they could sit on the terrace and enjoy the view of the ocean. Their first meeting was scheduled for the next day with Belvedere's lawyer, Juan Durante. When they arrived at his offices, they found what appeared to be a boutique law practice, with well-furnished offices but not a large staff: maybe two other lawyers and four assistants to handle the admin work. Juan was a short man, slight of build, very precise in his dress and manners. He wore a suit and tie which struck Alastair as odd considering the climate. They went into one of the conference rooms where coffee and sweet rolls were waiting for them. After a bit of small talk, Cisco opened up the discussion.

"Senor Durante, we have compelling evidence that Jason Belvedere was part of a money laundering operation here that operated for more than ten years."

"So you say; I can't argue the point. I never met the man. He had me register companies as subsidiaries over the years, and then at some point, dissolve the corporations. Their life time was about three to four years."

"You also did other work for him I understand," said Cisco.

"I handled a trust fund for him that made monthly payments to his wife and son."

"What about Ms. Marjorie Monette?" asked Alastair.

"She was listed as a correspondent who had authority to communicate with the local bank in New York as required. Upon Belvedere's death, she was also to participate in a trust fund. Some time back, I received a letter and copy of Mr. Belvedere's death certificate from Mr. Adamo in New York and opened up a trust fund for her as instructed. He also advised me that there was a will which would be probated three years after Mr. Belvedere's death."

"Do you have a copy of the will?" asked Cisco.

"No, only the death certificate."

"How many accounts did Belvedere have in the Caymans?"

"I don't know the total number. I can tell you that there were at least two: one for the trust fund and another that just sat there. In anticipation of your next question, I never knew how much money was in either account. As I said initially, I never met the man. I registered and dissolved subsidiary companies for him, but I never knew who was putting funds into them."

"How were you compensated?"

"I had a yearly retainer; one hundred fifty thousand dollars."

Easy money, thought Cisco, *move some paper around and get handsomely paid for it.*

"A final question please, what kind of legal work did you do for him," asked Cisco.

"As I said I registered and dissolved the subsidiary companies. When he set up the first one, I gave him advice on the structure and legal issues involved. Other than that, I set up the trust funds for his wife, son, and then Ms. Monette. We never had much day-to-day contact. For what it's worth, he paid my retainer in quarterly installments."

Cisco was a bit disappointed. He had hoped that Juan Durante would have played a more significant role in Belvedere's business operations, but not the case. His was pretty much an administrative function with little involvement or interest in Belvedere's actual business. His role didn't involve moving money. No great loss though, as they were here mainly to meet with the banking authorities and gain access to Belvedere's accounts with Global Caribbean Bank.

Chapter 45

The meeting the next day with the banking authorities was the main event for the team. When they arrived in the conference room, they found twelve people from the bank's government regulatory office there and none of them were prepared to talk, let alone introduce themselves. It was a hostile environment.

Gordon Marella would have no part in it. He told the team to pass him their business cards, then he went around the room giving them to the government regulators—————and insisting on receiving one from each of them in return. When he finished, he asked, "So who's in charge from your side?"

"I'm the senior man," said George Elliott, who had what is best described as a mid-Atlantic accent. He had been in the Caymans for a number of years but still retained vestiges of his British accent. A pleasant blend of the two places.

This exchange pretty much set the tone for the meeting. Marella was not prepared to make his presentation, then just walk away, and wait for them to make a decision. The banking regulators already knew the FBI was serious, but now the 'rules of engagement' were firmly set.

Gordon started the meeting by thanking them for making time for their team and by introducing them. Alastair and Dick Strong were new faces. Cisco was well known to them and had a reputation for being competent and tenacious. The fact that the senior agent from the Miami office was there and heading the team was not lost on the regulators.

"Mr. Elliott, we have conclusive evidence that a money laundering operation has been flowing through your bank for the better part of ten years. This is not a one-shot operation fueled with drug money but a well-organized operation that has been in play for a long time. We have a comprehensive presentation of the operation for your review. However, I'm reluctant to present this sensitive information to such a large group, but I will do so if I have your assurance that it will be held in the strictest confidence. It's in both of our interests that this does not find its way to the media. At some point later on, we may be able to manage the narrative with the media, but in these early stages, we must keep in close-held while we complete our investigation."

George Elliott looked over to one of his aides and the two men walked to the corner of the room to speak privately. When they returned, eight people were sent from the room, leaving only four.

George explained: "Please understand that I trust these people, but as we are in the initial stages I want to keep our side on a need-to-know basis. We'll expand our group as this develops. The duration of the money laundering operation is troubling to us. I don't think we've seen anything like this before. How did you come upon it?"

"I'd love to say it was the result of years of surveillance and analysis but like many crimes, they come to you. Peeling back the layers of the onion, so to say, took us deeply into the operation. It started with the murder of an individual in the parking lot of a golf course in New York State. The police were not able to close the case and the widow of the murdered man retained Mr. Stewart's agency to look into it. They identified the killer or hit-man as they like to say in New York and one thing led to another."

"It sounds like there's a good murder mystery book there, Mr. Marella, you should write a novel about it. It could also be a great television series," said George.

"I'll leave that to Mr. Stewart and his investigators; they broke the case open."

Cisco addressed the group and took the better part of two hours laying out in detail how Jason Belvedere ran his operation. The presentation was compelling and its importance was not lost on the banking regulators. Cisco showed each of the subsidiary companies and the amount of money transferred to the parent companies in the States. When he finished, nobody spoke for a few minutes. The information was overwhelming. There was no way Global Caribbean Bank or the Cayman Islands government could sidestep the evidence.

George Elliott spoke up. "How many shadow investment companies were involved over the years?"

"Five that we've identified so far. Some of them participated in multiple projects. But we don't yet have the investors' names and as you know, that's why we're here. We believe they may have invested in one or all of the shadow companies."

"I think you're correct in that assumption," said George Elliott, "Different investment company names but many of the same players. I don't think the names in these companies will identify all the top people in their organization. They usually have a buffer between them. But as you say in the States, you should be able to flip some of them.

Maybe I'm getting ahead of myself. Today is Tuesday; can we meet next Friday at two PM? I need to discuss this at the ministerial level here, and obviously with my bank. It will take a few days to sort this out on our side. In the meantime, take a break and enjoy our beautiful island and mild weather. You could fly out and come back on Friday, but I think it's important that you be here in case I need to bring you into any of our internal meetings. I can't commit to anything at this point, but I don't think we'll be wasting your time by you staying on."

"We'll standby," said Gordon. A few days in a great hotel would be very welcome."

"Don't get too comfortable, I think we'll be pulling you into some of our meetings," laughed George.

When the team returned to the hotel, they met at the bar to discuss the status. "I think we're going to get there," said Alastair, "They could have slow-rolled us and sent us on our way. Cisco, your presentation was excellent. It made it hard for them to dodge the facts."

Cisco replied, "The fact that this was a long running money laundering operation is a major embarrassment for the government. They'll have to step up and cooperate with us and will force the bank to play. I agree with you; we'll get the names of the players," said Cisco, "and once we have them, we start building our case. It will be a lengthy process. The wheels of justice turn slowly, but in the end, we'll prevail."

"I was thinking about the timing said Dick Strong. "We won't hear anything for a fair amount of time as the case is assembled. No quick charge up the hill and plant our victory flag."

"Actually, I think you'll be quite busy, Dick. Your office did the forensic analysis of Belvedere's accounts, I think you'll be spending a fair amount of time with the Department of Justice assisting them. But first, we need to get through this week. What do you think, Al?"

"I agree. I wish we could go in with our guns blazing and arrest them all and let them rot in jail while we built the case but that would be putting the cart before the horse. My boss during my days in the Miami Field Office was always preaching patience; play the long game."

"What do you think George Elliott is doing now?" asked Dick.

"Oh, I think he's running this up the flagpole and scaring all the government ministers. Ten years and running: that's probably a record here for a money laundering operation. After that, I think they'll meet with Global Caribbean and kick their asses," laughed Cisco, "Ten years and the bank never got suspicious? They were probably making too much money to notice anything might be wrong."

"Do you think they'll shut them down?" asked Alastair.

"I doubt it. They're a long-established bank," replied Gordon, "so they'll probably just throw a couple of guys off the ledge, maybe a director or two also."

Nothing happened on Wednesday, so the team spent the day catching up on their e-mail traffic and lounging by the pool. *Not a bad way to go,* thought Alastair, *I can get used to this.*

Early on Thursday morning, George Elliott called Gordon Marella. "Can we meet with you and your team? I'll pick you up at 11:30. Our Minister of Finance would like to discuss the case and review your presentation. We'll meet over lunch."

Interesting, thought Alastair, *If they were going to dust us off, they would just call George Marella in and be done with it. I wonder if they're trying to mend some fences or maybe the man just wants to hear it from us. If this ever went public, they'd be cleaning up the mess for years.*

Chapter 46

They met in a well-appointed conference room adjacent to the Minister's office. It was probably for his own personal use. At the back of the room, a lunch had been set up for the meeting. A variety of juices, coffee, tea, and an assortment of fruit and small sandwiches.

"Mr. Marella, I'm Pedro Martinez, the Minister of Finance, thank you for staying on and meeting with us."

"It's my pleasure sir; I think we share a common interest in this matter."

"George has provided me with a comprehensive briefing on this issue but if you would indulge me, I would like to hear it again from Agent Riviera. He is well known to us and enjoys an excellent reputation."

"Certainly Minister."

Cisco had the presentation on a thumb drive and proceeded to load it onto the conference room computer. Knowing that Minister Matinez had been briefed by George Elliott, he did not dwell on the background but concentrated on the mechanics of the operation. When he finished, the Minister said, "Ten years, ten years and nobody raised a red flag. I want this shut down and have processes put into place so it never happens again. Am I clear Mr. Elliott; does your bank understand the seriousness of this matter?"

"Yes sir."

"I know this is painful sir," said Cisco, "but with your permission, we would prefer to let the operation continue for a while as we build our case. If we close it down now, we allow the criminals time to maneuver and hide."

"In British parlance, George would call that ducking and diving," replied the Minister.

"For sure," laughed George, "you're spot on."

"All the more reason to keep this under wraps," said the Minister, "If the bank does not support this, I'll revoke their license and we can read about them in the history books. George, make sure this happens. No secret calls to clients from the bank late at night. I will not allow them to embarrass this government. They need to understand how critical this is for them. Also, I do not want a room full of people on Friday. If this does get out, I want to have to deal with only a very few people to find the leak."

"I'll make it happen Minster." replied George.

When they got back to the hotel, Gordon and Alastair sat in the spacious lobby. Afternoon music was provided by a trio consisting of piano, bass and drums, playing familiar tunes. Over coffee, the two men talked about the developments.

"This is probably as good as it gets, Al," said Gordon. "I thought we'd have to fight them bloody hill by bloody hill. It's always hard to understand the secrecy issues here. Clearly, the banks want to protect the privacy of their customers but it all falls apart when a criminal element is introduced. With all the drug activity these days, it's even worse. Some of these guys are awash in money and don't know what to do with it. For a bank, they're like a kid in a candy store. I think the government knows they have a problem and are struggling to control it."

"I would have loved to be a fly on the wall when the Minister met with the bank. I bet it wasn't pretty. The comment the Minister made about Cisco was interesting: they seem to have a lot of time for him."

"Cisco has been a great find for us. He came to us just after you left for New York. An energetic kid almost to the point of being brash. He's a University of Miami grad; Degrees in accounting and finance. We didn't really appreciate what we had until he was the lead investigator in a case involving a stolen car ring in Florida. After that his ticket was punched. He's had the opportunity to transfer to the Bureau in Washington but he's a Miami guy with an extended family, so he doesn't want to move. They bring him up to Washington from time to time and he also works cases for them out of our office. I love being around him. His energy and enthusiasm are contagious."

"How do you think this will play out on Friday?" asked Alastair.

"It's their show. Cisco can go through our case findings again if the Minister wants, but I suspect we'll just sit there and take notes. I think he's already beat them up when they met the other day. On Friday, I think we'll exchange names and contact information to help us as we move forward with our investigation. My main concern is that the bank keeps a tight lid on what they tell us, as we have a long way to go to build the cases, which have to be solid. I don't know how many bad boys we'll be dealing with but I'd bet you a paycheck it's around ten. So, we need to see who they are and where they fit into the pecking order. We'll try to flip some of them so we can move higher up the food chain, but this all takes time. The Department of Justice is very process oriented and that's good, but it comes with a time penalty."

'I wonder if they'll try to put this laundering model in play again now that Belvedere is gone," said Alastair, "That may be the bank's get out of jail card with the Ministry if they continue to cooperate."

"Yeah, that's a good point. I can see the families coming back with another player like Belvedere. Wow, would that make for a solid case! If it isn't mentioned from their side, we need to address it. I wish we had someone buried in the mob organizations in Miami or New York who could tell us if they try to start up again."

"What about the guy Cisco talks to here?" said Alastair, "He seems to have a good feel for what's going on."

"That's a good idea. Also, the bank and Ministry can tell us if anyone is registering subsidiary companies here. They have to have them in place to send the money north. I'd love to find them trying to roll out a new operation, then we could freeze the funds and really hurt them."

About that time, Cisco and Dick came over and joined the group. No more shop talk, they needed to deal with major issues, like the Buffalo Bills and Miami Dolphins! Everyone was relaxed, they knew they were headed in the right direction.

Chapter 47

The meeting at Global Caribbean Bank was scheduled for ten o'clock. However, when Gordon, Alastair, Cisco, and Dick arrived, the Minister and his team were already there. There were a lot of open files on the table suggesting that the bank and ministry had been together for some time. Gordon and Alastair looked at each other, both thinking the same thing. *Is this deal coming unraveled?*

Pedro Martinez, the Minister of Finance sensed their concern and smiled. "I wanted to talk to the bank ahead of our combined meeting to review the material they plan to provide. Rest assured; you'll have their full cooperation. Let me turn the meeting over to Gustavo Bennett, Vice President of Compliance for Global Caribbean."

Gustavo was nervous. It's not an everyday occurrence that you have a government minister looking over your shoulder. "We've prepared a dossier of all the subsidiary companies that participated in this scheme over the years."

"I would use stronger words, Mr. Bennett," said the Minister, "but carry on."

"George Elliott, my two assistant vice presidents and I are the only people in the bank who are aware of this problem. We fully recognize the need for secrecy."

"It's very important Mr. Bennett," said Gordon, "because we don't believe that the people behind this money laundering operation know that anyone is aware of their game. Given the long running, and frankly successful record of this operation, we think they may try to continue laundering money through your bank.

They may have already started for all we know. Our assessment is that they'll keep the model intact and introduce new players. The best indication we will get about this is from your side. That is the registration of a subsidiary company. We've met with the lawyer here who handled the registration of the subsidiaries, Mr. Durante, and he'll cooperate with us. Maybe they'll come back to him to register a new subsidiary. Between Mr. Durante and your bank, you're the first line of defense."

"We understand, Mr. Marella, but is there any way you can also get information on any new activity from your side?" said Gustavo.

"I wish we could, but the origin of the operation is still a mystery. For example, how did a person from upstate New York connect with the mob and start the money laundering scheme? Maybe they saw his first two property development programs and convinced him to work with them. We just don't know. Furthermore, assuming they do start this up again, it could be anywhere on the East Coast. The first one was run out of Endicott, New York. Who knows where they'll set up shop the next time? That's why support from your side is so important."

"We know Attorney Durante and we'll work closely with him," said Gustavo.

Well, thought Alastair, *maybe we can find these guys if they decide to set up shop again. This is a real surprise. I never expected this level of cooperation.*

"Regarding the subsidiaries, let me give you six files. These are the subsidiary companies that were used in the operation. In total, we have eleven names. Some of them are in multiple companies. We also have addresses but don't know where they fit into the organization in your country. I believe you can sort that out."

"I'm curious," said Cisco, "How much money flowed through these companies over the years?"

After a painful silence, Gustavo responded. Over six hundred million dollars."

"Amazing," said Gordon, "just amazing. He looked over at Dick Strong and whispered, "that's the amount you briefed earlier."

Cisco looked briefly at the files and nodded to Gordon, indicating that many of the players were known to them. *Now we can start building our case,* thought Cisco.

Mr. Bennett, how many accounts did Jason Belvedere have with your bank?"

"Only two. One account dealt with the development projects. As money came into the subsidiary accounts, he would take out a portion and deposit it in his other account. It's hard to say what these deposits represented. It could be his share of the profits."

"And maybe he was skimming the subsidiary accounts," said Cisco.

"Mr. Riviera, I have no specific information on what Mr. Belvedere was doing. Certainly he could have been taking unauthorized funds from the subsidiary companies. All I can tell you is what happened, not why it happened."

"Fair point," said Gordon, "tell us about the second account, how much money was in it?"

"The second account was used for trust fund payments. It would periodically be funded by the other account. It never had more than one million dollars in it."

"And the first account?" said Cisco, "How much was in that?"

Gustavo Bennett hesitated for a moment before answering. *Here we go,* thought Cisco, *stand by for another big number.*

"It currently has thirty four million in the account," replied Gustavo.

Gordon and Cisco looked at each other thinking the same thing. The amount of money was staggering. It was a well-organized and established operation and over time produced dramatic returns. It seemed that Belvedere took his profits in the Caymans and parked the money at Global Caribbean Bank. They were sure he was also skimming the subsidiary company accounts but couldn't prove it.

After the meeting, Minister Matinez asked Gordon for a side meeting. "I want to make sure that you're satisfied with the outcome. I'm committed to resolving this violation of our banking regulations, and make sure it doesn't happen again."

"We have everything we need at this point, thank you. I'm impressed with your level of support and also Global Caribbean's cooperation. I'll keep you informed as we move forward. It will be quiet for a bit as we assemble the case."

"I understand. You have my number if you need it."

When they got back to the hotel, Gordon called Special Agent Dye in Washington. "Lou, we got everything we asked for. It couldn't have gone better. This is a serious embarrassment for them as the operation was in place for so many years. They want it cleaned up. Would you set up a Zoom call next week with the whole team? And, we'll need to bring in the Department of Justice also."

"Great news Gordon, finally I can see the end. I'll set a meeting for Wednesday next week, that will give you all a chance to sort out the next steps. Safe trip home and job well done."

After the call, the team sat on the veranda by the pool discussing the meeting with the bank. "You know, there is still an open item we need to close out," said Alastair.

"What do you mean?" replied Gordon.

"When Belvedere first started his project development business, he ran two clean developments. No play in the Caribbean that I can see."

"It was fully disclosed in his tax filings," said Dick Strong, "I don't have the files with me but I remember reviewing that."

"So, what did he do with his profits?" said Gordon.

"They must be parked somewhere in New York or maybe Miami," replied Alastair, "I know his wife Marion told me they had a joint account with Key Bank in Endicott. It was used for daily expenses and I bet Belvedere drew a salary from it also. Maybe there are other accounts."

"I'll give Henry Abbott a call at the Binghamton field office and have him speak with the bank. He may have to get a court order but it shouldn't be a problem."

"You know guys," said Cisco, "Belvedere may have done us a huge favor."

"I know where this is headed." laughed Dick Strong, "Dirty money."

"You got it," said Cisco. "Maybe the New York money from the first two projects is legit, and all the money in the Caymans is dirty."

"It will sure make it a lot easier unravelling his finances," said Dick, "Thank you Mr. Belvedere!"

Chapter 48

The Zoom meeting on Wednesday was 'all-hands-on-deck.' The FBI offices in Binghamton, Miami, and Washington, the AG's office, Endwell Investigations, and the Binghamton Police were all online. Special Agent Dye also had two attorneys from the Department of Justice on the call. Everyone could see the investigation was coming to a head now that the Department of Justice was involved. They were the final link in the case.

"Gordon, why don't you start us off by summarizing the meetings in the Caymans. I hope it didn't get in the way of scuba diving and beach time."

"It was a squeeze, Lou, but we managed to get it all in," laughed Gordon, "We now have all the subsidiary companies identified plus eleven names in back of them, along with a summary of how much money flowed through them over the years. By the way, it came to over six hundred million dollars!"

There was a collective gasp from some of the group. Nobody expected this much money to be involved. Maybe a hundred million but six hundred million?

"I know this sounds impossible, but remember the laundry was operating for close to ten years and it adds up," said Gordon, "Those figures are from Global Caribbean Bank. It gets better; Belvedere also had two accounts of his own with the bank. One was 'funded' for want of a better word out of the subsidiary companies while the other was used to make trust fund payments with money from the first account. The accounts adds up to thirty four million."

"We're in the wrong business," laughed Special Agent Dye.

"I know we'll be going after the bad boys, but will the FBI and DOJ take any action against the bank?" asked Lieutenant Hendricks.

Martin Goldberg, one of the DOJ lawyers spoke up. "We need to dig into this, but my sense is we'll let the Cayman Islands government deal with them. We would have to prove that the bank knew of the money laundering operation, and supported it. Given that they're an offshore bank, I don't think we could get the evidence we need to prosecute them unless the Cayman Islands government throws them under the bus. From what I've seen of these cases in the past, it's more a lack of oversight on the part of the bank, not an active involvement in the crime. The bank was making money and that's probably all they cared about. The Cayman Islands government will take some action against the bank but I can't see them being shut down. Maybe a stiff fine and some people lose their jobs."

"Do we have enough to go after the eleven guys?" asked Warren Hackler from the AG's office in Albany."

"We sure do, but we need to develop a strategy as we move forward. We could easily go after the eleven guys at once, but first I think we need to understand where they fit in the organizations. I think some of the lesser guys can help us take down some of the bigger ones. We'll be going after serious jail time here and that should be an incentive for some of them to flip."

"We need to be careful how long we take over this before we pull the plug," said Gordon, "We usually refer to this period as 'shelf life', because sooner or later the word leaks out and we could lose our advantage. I should have mentioned this earlier, but we have an agreement with the bank and the Cayman Islands government to let the operation continue to run. Clearly, there will be no more development projects from Belvedere but we think they may try to continue with a new player. We have no idea who it will be, or where it will surface, but for now they don't know we're on to them, and they may try again with a new cast of characters."

"How will we know if they try again?" asked Warren.

"The bank and the government are on high alert for any new subsidiary company registrations. Also, the attorney Belvedere used in the Caymans is cooperating, so if they come back to him to register a new subsidiary, he'll alert us. As you can see this is sort of a sting operation. If they do try it, we can freeze any funds and really hurt them," said Cisco, "but as Gordon said, we have to be aware that we can only keep the lid on this for so long. Sooner or later things always leak. If that happens, we could have a problem. People disappear."

"Okay, we'll come back with an analysis of the eleven names. They're probably mob guys from Miami and New York City, based on a quick look. We'll place them in their organizations and this will tell us how we want to go after them. I'd love to make a splash and bring them all in at once, but we need to decide if we're hunting with a rifle or shotgun," said Special Agent Dye, "Once you have the pecking order, how long will it take you guys at the DOJ to finalize the case?"

"We'll work all eleven at the same time," said Martin Goldberg, "I guess that's the shotgun approach at this point. If something starts to go south on us, we want to be able to react quickly. If the lid stays on the investigation, we can be selective if we want; sort of the rifle approach."

"Let's hope we get lucky and they try to run the same laundry operation with new players. If that happens, it will be the icing on the cake; it won't get in the way of the eleven indictments," said Gordon.

Special Agent Dye summed up the meeting. "This will pretty much be an FBI and DOJ show for the next few months. I'm not trying to cut anyone out. You were all integral to our success. We'll keep the secure portal active and post a weekly status on it. Also,

I'd like to have a quick Zoom call every other week to make sure everyone is up to speed. This will move slowly at first and then quickly take off. We need to be prepared. Any questions?"

For the next few weeks while the FBI was busy assembling an organization chart to show where the eleven names fit, and the DOJ was working on the indictments, the portal would be light on information posted and the Zoom calls likely to be more social than business. But It would be essential, to keep the group intact.

About three weeks after the all-hands Zoom call, Gordon Marella got a call from Juan Durante, Belvedere's lawyer in the Cayman Islands.

"Mr. Marella, I just received a request to register a subsidiary company for a US corporation. The name of the company is All States Development and the company is incorporated in Delaware. Doesn't this sound familiar? I've never done business with this party before, but the fact that they called me to register a subsidiary begs the question."

"Sure sounds like the same song, second verse, Juan. Can you send me the details on the company, we'll need to run it down?"

"I'll send it to you this afternoon. Should I go ahead and register the company?"

"Absolutely. But stretch it out in terms of the time it takes to register them; try to add on a few weeks. We need to complete an analysis of the names the bank gave us. Let the bank know about this development and also Minister Martinez. For now it's business as usual. Once money starts to show up in the subsidiary company, we can take the next steps."

After the call, Gordon and Cisco discussed this latest development. "I wish there was a way we could get these guys to put a load of money into this new subsidiary. I'd love to hit them hard," said Gordon.

"Let's just hope it's a big project that needs a lot of money up front," replied Cisco, "The case is really starting to take off now. Showtime!"

Chapter 49

The FBI analysis of the names behind the subsidiary companies confirmed that it was a New York City and Miami mob operation. Two different families, yet working together. Six names in New York City and five names in Miami. Of the eleven, four of them were high up in the families. The remainder were probably lower level soldiers who ran the day to day operation. They would be the targets to flip.

Alastair called Marion Belvedere to update her on the case. It was something he did not look forward to, as the news about her husband was never positive. However, it was important to her to know everything so she could reach closure. "Marion, you mentioned once that you and Jason had a joint checking account at Key Bank in Endicott. Did he have any other accounts there or anywhere else?"

"I don't know about any other banks but he did have another account at Key Bank in his name. One time a statement came in the mail and I thought it was for our checking account. I asked him about it and he said it was for his business. It wasn't a checking or savings account; I think it dealt with investments and things like that."

"Do you know how large the account was?"

"Not really, I had opened the letter thinking it was our checking account but had not looked through it when I showed it to Jason."

"Okay, the FBI will get a court order to look into the account."

"Oh dear, what was he up to?"

"Try to not worry about it. The investigation uncovered accounts in the Cayman Islands, and they want to find any accounts he had in the States. It looks like he was involved with some gangsters in New York City and Miami. Something went wrong and they had him killed."

"Al, is this really happening? When is it going to end?"

"Soon. They've identified all the men and are building a case against them. The man who killed Jason was working for them and as you know, he was arrested."

"You mean he committed murders for them?"

"Yeah, he was a contract killer. Marion, this investigation still has a long way to go. It may be months before it's settled. We believe that some of the money Jason made may in fact be from legal enterprises, and as such would go to you and Steve. However, I believe most if not all of the money in the Cayman Islands is from a money laundering operation and will be recovered by the government."

"I don't care Al; I don't want any part of any criminal gains. They can take it all."

When Gordon Marella received the information about the new subsidiary registration from Jaun Durante, Belvedere's lawyer in the Caymans, he was in for a surprise.

"Hey Cisco, check this out. This just came in from Juan Durante. The new company, All States Development has a Miami address, and it's not too far from our office. Let's drive by and see what it looks like."

Cisco looked at the address and laughed. "There's not much over there other than a bunch of strip malls. I guess our boys are starting small and plan to grow the business."

When they went to the address, they ended up at a beauty parlor. Mandy's Salon appeared to be a viable business with customers and beauticians.

"I love these guys," laughed Cisco, "starting out small in a beauty parlor to save money and grow the business. A real success story; makes me proud. Is this a great country or what!"

"How about just a mail drop," replied Gordon.

"No wonder you're the lead agent," laughed Cisco, "a keen eye for the obvious!"

Gordon briefed the team during the next Zoom meeting. "Our friends in Miami and New York have registered a new subsidiary company in the Caymans; All States Development. Like the others it's incorporated in Delaware but this has a Miami address. Cisco and I went over to see what it looks like and it's a mail drop in a beauty parlor located in a strip mall."

"This time it could be different," said Cisco, "We don't think they're using an outside source like Belvedere. It looks as if they've borrowed Belvedere's game plan and are doing it themselves."

"Eliminate the middle man?" asked Detective Adams.

"Exactly. Belvedere cost them a lot of money when the EPA blocked his last development. That money is gone. Also, we're pretty sure Belvedere was skimming the accounts and that really gets the mob's attention."

"Has any money flowed into the new subsidiary in the Caymans?" asked Alaster.

"Not yet. Belvedere's attorney in the Caymans, a guy by the name of Juan Durante is handling the registration. He's dragging his feet to give us time to sort out the players and the families. It will be a couple of weeks before the registration is filed."

"Once the subsidiary is funded, do we go after the money then?" asked Lieutenant Hendricks.

"Not yet," said Special Agent Dye, "The DOJ wants them to make the intra-company transfer up here and then we shut them down. It's important that they complete the transfer cycle. Once they do that, we'll charge the eleven guys. By the way, the names on All States Development are names we already have."

Nobody, other than the Department of Justice had thought about having All States Development complete the transfer to the

US company. *Sure, it has to be that way,* thought Alastair, *Once the money ends up at All States Development in Miami, the money laundering cycle is complete. Seal the deal.*

"If I'm following you," said Lieutenant Hendricks, "once you go after them when the transfer is complete, you'll have to arrest the eleven guys too. Seems as if it all has to happen at the same time."

"Has to be," said Special Agent Dye, "We can't risk anyone getting away. It will all happen on the same day.

We've eyes on them now and have teams in place in both cities. When we pull the plug, we'll freeze the money transferred to All States Development, and arrest the eleven guys; it's the shotgun approach."

Chapter 50

About two weeks after the Zoom call, the All States Development subsidiary was registered in the Caymans. Shortly after that George Marella was advised by Global Caribbean Bank that money was being deposited into the subsidiary company, not as one large deposit but several smaller ones which continued for about two weeks. When they finished, it was over twenty one million dollars. The FBI arrest teams were on alert, knowing that the money was going to be transferred to All States Development in Miami.

Although the FBI knew that Third Dominion Bank in Miami was the bank of record for All States Development, they didn't contact them. They wanted to see if Global Caribbean Bank would leak any information to them. They did not. Once arrests were made, the Department of Justice would be investigating Third Dominion. Unlike Global Caribbean; serious fines could be levied against them.

Late on a Friday afternoon, after Endwell Investigations had finished their weekly wash-up of agency business, Alastair got a call from Lieutenant Hendricks. "Al, the FBI arrested all eleven of the guys today. The Department of Justice also froze the funds transferred to All States Development in Miami."

"How much was frozen?"

"I think over twenty one million."

"Damn, the amount of money is staggering. It has to be drug money don't you think?"

"For sure, you can't generate that kind of money from gambling, prostitution, loan sharking, and stuff like that. I bet you eighty, maybe ninety percent of the money is drug related."

"Hard to get your arms around it. Do we have to do anything more at this point?"

"I don't think so. The DOJ might call us to testify at some point, but I think all we need to do is sit tight and follow the action. Todd and Tony asked the same question. Lou is going to call an all-hands meeting sometime next week, so we should get a better feel then."

"It's over, Al! We can read all about it in the papers."

"This has been quite a ride, Elton. I never expected this kind of activity when I came back and opened the agency. I thought I'd be chasing deadbeat husbands and insurance scams. I feel like I'm still with the FBI."

"I know what you mean. When I came here from the NYPD, I did it for my wife and kids. I never expected cases like this. I've been down this road twice now with the FBI dealing with complex cases involving different agencies. As you said, quite a ride."

On Monday, Alastair called the team together to let them know that the case was finished and in the hands of the Department of Justice. "We have an all-hands Zoom call on Wednesday. Special Agent Dye will update us on the status, but from my conversation with Lieutenant Hendricks, I don't see any more play in it for us. The DOJ is running with the ball now. We might have to testify at some point, but I doubt it. I need to get a reading from Dick Strong at the AG's office regarding the money Belvedere has at Key Bank. It seems like it was from the first two projects Belvedere ran and if so, that may be clean money and can be part of Marion Belvedere's inheritance."

"How much money are we talking about?" asked Gil.

"I don't know. Agent Abbott got a court order to access the account. We can ask him on the Zoom call.

"Al, when I was going through our accounts the other day," said Chantal, "I saw that Mrs. Belvedere is no longer on our books and hasn't been for some time. Were there any issues between her and the agency?"

"Not at all; when the cops arrested Armand Haughton, I stopped billing her. Our job was finished. Since then I've kept in touch with her to keep her up to speed. Her husband really hurt her and their son; I wanted to try and help them."

The Zoom meeting on Wednesday was almost a social gathering. Everyone was relaxed and happy with the outcome. Martin Goldberg briefed the team on the indictments. "We've arrested all eleven of the bad boys and they're presently in jail in Miami and New York City. Given the amount of money and number of years of the money laundering operation, the judge denied bail. Some of these guys are flight risks; so we should be able to keep them all locked up. It's being challenged by their lawyers, so we'll have to see where it goes. The DOJ froze the assets of All States Development, that's over twenty one million dollars which they'll never see. Our case is strong and we're asking for a speedy trial. As you can imagine, the other side is trying to string it out."

"What about the companies that purchased the development projects once they were completed?" asked Alastair, "they bought a development financed with laundered money. Do you have any recourse."

"I don't know yet," said Martin, "we would have to prove they knew the money behind the development was laundered and probably came from the drug trade. My boss wants to shake their tree, so to say, and see what falls out. If nothing else, their due diligence was rubbish. They probably turned a blind eye as the deals were very attractive. We may be able to levy some fines but I think we'd be hard pressed to prove they knew about the laundered money. We'll see; they're on the hit list."

"A question for Henry Abbott and Dick Strong," said Alastair, "How much money was in Belvedere's account at Key Bank, and is it clean? I'm thinking about what Mrs. Belvedere and her son might inherit."

Henry spoke first, "He had almost eight million in the account in a mix of money and investments."

"Looking at the time line," said Dick, "the money was deposited before Belvedere started his adventures in the Caymans. It's a DOJ call, but I believe it's clean."

"I agree," said Martin, "We'll have a position before the will is probated. It looks pretty straightforward to me."

The meeting carried on for about twenty minutes more. Most of the questions were general in nature with nothing to indicate a problem with the case. It was more of a Question and Answer session as the FBI like to say. Special Agent Dye let the conversations continue, as it was great to see the group working together.

"Before we close the meeting I want to take a minute and thank you all for your excellent work. This is a big score for us. We've shut down a long running money laundering operation and decimated two established crime families. Sure there will be new players to fill in the empty spaces, but we've made the game much harder for them. I'm so impressed with the team effort. Everyone played a role and contributed. I know I said this earlier, but Al Stewart and his team opened up this case, and look where we've ended up. Al, many thanks to you and your team at Endwell Investigations."

After the call, as George Marella was headed back to his office from the conference room in the Miami office, he received a text message from Pedro Martinez, the Finance Minister in the Cayman Islands. It was brief: I understand arrests have been made. Thank you.

Epilogue

Over the next year and a half a series of trials was held. Three of the defendants cooperated with the Government, and their testimony from the inside of the organization assured the convictions of the major players, and stiff sentences were handed out – the icing on the cake for the Government.

When Belvedere's will was probated, Marion found out a third person was listed as a beneficiary. She didn't contest this and insisted that she not be told the person's name. Knowing the full extent of Jason's personal and business life was already very painful for her; knowing the name of the other person in Jason's life would serve no purpose, and only add insult to injury.

Alastair had always suspected Marjorie Monette knew more than she told them. She and Belvedere had been together a long time. She never received any money from him other than the will. Maybe they did get it all when they met with her. George Adamo was a surprise as once he decided to cooperate, his testimony tied a lot of ends together. Alastair felt that Marjorie was the holder of the secrets; but not the case.

And at Endwell Investigations, it was a welcome change to return to a more normal routine. The case load continued to grow steadily and the prospect of another investigator was being discussed again. Alastair decided he would cap the size of the agency at four investigators and of course Sherlock, finder of lost cats!

The End

If you've enjoyed this novel, please write a review. They are very important for self-published authors like me.

https://www.amazon.com/More-Than-Murder-Endwell-Investigations-ebook/dp/B0CQDLRNN4

More than Murder is the third book in the Endwell Investigation series. Here is an excerpt from the first book.

Full Circle

Chapter One

   Raymond Leonard was twenty-three years old and autistic, high functioning but not able to live on his own. However, he was able to interact with other people and maintain social relationships. He lived with his mother and father on Binghamton's west-side and worked at The Sheltered Workshop in town. His brother was a senior at Northeastern University in Boston majoring in statistics. He planned to stay in the Boston area after graduation.

   It was a safe and comfortable life for Raymond. He had his family, his job and his home. His parents helped him to develop his independence. They knew that there would come a day when they would not be able to look after him. Along with his father, he managed the day-to-day household expenses. He had a number of other jobs around the house, all designed to help him understand what it took to run a house and be independent. Although he did not drive, he did most of the grocery shopping for the family. There was a Weis supermarket about five blocks from the house. He had a backpack and roller cart he used to carry the groceries. He enjoyed the structure of shopping. Make a list, go to the store, buy the groceries, take them home and then put them away. The completeness of the task was appealing to him. A defined beginning and end.

   He was also a bit of an explorer. His trips were not always a straight walk to the store but a wider-ranging walk about the town. When he was little, his mom had always pointed out the trees and flowers when they went on their walks, and he still liked to look at them.

   The season was well into fall. The clocks had been turned back and the days were much shorter now. There were plenty of leaves still on the trees but their earlier vibrant colors were now dull and they would soon fall. Raymond had decided to take a walk to look at the leaves on the way to the store because he'd heard his mom say they'd soon be gone.

   This evening, he walked through an older part of Binghamton that had seen better days but where the trees were fully grown. The city was trying to improve the area and some of the abandoned houses had been torn down.

   He was passing two empty lots, side by side. They had been there for some time and were overgrown, neighborhood junk starting to accumulate. He casually stopped and walked in a bit to look around. But the vegetation was dense and in the fading light he couldn't see much. As he was leaving the lot to continue his walk, he saw three men having a heated conversation in the back of the lot. He saw flashes and heard the sound of gunshots. Two men had been shot and he saw it happen!

Raymond was terrified. *What just happened?* he thought. Then he saw a man with a gun coming toward him. Without knowing what he was doing or where he was going, he quickly ran out of the lot, crossed the street and headed towards the downtown area. *I have to get away! This is a really bad man,* was all he could think.

But Raymond was not the only one on the street. Reilly Harrington, who was from Rochester, had arrived at the bus station earlier and was on his way to the same lot to pick up a backpack full of drugs. He had been sober for some months now and was trying to get away from the drug life. However, the lure of some quick money was hard to resist. So, he thought, one more trip as a drug mule for a dealer in the Rochester area and then close it out. Reilly made most of his trips in upstate New York, with occasional runs to New York City. Being a drug mule supported his meager lifestyle. He knew this type of work was reckless and dangerous. Sooner or later it would come crashing down on him.

When he arrived at the lot to pick up the drugs, Raymond was already gone and all he saw was a guy running down the street with a gun. It wasn't anyone he knew. *Whoa, that's not one of the dudes I'm supposed to meet. Where are my guys?,* thought Reilly. He knew something was wrong. Really wrong! He went up to the lot and looked in but couldn't see much. He went into the lot about ten feet and then he saw the two guys he was supposed to meet, both dead. *I got to get out of here now! Somebody must have heard something. I don't want to be around when the cops come.* He quickly got out of the lot and headed downtown. He headed back to the bus station looking for the next bus to Rochester. *Someone robbed those guys and killed them. He'll shoot me, to, if he knows I was there.*

Raymond had stopped running now. He walked at a rapid pace but where to go? He came to the bus station and saw three buses loading and unloading. *I'll take one of those buses. I have to get out of here now. If the bad man finds me, he'll hurt me!*

Raymond had the grocery shopping money and some of his own. Not much, maybe sixty dollars total. Small bills and change. He went up to the ticket window and just looked at the agent. He didn't know what to say. Where should he go? He looked back at the buses at the gates and thought, *one of these I guess.*

He was looking at the Rochester bus when the ticket agent said, "What's it going to be my friend?"

"That one, Rochester," replied Raymond.

"Can't do that, it just came in from Rochester and will depart in ten minutes for Monticello and then on to the city. There is a Rochester bus coming from the city in thirty minutes." New York City was usually referred to as the city by the upstate folks.

"Want that one?"

"Okay," replied Raymond. "I'll take that bus."

"It'll go from Gate 3 over there; we'll make an announcement soon."

Raymond bought a ticket and took a seat near Gate 3 where he could see most of the doors in the terminal and waited for the bus.

Reilly Harrington came into the bus station about ten minutes after Raymond sat down. He went up to the ticket window. "When's the next bus to Rochester?"

"The driver just called in with a status. He's about fifteen minutes out. Want a ticket?"

"Yeah."

Reilly paid for the ticket, sat down to wait for the incoming bus. *What is going on? That's it, I'm finished with this life. If I'd been in that lot ten minutes earlier, I'd be toast. It's over! Maria is right, sooner or later you die in the drug business. I'm going to continue to stay sober this time and not go back. If the killer knows I was nearby, he'll find me and kill me for sure.* Maria Suarez was Reilly's on-again-off-again girlfriend. Reilly wanted a more committed relationship but she would not get too close to him given his life style. She was there for him but would not let the relationship develop. She worked as an administrator at a not-for-profit that supported halfway houses in Rochester and Monroe County. Mainly for people recently released from prison or enrolled in rehabilitation programs.

Reilly texted his dealer in Rochester. They had a codeword system to let him know he had picked up the "package" and also if he had trouble. Reilly used a burner and sent a text with the codewords for a problem. It said, "gone south 11:50" which was the code for a broken deal and the arrival time in Rochester for his bus. He took the sim card out of the burner and broke it into small pieces. He knew he'd have a reception committee waiting for him when he got to Rochester. *These guys have only one way to deal with problems—violence! They're not going to be happy campers,* he thought.

As he was sitting in the station lobby, he noticed Raymond sitting not too far away. He looked agitated and clearly in a very nervous state. He was constantly rocking forward and back which Reilly knew was a coping mechanism for extreme stress. *Well, I guess I'm not the only guy with problems. This dude is hurting,* he thought. Reilly kept looking at Raymond. It was odd; he was not dressed as a typical guy would be at his age. The clothes were clean and not worn but there was a style and color disconnect. Sort of like his mother was still buying his clothes. The colors and styles were a bit dated. If he was aware of it, it didn't seem to bother him. At that point, they made eye contact. Reilly felt sorry for the guy. He smiled and made a small hand wave gesture. Raymond didn't respond but kept looking in his direction. *Strange dude,* thought Reilly, *wonder what his problem is?* He guessed he was five to ten years older than Raymond. Neither one knew that the other had been way too close to the murders.

When they started to board the Rochester bus, Reilly was one of first to board. He took a seat by a window. The bus was about half full. He saw Raymond still outside. He was letting the other passengers board ahead of him. *Is this guy going to get on the bus? He really seems confused,* he thought.

About that time the bus driver was coming out of the terminal with the passenger manifest and spoke to Raymond. Reilly couldn't hear what was said but imagined he was telling him to board the bus if he wanted to go to Rochester. Raymond got on the bus; spotted Reilly and sat down next to him. *What the hell, plenty of empty seats, why sit next to me? What's your game?* They settled in to their seats and were off to Rochester. Reilly could sense Raymond constantly looking at him as he kept rocking back and forth.

Finally Raymond said, "I'm Raymond. I'm going to Rochester."

"Well, you're on the right bus. Is someone going to meet you?"

"I don't have anybody."

"Where are you going to stay?"

"I don't have anybody."

"You already said that. You can't just get on a bus and get someplace at midnight without a place to stay and a plan."

What am I going to do about this guy? thought Reilly, *I just can't cut him loose at the bus station at midnight. Nothing good will come from that. Maybe I should keep him for the night and then get social services involved tomorrow. I'll call Maria and see what she thinks. Something's not right with this guy and I don't understand it. He's not a threat but he acts sort of strange. Christ, when is all this shit going to end? The Rochester dealers are going to be really pissed off at losing their dope and will try to blame me for it. I can see that coming. Now I got this weird dude who doesn't have a clue about what he's doing.*

To read more of this story please go to the link below.

https://www.amazon.com/Full-Circle-Endwell-Investigations-donohue-ebook/dp/B0B1ZDCCKR

For a free short story and information about all my other cozy mysteries, please visit my website:

https://upstatemysterycom

Or you can visit my Amazon page.

https://www.amazon.com/

s?k=fj+donohue&i=stripbooks&crid=34Y5WAN6PY

Thank you !

About the Author

I'm a retired International Sales Director having worked in the commercial and military flight simulation industry for over 30 years. I lived in Brussels, Belgium and Bonn, Germany for 8 years and met my British wife in Brussels. Before my career in the flight simulation industry I was an Armament and Electronics Maintenance Officer in the USAF. We have 3 children and 7 grandchildren. Home is a small town in central New York State where the novellas are set.

I am a volunteer mediator and Lemon Law arbitrator. In the novels I may have one of the characters involved in a Mediation or Lemon Law arbitration.

An underlying theme in my novels is people helping people. In spite of the difficulties and crime that may surround us, there is always hope in friendship and good neighbors.

Milton Keynes UK
Ingram Content Group UK Ltd.
UKHW011832260224
438492UK00001B/93

9 798224 101160